The Woman in Room 19

Ann Girdharry

At the Pool

Drowning is not a pleasant way to die. I see the terror in their eyes. The water churns as they claw for the surface. Air billows from their lungs. The drugs in their system are doing their job. Likely they can't think straight and their limbs aren't working properly. The bubbles were huge at first and now they're becoming smaller, almost delicate. Despite the flailing arms, that body is going nowhere but down.

I could help. The pool isn't so deep and the water is perfectly clear. I could take a breath and dive and reach out my arms. Except I won't. Would you? Would you save someone who has taken away everything you hold dear?

It's almost over. As my gaze locks onto theirs I know they have understood. This is the end.

In the final moments their hair wafts gently and there are no more bubbles. I force myself to watch until their eyes glaze over and their hands relax. Only then is the nightmare over.

Chapter One

Shannon

Shannon nestled into the corner of the sofa and closed her eyes. She sighed, enjoying the quiet of the lounge. It was time to concentrate on the good and push away the bad forever. She didn't need to dwell on the dark times anymore, she just needed to concentrate on being hopeful and excited. This was a new beginning and nothing and no one could spoil it. She placed her hand over her belly and sent a silent prayer to Heaven. This new life inside her was all that mattered.

A few hours earlier she had broken the news to her boss and he had taken it well, she had to give him that. After all it wasn't every day your first ever employee, the one who started out with you at the beginning when you were nothing and nobody, suddenly announced she needed a year off. A year to think about things, take it or leave it.

Her boss, Donald, had nodded and swallowed then nodded some more. Then he had wished her well. Donald had been so good to her over the past few months. What had happened had not been his fault, it had been hers, and now it was time to leave it behind.

Shannon leaned back against the cushions. She had loved her job as receptionist at Donald's Design Agency. She had started at age eighteen when Donald had only one client to produce publicity for. Now he ran a top media agency, and

Shannon was queen of the reception as well as organising plush hospitality for their high-profile clients.

Where she used to dash out to get sandwiches from around the corner for Donald's meetings, she now booked breakfast at The Ritz or dinners at The Savoy, and tickets for Wimbledon finals matches. She was surrounded by staff with strings of qualifications but Donald always made sure she got respected. Everybody knew she was his favourite. Donald had moved up in the world and she had moved up with him.

She had once been friendly and efficient, but the truth was Donald and the entire staff team had been putting up with her mood swings for a long time. Her colleagues had given her a lot of sympathy. They had suffered her sobbing fits, her flights to the restroom, her sudden breakdowns at her desk, and goodness, even some long-term clients had been looking after *her* and handing out the tissues as she dabbed at her eyes.

Shannon had felt bad walking out but perhaps everyone else had given a sigh of relief. Donald had gone out of his way to be understanding.

'Let me know what you decide,' Donald had said, as he ran his hands through his greying hair. 'I really hope you come back but don't worry, I understand. The baby is the priority now.'

The baby certainly was.

The desire to become pregnant had dominated her life for at least five years. Over the last three, she had been driven crazy by the doctors, the tests and the procedures. She and her husband, Jared, had been pushed to the edge by rounds of fertility treatments, and their marriage had been cracking at the seams. Damn it, *she* had been cracking at the seams. After all the failed treatments, adoption had been the only route left. Then it all changed and now she was pregnant at last.

Now she could look forward to welcoming a brand-new precious life. It was all she had ever dreamed of.

She grabbed an apple, took a bite and smiled. No more chocolate or biscuits, only healthy snacks from now on. Selecting an old comedy programme, she put her feet up on the coffee table and laughed her way through several episodes. It wasn't until sometime later that she realised no dark memories had intruded. That thought almost made her cry but she pushed away the tears. This was her time to be happy.

When Jared came home, Shannon was still relaxing on the sofa.

'Glad to see you're taking it easy,' he said.

He leant over to kiss her and his dark hair flopped into his eyes. At over six foot, with an athletic build, Indian good looks and liquid brown eyes most women would die for, her husband was the sort of man who attracted a lot of female attention. It was more than his looks that people liked. Jared had a warm nature and women tended to instinctively trust him. He still pushed all the right buttons for her, though she knew she had made him suffer with her roller coaster feelings. If she had been on the receiving end of emotions like hers for the last three years, she would have found it hard to stay so devoted.

He topped up her water glass and poured one for himself.

'I cleared out all the crisps and sugary snacks and put them in the bin,' she said.

Jared laughed. 'And what if you get cravings in the middle of the night for, I don't know, your favourite chocolate-covered biscuits? Am I meant to go get some or refuse?'

'That's a good question. I've no idea.'

'Would you like me to bring you anything from the kitchen?'

Here she was, an independent and capable woman. She had not expected Jared to turn out to be hyper-protective but that was what seemed to be happening. In fact, since the world-changing moment, she could hardly lift a goddam paperback novel without Jared rushing to do it for her. She really did not deserve him. 'I'm fine thanks.'

'Did you tell Donald the truth?'

Jared's comment took her by surprise. A wave of anxiety suddenly gripped her. She fought to control it, bunching her fists so Jared wouldn't see her hands shaking. Perspiration peppered her lip.

'What truth? I don't know what you mean.'

'Huh? I mean did you discuss with him about giving up long-term? You know, beyond maternity leave?'

She took a big breath in and breathed it out long and slow. *Get a grip. Don't let the past suck you down.* 'Sort of. I explained I needed space, and the pregnancy was the absolute priority, and Donald was great. He's totally fine with me taking as much time out as I want. He's such a dear.'

'Sure he is. You can twist that man around your little finger. If he wasn't almost twice your age, I'd be jealous.'

She wiped the sweat from her lip. 'Don't exaggerate. Donald's not that old and you're being silly. Anyway, he's married with a daughter who's old enough to start driving lessons.'

'I'm only kidding. Here, take a look at this.' Jared shot her a boyish grin.

He edged up close and took out his phone and as he swept his hair out of his eyes, his gaze fell to her stomach and he gave a quick laugh. Jared's shoulder nudged hers and he showed her his phone screen.

'What are you so pleased about?' she asked.

'Apart from being an expectant father? Nothing much.'

She snuggled closer. On the screen was a photograph of a stately home with a grand façade. The sort of place a lord or a duchess might live in.

'Ooh, that looks lovely,' she said. 'Is it the place they used to film Downton Abbey?'

'Looks a bit like it, doesn't it. Guess what, I've booked us a luxury break.'

Wow. Jared wasn't usually so romantic. She raised an eyebrow.

'What?' he said.

'Nothing, it's just unexpected but very, very nice. Looks expensive.'

'I know you didn't want to fly but I wanted us to go somewhere amazing and unforgettable to celebrate the start of our new family.'

Gosh, it had been easy to forget Jared had been just as desperate as she was. She could see his lip quivering.

He scrolled through the pictures. 'They've only got forty rooms and it's rarely open to the public. It's in the middle of the Sussex countryside. They've got spacious grounds and outside and inside pools. It's perfect because it's going to be a heatwave and with our pool out of order it will be great to get out of the city.'

It definitely would be. Their house had a private spa and just when they needed it most, the pool had a maintenance problem.

'Their chef comes from a five-star restaurant in Paris. They say the cuisine is meant to be one of the highlights,' Jared said.

'I love the name, Sussex Abbey.'

'Believe it or not, it used to belong to a lord and lady. And guess what? I asked for our room to be your lucky number.'

Nineteen. The date of her mother's birthday. Cuddling up to her husband, she breathed in the musky scent of his cologne. Sussex Abbey seemed perfect for a fresh start.

'It sounds wonderful, darling.'

Chapter Two

Natasha

Natasha laughed as the wind whipped through her hair. It was exhilarating, speeding along a country road with Harry's car open to the sun. Harry loved sports cars and this one was a beauty.

'I could do with a cold beer,' Harry said. 'Better still if it's served to me poolside.'

He was in a great mood and so magnetic when he was like this – carefree, with his blond curls wild and tossing in the breeze. He turned to her and she got a full hit of his eyes which were as blue as the sky and as sparkling as sapphires. When Harry turned those eyes on women, it made them lose their reason. He had had exactly that effect on her. When she'd first met him she had been young and impressionable and she had fallen madly in love. Knowing the other side to Harry's nature hadn't taken the edge off his appeal, even when it should have, and she had remained in love with him for years.

Cutting him a smile, she wriggled her hips.

'Ooh Natasha, are you teasing me?'

Of course she was. Harry was gorgeous to look at though his real power came from the way he oozed charisma and masculinity. He could have any woman he wanted. Men too, if that were his thing, because when Harry turned on the charm people threw themselves at his feet. It's what attracted her to him in the first place because who can resist that kind of power?

Harry turned up the music and started singing at the top of his voice.

She took off her shiny red stilettoes, careful not to scratch them, and stretched her toes. The car, the expensive shoes and dress, and Harry's casual attire which cost a fortune, had all been picked for a reason – to make an impact. To say they were the couple who were making it. To show they were the ones with an effortless lifestyle and a bank account to match. It was all about creating the right image. She and Harry were good at it and they could carry it off with style. That was why people liked them and it was what helped them get close to their targets.

Harry turned the volume up another notch. Of course, he was going through his favourite playlist and it was one which she pretended to like. She even knew the words to most of the songs and could sing along as if she loved rock and roll. Living with a man like Harry, you got to learn tricks like that.

When the hotel came into view she let out a gasp. 'I can't believe it, it's absolutely gorgeous.'

'Isn't it. Welcome to the majestic and historical Sussex Abbey.' Harry pulled into the parking area. 'A paradise fit for my darling.'

They took a few moments to appreciate their surroundings and to be seen by anyone who happened to be watching. She leaned in to give Harry a luscious kiss.

Sussex Abbey had once been the home of a British family who had made their fortune by riding to war at the side of the king. The days of the knights were long gone. It now belonged to a leisure company who had kept the charm of the white stone building and ornamental gardens, right down to the hedges clipped into the shape of animals and the marble steps leading to the entrance. There was a grand conservatory attached to one wing of the house and a modern extension at the back which housed an indoor spa. On the website there had been pictures of the other side of the Abbey with its raised decking area and an outdoor pool overlooking the grounds.

This was where lords and ladies had ridden out on their hunting and shooting parties. They had been entertained at fine banquets, waited on hand and foot by a small army of servants. Looking at the grandeur made Natasha giddy, as if she could pretend to be a real lady. Here, she would be able to eat and drink whatever wonderful offerings came from the chef and she would be pampered by staff who would behave as if she and her comfort were all that mattered to them.

'Are you ready for it?' Harry said.

'Always.'

The adrenalin ran through her veins. It wasn't just the thrill of the job they were there to do which got to her. It was also the poverty-stricken little girl inside who was excited because she still couldn't believe who she had grown up to be.

'Then let's go, babe,' Harry said.

Shaking her hair and arranging the dark tresses over her shoulders, she let out a laugh as he took her hand and they headed for the entrance.

This was almost her favourite part. Full of possibilities, of not yet knowing who they would pick and what they would be like.

As they crossed the reception area, she felt the humble gaze of the staff and their appreciative, ready-to-serve expressions. This was class. This was what it felt like to succeed, to be part of the elite. Her past was far behind her and she and Harry were unbeatable.

Chapter Three

Jared

Jared hummed a little tune to himself as he prepared supper. His mushroom risotto was one of Shannon's favourites and he loved to make it for her. He loved even more how she looked so content and preoccupied. At last, against all the odds, they had made it. He had sent silent gratitude skyward for the miracle, for how he had given up only to be saved when no hope was in sight. The important thing was they were going to be parents and the past years of desperate trying were over. Now all they had to do was look forward to a rosy future.

'Would you like a slice of lemon in your water?' he called through to the lounge.

'Oooh yes, and ice please,' Shannon said.

'Coming right up.'

He returned to the kitchen to wash the salad and chop the mushrooms. They were lucky they could afford the break at Sussex Abbey even though Jared had taken the decision to make it on his own and not be part of his family's multi-million-pound business empire.

'What are you making?' Shannon called to him.

'It's a surprise.'

Her light laugh made him smile and then he heard the sound of the television in the background as he turned his attention back to the cooking. This was how he liked life – simple and easy and not spoiled by family feuds.

To the horror of his father, Jared had studied creative writing instead of management and now he worked as a ghostwriter which meant he earned a modest wage rather than the sums he would have if he had decided to take up the family business at his father's side. Still, it didn't stop Jared occasionally dipping into his family's funds but he had his own strict rules because he only did it for Shannon. Their house, the break at Sussex Abbey, they were for her and her comfort. And for their number one priority. The baby.

Jared knew his father kept money on open access to him because he was hoping that one day Jared would give up and come crawling back. Jared was determined that would never happen. Though on his and Shannon's combined salaries there would be no way they could afford either their west London townhouse or expensive weekends away.

A while later, they were sitting at the dinner table. Even with the ceiling fan on it was hot in the room.

'I've been reading up about Sussex Abbey,' Shannon said. 'It's twice been used for a film set and I've ordered the DVDs so we can watch them.'

'Cool.'

'They host a lot of celebrity weddings and last year the only weeks open to the public were one at Christmas and one in the summer. The week we're going is the only time this year it's been open for booking. All forty rooms went in less than an hour. How did you manage it?'

A jolt of guilt shot up his spine and he almost sloshed Shannon's risotto onto the tablecloth rather than onto her plate. 'Oh, Lilith told me about it.'

'Didn't she want to go there herself?'

'She said she was too busy.'

'Shame. But it was nice of her to recommend it. I guess your work with her must be coming to an end soon?'

'Sort of. I'm taking it slowly for the wind down, you know how it is.'

Shannon gave a sympathetic nod.

When a ghostwriting project was nearing completion it was often a difficult moment because clients got so attached to Jared and he got attached to them too. In writing someone's life story, he got close. They told him about their dreams and their disappointments. It could be a very intimate process and it was one which Jared deeply respected. Although he wrote about successes, he had discovered in his work that often the path to success had not all been roses.

His current project with Lilith was one of the more challenging ones he had tackled. Having set up her own fashion enterprise from her bedroom at age fourteen, Lilith was now early thirties and earning six figures a month. She was surrounded by admirers and assistants and had a massive social media following. The surprising thing about her, and which no one would ever guess, was that Lilith had had a deprived childhood. What Jared found even more surprising, was that Lilith was lonely. She told him she had enjoyed plenty of relationships but she had never found anyone who was special.

In their time together, Lilith had told him about her old neighbourhood which had been full of drug problems, and about her five siblings two of whom she had lost to overdoses. Then there was her father who ended up in prison. Jared had learned that Lilith's life philosophy was take every opportunity which comes your way and Lilith saw him as one such opportunity not to be let go easily.

The chemistry wasn't only on her side. Jared felt it too. But he would never act on it. He would never cheat on his wife even after so many passionless rounds of lovemaking with the sole aim of producing an offspring. There had been no light at the end of the tunnel. Then ten weeks ago Shannon changed everything with her wonderful news.

'This tastes lovely,' Shannon said. 'I think I want to eat risotto every day until the baby arrives.'

'No problem. I just wish we'd got air conditioning. Do you think we should get some installed? It's going to be too hot to sleep much tonight.'

Shannon wrinkled her nose. 'And have a load of guys traipsing through the place making noise and mess? I don't think so.'

'Right.'

'I want a nice cosy nest where I can be quiet and peaceful and anyway, we can cool off at Sussex Abbey.'

He clinked his glass with hers. 'I'll drink to that.'

They had moved onto dessert when Jared's phone pinged. One glance at the screen told him it was his brother, Raj. Jared pressed his lips together.

'Who is it?' Shannon asked. 'Is it Raj?'

She had an uncanny knack of reading his expressions. He raised an eyebrow and Shannon wafted her spoon.

'Yeah, I can tell it's him by the way your mouth is all screwed up. I thought he tried to call yesterday too? Is that the second time he's contacted you?'

Jared shrugged. 'Maybe. He can wait.'

The last thing he wanted was a conversation with his big brother. Raj was the golden boy who had joined their father in managing the family business and Jared and Raj could never agree – about anything. Whatever his brother had to say it could wait, and preferably for a very long time.

'Tell you what, why don't I clear this lot away and then we can talk about the nursery,' he said.

A while later and they were on the sofa, with Shannon's legs resting across his lap. Jared felt so happy it was as if his chest could barely expand enough to fit it all in. They chatted about Shannon's idea for creating a nursery next to their bedroom. What colour should they paint it – yellow, blue, or lilac? And should they keep the sex of the baby a surprise or not? The idea of it made him tingle from head to foot.

Over the last few weeks he had had the feeling Shannon was drifting away from him but tonight they were back to their old closeness. One thing was certain – it was time to build bridges and reconnect after too much pressure and frustration. He wanted to keep their new-found intimacy at Sussex Abbey. By the time they left that place, he wanted their relationship to once again be perfect.

Chapter Four

Harry

Harry tugged down the sleeves of his dinner jacket and checked his reflection in the mirror. Sussex Abbey had a good vibe. The staff had just the right amount of deference. The rooms were spacious and pleasing to the eye. The grounds were so extensive it felt as if the hotel was cut off from the outside world. Cocooned from stress and mundane concerns. The parking area had been full of top-end vehicles and chauffeurs, and he knew the clientele would be exactly the calibre he was looking for. He could hardly wait to get out there and mingle. Brushing a speck of dust from his shoulder, Harry gave himself a smile.

Natasha was in the bathroom preparing for the evening. She always took ages with her make-up and he had long ago understood there was no point in trying to hurry her. She would come out when she was ready and not before.

He took a swig of water. There would be cocktails in the lounge where they would first set eyes on the other guests, before enjoying a sumptuous evening dinner. This time he was after a high-ticket number.

When Natasha finally emerged, his breath caught in his throat.

'Ravishing,' he said, as he planted kisses on her bare shoulders.

With her pale complexion and grey-green eyes and dark hair, she was stunning in an emerald satiny number that showed off her curves. The guys were all going to be drooling over her, but you know what? She was his and she always would be.

'That colour suits you beautifully.'

She blew him a kiss, her red lips a perfect pucker, which was all the reward he needed. For now.

'Then let's go and give this lot a run for their money,' he said.

'Are we after jewellery? There's bound to be a big number item coming out, most likely being saved for the gala night.'

Hotel safes were a breeze for him, even the one in the manager's office which most people didn't bother to use anyway.

'I'm not sure yet. This crowd are bound to have plenty of holdings and investments and collectibles. Let's see what comes up as the best option. Maybe it will be jewellery or art if we can get an invite to someone's house. Why not try something different for a change and mix it up? Let's keep our eyes and ears open.'

Natasha nodded and she swept up her clutch bag. That was his girl – always ready to get to work.

A few minutes later they walked into the lounge, with Natasha linking her arm in his. Harry took a deep breath. My god, it smelled of luxury – a clean, fresh aroma. One which you could only get from a lot of labour and the myriad of staff who serviced this place.

He knew ninety percent of the men would be looking Natasha's way and maybe the other ten percent were looking at him. First impressions were so important and it was their job to give everyone a good eyeful of them being the devoted couple.

A waiter approached and they ordered drinks and Harry made sure everyone saw him captivated by his own wife. He didn't really have to act because he loved the way her hair fell across her shoulders and how her dress gave the illusion that with a flick of his hand it could fall. Even the way she held her cocktail glass was entrancing and made him imagine her delicate fingers caressing him. What a fortunate man he was.

He took small glances around the lounge and let his expert eye assess the prospects. There were a lot of elderly couples who were very likely up to their eyeballs in riches.

One of the couples snagged his attention because although the man was a usual type for his age, which meant he was self-important and bored, the woman was much more interesting because Harry could catch her haughty manner even from the other side of the room. Mentally, he gave them a tick because it wasn't always just about the money. As well as the winnings, playing with a proud woman and bringing her down was something which gave him a kick. He steered Natasha away from their direction. It never paid to appear too eager.

There were a few younger couples and it was child's play picking out the ones with inherited wealth because they blasted it out. There was no mistaking their air of smug entitlement. It came from being born with your hand in the honey pot. Although he and Natasha had worked hard on their sense of presence they could never completely mimic the superiority which came from family and land and investments passed from generation to generation, though he knew he and Natasha were good enough to fool most people. Amongst the younger ones, there was only one couple he would peg as being self-made business people. Harry knew he would avoid them. They looked far too sharp and perceptive.

He had to stop himself from appearing too hyped. He could feel a buzzing in his chest and it didn't come from the slurps he had taken from his margherita, no, it came from the excitement of sensing out his next victory. This was what he was good at. He had learned the tricks of the conman's trade from his uncle, who had excelled at the craft. The assessment of clients was the most important step and rubbing shoulders with his potential victims made life worth living and the taking all the more worthwhile.

When one of the younger women caught his eye, he returned her hungry gaze. She was a redhead and she was after a quick adventure, that's what her eyes told him. With one glance he returned the invitation and let her know he was up for it. He always had a thing for redheads. How much was she worth? How much was the man she was with worth? How much of their money was liquid assets which Harry could get his hands on? What priceless item might be tucked away in their family home? Or their safe?

Getting close to people and coming away with a chunk of their wealth was what kept him and Natasha living in luxury. He had learned from the best and now Harry considered himself to *be* the best.

Natasha gave him an adoring look as she sipped her cocktail. Women were his greatest weakness, he had to admit, and his uncle had always warned him that if anyone could bring him down it would be a woman. Though Harry listened to every word his uncle said, Harry considered himself too smart for that little piece of advice.

He put one hand in his pocket and aped the casual-rich attitude he had studied, for instance the attitude of an Eton graduate he had met several years earlier and befriended, then yachted part-way around the world with before stealing a chunk of the man's inheritance. That one had been fun. The yachting and the party nights and the wriggling himself into the man's confidence. He could not say he had been sorry to steal from the guy because he wasn't, though neither had it been vindictive. It was simply the way Harry made money.

Across the room, the redhead was giving him another lustful gaze. This time Harry licked his lips. He sighed. If he had time, he might indulge in a little adventure with her but only if it didn't interfere with his prime objective. Wasn't it nice to have options. *Harry, my man, how can life get any better than this?*

Chapter Five

Natasha

A few hours earlier, once the porter had brought up the bags and left their room, Natasha threw herself on the bed. She squealed. The covers were so soft and they had a wonderful scent. There were rose petals scattered across the silky pillows and she scooped them up and crushed them to her face.

'Oh, these are gorgeous. And did you see the free chocolates on the table?'

Harry gave her an amused look. 'Uh huh. You know I can buy you however many flowers and chocolates you want from anywhere in the world, don't you. And have them delivered by midnight.'

'I know *but it's not the same.*'

She opened the chocolates and let one melt in her mouth. Harry was used to her delight each time they checked into a top-class establishment. Behind closed doors, he didn't mind. In public it was a different matter.

'I'm going for a look around,' she said. 'Do you want to come?'

'Not really and please remember to act the part, not rush around wide-eyed.'

'You know I wouldn't.'

She pouted. It was annoying having him reprimand her out loud. How dare he. He should know better because she would never behave in any way that detracted from their cover. She was as much a professional as he was. She liked to do a tour to gather intel on their surroundings and she always tried to hide from Harry how, even after all these years of success, she still found it hard to feel like she belonged. Damn him.

Their room was on the first floor with a wonderful view over the grounds at the rear. The gardens were lovely and there was a raised decking area and pool, then lower down there were huge manicured lawns and lots of roses and flowering shrubs. To one side of the hotel, the glass panes of the conservatory reflected the sun and what looked like a giant palm was reaching for the skies. How tropical. That would be the first place she would visit.

There were no hotel bedrooms on the ground floor. There were twenty suites on the first floor, including theirs, and twenty on the second. Only the best of the best would be staying here this week.

Downstairs in the lobby, the hotel staff gave her nods and polite smiles and the manager came over to enquire if everything was to her satisfaction. Her stilettos made a pleasing sound on the tiles as she crossed the foyer. The wooden wall panelling echoed the original mansion style. She passed a drawing room, several guest lounges and then a library.

At the breakfast room, a couple were sitting in the sunshine. They were enjoying an afternoon tea and had a mouth-watering array of cakes laid out on their table. She made a mental note to invite Harry for tea one day, or if he didn't want to come, she might go on her own. Further down the corridor she spied a sign for the spa. She would explore that another time.

It didn't take her long to find the conservatory. It had been added to the house during the Victorian era under the direction of the then lord and owner who had been an avid explorer. She had read how he had wanted a place to store and show off his plant specimens from the new worlds.

When the door closed behind her, she was surrounded by luscious ferns. Water *drip-dripped* somewhere in the background and delicate green light filtered through leaves. How lovely. This was somewhere she could sit for hours.

She walked slowly, noting the benches tucked into nooks amongst the foliage. How special it must have been to be the lady of the manor with your own private bit of paradise.

She would have liked to sit and enjoy it, except Harry would not forgive her if they were late for dinner. Reluctantly, she left, and took the rear door which brought her out near to the pool area.

This was wonderful too. The water was a beautiful blue. It was surrounded by decking, loungers, sunshades and tropical plants in giant pots. A few guests lounged around the water. Oh yes, she could imagine Harry and her reclining in the sun, cool drinks by their side. If only she had time for a dip, though it could only be in the shallow end since she panicked whenever she was out of her depth. In fact, she had always been terrified by deep water.

She skirted the decking and made her way down some steps to the garden where she trod carefully across the lawn, her spikes sinking into the grass. Damn. She could not be sure Harry was not watching from their window above, otherwise she would have liked to take off her shoes and feel the grass under her feet. Of course that would be totally out of character for the person she was supposed to be – a cultured woman, upper class, sophisticated at every turn. She sighed and bent her face to a red rose, inhaling its sweet scent. *In another time and another place you'll go barefoot through the roses*, she promised herself.

Several hours later, Natasha was in her emerald green dress and heading into the lounge on Harry's arm. He was so dashing, everyone was looking at her as if she were a princess.

She scanned the guests. She knew better than most how beauty was only skin deep. All the manicures and spa treatments in the world couldn't change what sort of person you were inside. Were any of the people in the lounge living worthwhile lives? Was she? She gave herself a little shake. *Come on, Tasha, get focused. Stay on the ball.*

The women were all very elegant in their designer evening wear, and their expensive jewellery caught her eye. The men were more muted in their suits, though a number of them had abandoned jackets in favour of open-neck shirts, most likely a concession to the heat. Some people were lounging on the sumptuous sofas and others were chatting in small groups. She and Harry took their time before they started mingling. As usual she followed Harry's lead. He had a nose for the work and she knew he would want to take things slowly.

She liked the rustle of silk gowns and the muted conversations, interspersed with the *chink* of glasses. This was what money bought you and she would never tire of it. Everything had an air of ease as the waiting staff moved gently through the crowd, attentive to every need.

She sipped her cocktail. Pina colada was her absolute favourite and she liked to think it was both fun and classy. She still remembered the first one Harry had bought for her when she was a giddy teenager and he had been the charming prince who had saved her from a life of misery. That pina colada had had a pink umbrella and a red cherry on a stick and she had loved every drop of it. Their evening had been a whirl of thrills and she had loved Harry from their first kiss. If only their relationship could have stayed as sweet.

Although people appeared to either be bored or be engaging in polite conversation in a very English manner, there

23

was a lot of showing off going on. She could see plenty of strutting and jostling for position on the success and wealth map not just from the men but the women were at it too, flaunting their diamonds and gemstones. She fingered her own emerald necklace. It was a real beauty.

Observing the upper classes never ceased to fascinate her. She too was under scrutiny, even if it happened surreptitiously out of the corner of an eye or over the rim of a glass. It wasn't only what you wore, it was also how you wore it, and the dress, necklace and matching earrings were definitely a success.

Harry spent quite a bit of time flirting with a redhead from a distance and then he had moved on to an ash blonde. In the past, this would have made Natasha jealous but now all she felt was an odd detachment. Harry liked women and women loved Harry and somewhere deep inside she knew she was tired of this. Tired of who they had become.

By the time she finished her glass, Harry was in conversation with an elderly man with a goatee beard. Natasha had spent many years admiring the way Harry connected with people and made them feel at ease. Which story would he spin? Would it be the one about his business exploits and how he had more than once grown his own start-up and then sold it on for a fortune? Or the one where he had become an expert in offshore funds by investing his own family's wealth, and that he became so successful at it he now managed a portfolio for a couple of his select friends, though only because they had begged him to and because he had plenty of time on his hands and did it as a favour. Harry had a special way of drawing people close. The man with the beard, Samuel, was already being pulled in by Harry's charm.

When Harry finished speaking to Samuel, he drew Natasha aside. She felt a twinge of anxiety because she would put Samuel and his wife in their seventies and it reminded

Natasha of the last victims she and Harry had scammed out of a portion of their savings. *Please, not another elderly couple.*

'Do you want to see if we can sit with Samuel and his wife, Clarissa, at dinner?' she asked.

She knew Harry had sensed her hesitancy.

'Not so fast I haven't decided yet and remember, whoever I pick, we're only taking a small bite of the pie. They'll hardly notice and they certainly won't break a sweat about it.'

This had been true with the previous elderly couple they had conned. They had been massively rich with a huge private estate and forestry assets and farming land. She and Harry had only swindled them out of part of their wealth but the problem was Natasha had become attached to them. The four of them had spent several weeks together and she had not been able to stop herself having feelings because they had been so kind to her, especially the husband. A few months after she and Harry left, she heard the man had died. Natasha had been heartbroken.

'Don't start getting sentimental on me like last time,' Harry said. 'I promise you they will hardly notice the loss.'

Harry gripped her waist and dug his fingers in right on top of the last bruises, so Natasha nodded and smiled and blinked hard to stop herself from tearing up. She hoped Samuel and Clarissa turned out to be people she could despise and that way, she would be able to keep her distance. Professional detachment was what Harry called it and this time she must stop her heart from getting involved. It would not be good to risk Harry's displeasure again.

Next, Harry drew her towards a couple who looked as dull as they actually turned out to be. The woman was a lawyer and so was her husband and they had nothing interesting to say. Natasha wondered how people like that could possibly find enjoyment in life, dragging themselves through day after day of tedium, even if they were raking in the money.

It wasn't until later that Harry led her back to Samuel and Clarissa to start a real conversation. It turned out Samuel had been a merchant banker and Clarissa had inherited wealth from her parents. Clarissa was a proud woman. She had three strings of pearls and liked to toy with them as she spoke. Natasha could see why Clarissa had caught Harry's attention because he always liked to bring people down a little. It was one reason why Natasha and Harry had got away with it for so long, because haughty people never liked to admit they had been scammed. Rather than go to the police and be seen as naive, they preferred to stay silent. Harry had often told her how he wished he could be there when their victims found out. He wanted to see the expression on their faces, especially the proud ones.

She stopped herself from ordering a second cocktail. There would be wine at dinner and she wanted to keep a clear head and be ready to play her part with the conversation at the table. Samuel had already complimented her on the colour of her dress. It had not been a lecherous comment but rather a grandfatherly one and she was mentally steeling herself for the role of stand-in granddaughter.

'It's so secluded here,' Harry said. 'Tucked in behind the South Downs with all this lovely countryside around us. With the heat it's an ideal spot.'

'I've never known such a scorcher,' Samuel said. 'It must be due to global warming.'

Harry laughed. 'You're telling me and it's just the right moment to take it easy. My doctor should be happy, he's been trying to get me to slow down for years.'

'Your doctor?' Samuel said. 'At your age? What on earth for?'

Harry patted his chest. 'Stress can be a killer.'

Samuel and his wife exchanged a glance. Oh goodness, had Harry done it again? He had an uncanny ability to home in on people's vulnerabilities. It looked as if health was an issue for these two.

'And with my wife being a nurse,' Harry said. 'She makes sure I take regular time off.'

Natasha gave Harry an indulgent smile. 'With the hours you've been putting in, you bet I do.'

'I've always thought being a nurse is a very noble profession,' Clarissa said. 'And you can never quite tell can you when someone might be in need of medical help? It can happen out of the blue.'

Harry was nodding enthusiastically. 'Absolutely. Once we were on a flight to New York and a fellow two rows away collapsed. Natasha helped keep him alive until we could touch down.'

This was not true. Natasha had wanted to become a nurse although she had dropped out of the training part way through, and the airline story was a total lie, yet it rolled off Harry's tongue like second nature.

'Amazing,' Clarissa said. 'How nice it is to meet you. Perhaps you might care to join us for dinner? Unless of course you have other plans?'

When Harry did not reply, Natasha smiled politely at Clarissa. Harry's attention had been caught by another couple coming into the lounge. They were latecomers for the cocktails. The woman wore an off-the-shoulder dress. She had almond-shaped eyes and chestnut hair piled onto the top of her head. The man who accompanied her had a dark complexion and striking looks. When he spoke to a waitress, Natasha noticed the interaction seemed genuine and warm and the waitress smiled.

The corner of Harry's mouth gave the slightest of twitches. It surprised her because she knew it meant the new couple interested him. Strange. They didn't seem to have the right mix of wealth and allure to beat Samuel and Clarissa.

At that moment, the woman newcomer leant against her partner. Her partner put his arms around her as if to hold her up.

The man called out. 'Can someone please help? My wife needs assistance.'

'Natasha,' Harry said, 'I think this is your cue.'

She recognised the eager glint in Harry's eye. He took her arm to lead her across the room and as she leant against him, he whispered in her ear. 'Don't bungle it.'

So Harry was focusing on the new couple. Samuel and Clarissa had been dumped for much more interesting prey.

Chapter Six

Shannon

When Shannon walked into the cocktail lounge of Sussex Abbey, she felt so happy hand in hand with Jared. They had driven to the hotel after lunch and arrived in time for an afternoon siesta. All day it felt as if they were in their own bubble of joy.

And then, on her way into the lounge, her phone had buzzed. One glance at the screen and the bubble had burst. As she stuffed the phone back in her clutch bag, she felt a wave of panic. The colours of the room swam in front of her eyes and then she was on her knees. Jared's hands were around her as he stopped her falling face-first into the carpet.

'Can someone please help? My wife needs assistance.'

She closed her eyes. Oh God, no. First she had blocked the number. Then she had changed her phone. It wasn't possible.

A woman's voice sounded close by. 'I'm a nurse.'

'I think my wife is fainting,' Jared said. 'Please can you help her.'

'If she's feeling faint let her lie down, sir,' the woman said.

As he laid her gently on the floor, Shannon forced her eyelids open. Jared took her hand. 'Darling, what's wrong?'

Shannon could hear the tremble of fear in Jared's voice.

'She's pregnant,' Jared said.

'My name's Natasha and like I mentioned, I'm a nurse. I'm just going to check your pulse. Breathe nice and calmly. Can you tell me what you're feeling?'

'I suddenly felt dizzy and weak. Oh please, I don't want to lose the baby.'

'How many weeks are you?' Natasha asked.

Shannon didn't have the strength to answer and Natasha turned to Jared.

'Eleven,' he said.

Natasha leaned close. 'Have you had any bleeding? Perhaps earlier today?'

Shannon shook her head. Terror gripped her. What if the shock had been enough to cause a catastrophe?

'That would be a first indication,' Natasha said. 'And at this early stage there wouldn't be much the doctors could do. Keep breathing in nice and easy and out with a long breath. Could someone get me water, please?'

Cool water soon arrived and Natasha pushed a glass into Shannon's hands. 'Here, try to drink. When it's so hot it's super easy to get dehydrated.'

'But she's been drinking all day,' Jared said.

With trembling fingers, Shannon pushed back her hair and took a few sips.

'Please don't worry. I can stay with you until an ambulance arrives,' Natasha said. 'The paramedics will be able to check on you and your baby.'

Shannon could not help panicking and she was angry too. How dare *he* come back to haunt her, just when she had finally managed to forget about the nightmare.

'Jared!' She reached for his comforting hand.

'It's all right, darling, I'm here.'

They had been joined by the hotel manager. Staff had already ushered the other guests away and now the manager had his mobile phone to his ear. 'The ambulance is on its way, madam.'

'Thank you,' Jared said.

It seemed an age before the medics arrived and they were so kind. They took their time checking her over and reassuring her. There was no bleeding and her pulse was steady. When they told her the baby's heartbeat was strong it made her cry.

When she felt better, she blew her nose and her husband and a paramedic helped her to sit.

A while later, once the paramedics had packed away their equipment, and the hotel manager had assured her that he and his staff could be called on at any time of day or night, she started to feel a little silly. Natasha, the nurse, had stayed with them and a blond-haired man, who Shannon presumed was Natasha's partner, had waited in the background.

'Thank you for your help – you've been very kind,' Shannon said. 'I feel like an idiot.'

'Well don't,' Natasha said. 'I'm guessing this is your first pregnancy and it can be a bit overwhelming. Keeping hydrated is very important, though I'd advise you to check in with your doctor or midwife. We're here for the week and if you need anything you can always contact me. This is my husband, Harry, and we're staying in room ten.'

'Thank you,' Shannon said. 'We're on the same floor, in nineteen. We're here for the week too.'

Jared shook hands with Natasha and Harry. 'I'm Jared. Thank you again for your help.'

The man called Harry squinted his blue eyes. 'Wait a minute, you're not Jared Kavani, are you? Don't tell me, aren't you the king of the fitness clubs?'

'You must be thinking of my brother. He's the one who runs everything these days, I'm not involved in the family business anymore,' Jared said.

'Oh right,' Harry said. 'Great to meet you.'

Jared's hands were shaking as he picked up Shannon's clutch bag. 'My wife's given me quite a shock.'

'I'm so sorry,' Shannon said. 'And we've made you late for going in to dinner.'

'Please don't worry, I was happy to help out,' Natasha said.

'Tell you what, why don't we have dinner together,' Shannon said. 'It can be our treat. Go on, please say yes. It's the least we can do to thank you.'

There was a small silence and for a moment, she thought the other couple would refuse. Then Natasha grabbed Harry's arm and smiled. 'That's a nice idea, isn't it, darling?'

Harry spread his hands in a gesture of generous acceptance. 'If you say yes, then I do too, my dear.'

Shannon smiled. 'Great. It will be our way of showing our appreciation and we can have some fun. I mean, I'm feeling much better now and the three of you can drink even if I can't.'

'That sounds like an idea. Shall I lead the way?' Harry asked.

Shannon nodded. 'Yes, and it'll be lovely to get to know you both. Something tells me we're going to be good friends.'

Chapter Seven

Jared

On the way to the dining room, Jared hung back a little. He needed to catch his breath and settle his nerves. What he really wanted was a stiff drink because Shannon's sudden collapse had given him a scare. His first reaction had been terror at the thought of losing their child. They were heading for the twelve-week mark and the risk of any complications made him feel sick. With the air conditioning in the hotel, it couldn't have been the heat. And Shannon had been drinking steadily all day.

Shannon was back to her usual self, chatting with Natasha. How could Shannon bounce back so quickly? Thank goodness Natasha had been there to help, otherwise he would have felt completely useless. Wiping his hand over his brow, he followed the others as a waiter led them to a table.

Chandeliers hung from the ceiling of the dining room and the décor was entirely cream and gold. It was pleasing to the eye and the epitome of understated English style, though a little insipid for his tastes. The only vibrant colours came from the women's dresses.

They passed an elderly couple who were already seated and it seemed to Jared as if they had been wondering if Harry and Natasha would be dining with them, because the woman smiled at Natasha and indicated the empty spaces at their table. So Natasha was already popular. She went close and whatever she said, the elderly couple seemed to accept her explanation or excuse.

Moments later, Jared was at a table set for four and he sat between his wife and Natasha.

'Their chef is meant to be one of the best,' Harry said.

Natasha flicked back her hair. 'I hope so. Do you think he might come out to meet the diners?'

'I hope he does,' Shannon said.

Jared's jaw was tense and he massaged it with his fingertips and tried to clear his throat enough to speak. There was a strong risk that nothing would come out of his mouth except nonsense right now.

'Are you doing okay?' Natasha asked him.

Jared nodded. 'Fine thanks. Just getting my breath back.'

She was certainly a captivating woman. A little younger than the three of them and sort of mysterious. She had been very reassuring in the lounge and now she was being kind to him. There was a vulnerability about her too which was very appealing.

He would have preferred to have a quiet evening with Shannon but his wife was right, these two deserved his appreciation. And why shouldn't they have a bit of fun. They needed it, and it was his job to contribute to the success of the evening, not sit there like a stuffed dummy lost in his own thoughts.

The two women were soon chatting as if they had known each other for ages. It was amazing how women could do that and he could see Shannon liked Natasha. He wanted his wife to enjoy herself. The baby was fine and there was no need for them to panic. Sure, he had thought of this as a romantic few days together but spending time with new people might be good for them. Perhaps they had been focusing inward for too long and Natasha and Harry were full of energy and positive vibes. They were like a breath of fresh air.

'So what brings you to Sussex Abbey?' Jared asked Harry.

'A mixture of stuff really. It's too hot to work and I've been flat out for what seems like ages and in need of a break. Then Natasha spied this place had come up and she booked it on the spot. We've had our eye on it for a while and never had the chance to come here. What about you guys?'

'Sort of similar. I was told Sussex Abbey was a chance not to be missed. I grabbed it. London was getting claustrophobic and a week away seemed like a great idea.'

'Doesn't it. I couldn't agree more,' Harry said.

The idle rich, Jared thought. *One day I'll be strong enough to break away from this kind of life. One day I'll earn enough to pay for our weekends away myself, of course not at places like this but at nice spots that Shannon will enjoy just as much.*

Harry continued. 'We were in Antibes a few weeks ago. I don't know if you're familiar with that stretch of the French Riviera? It's such a lovely location, all blue sea and wonderful restaurants and private beaches. I spent a couple of days enjoying myself on a jet ski while Natasha went shopping.'

Jared had been there once as a child. He hadn't liked it much. He recalled his father being treated badly by a hotel concierge. At the time, Jared and Raj had thought it was discrimination. Money didn't always buy you respect.

'That's not too far from Monaco, is it?' he said. 'My mother likes it there.'

'Don't talk to my wife about Monaco or she'll want to rush there as soon as possible, she loves Monte Carlo. She's a big fan of a Japanese garden we came across a few years ago. Apparently it was designed by some famous Japanese guy for Prince Ranier. I'm more of a casino man myself.'

'I like gardens too,' Jared said. 'I've not heard of that one.'

'Ooh you must go there and I love their Princess Grace rose garden too,' Natasha said.

Harry cleared his throat. 'I told you, don't get her started on flowers and gardens or she'll never stop.'

The Caribbean had been another of Harry's recent trips and Jared responded quietly to the other man's conversation. A lot of it was showing-off talk but that was how it was around people with money.

Then they moved on to politics. He felt his usual reluctance to open up to another man. Harry showed himself to be entertaining and charming. He was well informed about investments and business. His wife adored him and Shannon seemed to like him too. So why did Jared hold back? He knew he was being stupid. He and Harry were a similar age but it was because Jared had spent too many years living up to the successes of his older brother and that even now he found it difficult to step out of Raj's shadow.

From across the table Shannon was giving him encouraging smiles. She had always been supportive and very understanding of his struggles with his family and likely she guessed he was, as he usually was around men, being guarded with Harry. Damn Raj.

His family situation was complicated. Jared was torn – on one side there was loyalty to his parents and on the other was the burning need to make his own way in life.

The aim of becoming a businessman had been set out for him at birth. Maybe even before birth. When he had revealed his desire to be a writer, his father had exploded and his mother had cried for days.

Jared took charge of the wine order for the meal, matching his choices to each person's starter and main course. It was one of his areas of speciality. Harry knew a lot about wines as well and the two of them discussed the various merits of French versus Italian. Harry didn't spar with Jared for top-dog position nor try to outshine him, not like Jared's brother would have done. Harry even helped to choose a non-alcoholic wine for Shannon.

When they got talking about business, Harry was curious about Jared's family empire.

'I read somewhere Kavani Fitness has kept seventy percent of their clients over the last ten years. That's an accomplishment. Competitors usually take away a huge bite of market share but you've nailed customer loyalty. Bravo. I often see articles about your father and his success.'

'People like writing about my father because he's such a rags to riches story. He came to England as an impoverished immigrant,' Jared said.

'And now he owns a chain of luxury health clubs and I'd say that's an achievement worth celebrating.'

'Right from the beginning my father always handpicked his managers. He has a good eye for character and treated that small circle of people like members of his own family. He said they were the key to his success. They never let him down – they worked long hours and they built the business up from the ground, they never cut corners or tried to cheat on him. Most of them are still with the company. Now my father takes a back seat and it's my brother, Raj, who's in charge.'

'And I understand you've expanded the business into holiday centres on the continent?'

'You're very well informed. Yes, there was an unmet need in the overseas leisure market. People wanted to be able to take a luxury break in Europe and learn to do sports activities in the sun, you know like sailing or windsurfing. It's not so much fun learning in the UK where it's colder. Having a dependable name like Kavani running an overseas operation gives people confidence when they book. It's working very well. That was one of my brother's initiatives.'

'Good for him.'

When the waiter poured the wine, Harry was very complimentary about Jared's choices. The flattery helped and Jared felt his insecurities fading into the background. He only wished Harry would stop asking questions about Kavani Fitness.

'You sound as if you're an accomplished entrepreneur yourself,' Jared said. 'I'd be interested to hear more.'

Harry chatted about his successes. The man had a whole string of business achievements. He was a real entrepreneur. Jared listened with genuine interest, although it wasn't until they were halfway through a delicious main course when Jared got a surprise he definitely had not seen coming.

'Let's not talk work all evening,' Harry said. He took a slug from his glass. 'I hope you don't mind me telling you this but Natasha and I have been struggling a bit recently. That's really one of the reasons we decided to take time out.'

Shannon put down her fork. 'What's wrong? I hope it's nothing serious.'

Harry reached to take Natasha's hand. 'It's a bit odd telling you this since we're practically strangers but I feel so comfortable with you and I can tell my wife does too. Well, the thing is, we've been trying for a baby for a while and nothing has happened so... our big news is we've finally taken the decision to start fertility treatments.'

Harry's gaze was locked with Natasha's and Jared felt his heart melt for them.

'That's an amazing coincidence,' Shannon said, 'because Jared and I took the same path a while back.'

Natasha's hand flew to her mouth. 'Oh really!'

'I can only be honest with you. I've got to say we've been through a struggle.' Shannon rested her hand on her belly. 'And this little miracle is the end of that journey.'

'I can't believe it,' Harry said. 'Meeting you has got to be one amazing stroke of good luck. How did we get thrown together like this?'

'There's quite a bit to tell and it's not all good, but it is optimistic,' Shannon said. 'I hope we can get to know each other and share stories.'

Jared felt instantly ashamed. This man was nothing like his brother. Here was the proof of that. Infertility was taboo in Jared's family and Raj contributed to it by constantly mentioning how Jared had no children whereas he already had three after three years of marriage. Jared had felt forced to keep their fertility treatments secret and pretend to his mother that they were not trying for a child because they wanted to concentrate on their careers. It had been a horrible lie, and even worse that they had to keep it going for years.

'If you ask me we were meant to bump into each other tonight,' Shannon said. She clinked her glass with Natasha's.

When Harry turned to him, Jared swallowed hard to try to get rid of the lump in his throat.

'Whether it's chance or good fortune it doesn't matter. We're here together,' Jared said. 'You're not alone. Like Shannon said, we've been on a difficult journey and support on the way is really important. I hope we can help you. If there's anything we can do to make it easier for you, we'd be delighted.'

He had already made his decision about Harry – this man would be getting all the support Jared could give him.

Chapter Eight

Shannon

Before dinner with Jared and their new acquaintances, Shannon took a few moments to visit the ladies restroom. She needed time to herself in peace and quiet. She left the plush drawing room where the paramedics had cared for her. The room had been closing in on her and she felt she could not breathe properly. The curtains with the gold embroidery, the shiny black shoes of the men, the tasteful artwork, it had suddenly felt oppressive. When she had felt faint, Jared's eyes had been huge with fear and it was clear he had been dreading the worst. Poor Jared.

It was only once she was locked in a cubicle that she was able to put her head in her hands and sob. The anguish ebbed and her heart stopped thumping. Again, she confirmed for herself, one more time, and as she had done so many times, that she was not facing the loss of the baby, even though the medics had been certain about this. Obsessive checking was something she had been doing several times a day ever since the positive test.

She wanted this baby so badly. Without it, life would hardly be worth living. Being childless was what had kept her awake at night, the cold hand which squeezed her heart. Dread of it still hovered around her. She could not help feeling that losing this pregnancy would be her just desserts. Her payback.

She breathed deeply again and then realised it was making her cry harder.

'Are you okay in there?'

The voice came from just outside the cubicle. It made her jump. It sounded like Natasha. Shannon didn't know she had been followed.

She sat very still and stared straight ahead at the cubicle door. This was awkward and embarrassing. How long had Natasha been standing there? Had she heard the sobbing? *Please, please don't let me have whispered any of my thoughts out loud.* Shannon put her hand over her mouth to stifle any more sounds. 'I'm absolutely fine. Really.'

'Are you sure?'

'Yes. I just needed a few minutes to myself.'

There was a silence and no sound of the other woman moving away. Shannon bit her lip. 'Please don't wait for me, I'll see you at the table.'

'Okay, well I'll let you have some privacy.'

'Thanks, see you in a few minutes.'

Once the door of the restroom swished shut and she was alone, the tears flowed again. She wrapped her arms around her chest. *Calm down, you're okay. It's normal; you're hyper-stressed. Nothing bad is going to happen to you or to the baby and you've got nothing to worry about. You do not deserve a disaster.*

Thank goodness Natasha had been there to reassure Jared. What were the chances of such a kind person being on hand, and of her being a nurse too?

Shannon was cursing the fact she would have to redo her make-up when her phone buzzed with another text. Instantly she went hot and then a wave of fear washed over her. Sweat drenched her back. Putting her hand inside her clutch bag, she grabbed her mobile and squeezed the plastic hard. Would he never stop? How had he got her new number? Would she ever be free of the nightmare? A sudden anger flared. She flung her sodden clump of tissue at the floor and stabbed at the onscreen keyboard.

Leave me alone. If you contact me again I swear I'll go to the police.

When she joined the others at the dining table, Shannon whispered in Jared's ear and told him everything was fine. With her hair redone and her make-up repaired, she hoped she looked unruffled.

What she wouldn't give for a glass of wine. Or two. She enviously eyed the glasses clutched by the others but it was out of the question.

She took her place and willed herself to concentrate on being present. She held Jared's hand and felt his reassurance and his strength. Leaning close to him, she breathed in his musky cologne, a scent she loved so much.

After a while, she found herself captivated by Natasha's light sense of humour. Natasha was lively and interesting and the conversation at their table was fun and Shannon warmed to the other woman's friendship advances. And why not? A good laugh was what she needed to take her mind off things.

Although she had been exaggerating out of politeness when she said it would be nice to get to know them, she found herself naturally falling in with the idea. She had got into a rut and this new couple could help her break out of it. Why not have a few entertaining evenings together. It would be good for her and for Jared, and for their relationship.

Harry was great too. He struck her as a dependable guy and he had a natural authority and a confidence about him. Yes, it was going to be fun hanging out with these two.

The chef had done himself proud. Everyone's starters and main courses were not only mouth-watering but also a work of art on a plate.

'I've had gourmet dinners from any number of celebrity chefs and this is one of the best,' Harry said.

Though she was sure that she had been in far fewer high-class restaurants than Harry, Shannon joined in the praise.

It was not long after when Harry dropped the bombshell about fertility treatments. It seemed incredible that Harry and Natasha would be following the same journey she and Jared had taken and she couldn't help thinking it was such an amazing vote of trust for Harry to speak so openly.

She knew her emotions were all over the place. Part of her was still so raw it felt like it would never heal and she was not in a state of mind to make judgements about anyone or anything, but from that moment it felt like there was something special between them. They were no longer four people who were spending a convenient evening together, they had become much more. She could tell Jared was eager to put their new friends at ease and so was she.

After Harry's comments, Jared opened up, something difficult for him to do. He talked about his passion for writing. He told amusing anecdotes about people who had hired him to write their life stories. He never broke his clients' confidences and he was quick to assure them that the story snippets he told had already been published.

Natasha and Harry lapped up Jared's every word, especially Natasha, who was leaning across the table with her lips slightly parted. Shannon always liked to listen to Jared's stories because it reminded her how much he cared about his clients and how they cared about him too. In fact, Jared had a long list of ex-clients who were now friends and liked to keep in touch and enquire about his wellbeing. Jared was in full swing when she again felt her phone vibrating against her leg. Her back tensed so hard it hurt.

Each little pulse of her phone made her go colder.

Then her phone stopped. It took all her concentration to recover and she had just about managed to when it started vibrating again. This time she pushed back her chair. Perhaps a bit too abruptly because Jared's gaze flicked towards her. *Oh no, I've worried him again.*

'Excuse me and don't let me interrupt.' She blew a kiss in Jared's direction and smiled. 'I'll be back in a few minutes.'

This time she headed for the library. By the time she pushed open the door, the stress had given her tunnel vision. She had hoped that at this hour it would be empty and it was. The room had muted lighting and smelled faintly of the books which decked the shelves. Dark wood panelling and a dark carpet gave it the air of another era.

Unlike the decoration, the furniture was modern. She took a seat facing a window and hunched over her phone, scanning the last texts. They were all from the same person.

She dug her nails into her own palms and took a few deep breaths. Her finger trembled as she stabbed at the keyboard.

Stop contacting me, she texted.

I can't stop thinking about you, said the reply.

She was about to type again when Natasha's voice sounded right behind her. She yelped in surprise and almost dropped her phone. Looking up, she stared straight at Natasha's reflection in the window. What the hell? The woman was standing right behind her. How could that have happened? Surely no one could move so stealthily. Oh God, had Natasha been close enough to peer over her shoulder and see the screen? Natasha's footsteps must have been softened by the carpet though Shannon had no recall of hearing the door of the library opening or closing.

'I'm sorry, I didn't mean to startle you. I said, are you all right?'

Shannon had brought her phone close to her chest and now she closed the case with a snap. 'Goodness, I was completely lost in my thoughts. I didn't hear you coming in.'

Natasha pulled over a chair. 'I really like this room. It's almost like stepping back in time. And the little lights in the garden look so magical, don't they?'

She nodded. 'I needed a few quiet moments. It's peaceful in here.'

'That looks like an important message?'

'It's from my sister, Rosie. She's going through a divorce and things are pretty rough for her at the moment.'

'Ouch, that sounds nasty.'

'It is,' she said, as she put her phone away. 'Have you any brothers or sisters?'

'One brother though we don't see each other much. I guess we've drifted apart.'

'What a shame. Rosie and I are really close.'

'That's nice. I hope I'm not disturbing you. I just wanted to check you were okay.'

Natasha took a book and slowly leafed through it. Shannon toured the shelves, pretending to be interested and then she stared out at the garden.

A while later, she suggested they go back to the dining room. She kept trying to work out if Natasha might have seen the screen. Shannon's neck and face felt like they were burning. *It's okay. She doesn't know. She didn't see anything.* Despite telling herself it many times over, Shannon felt shame scorching into her.

How the hell had she got into this nightmare? And the most important question was, when would he give up and what if he never did?

Chapter Nine

Harry

Harry lounged on the bed, a glass in his hand. He sniffed the cognac and made an appreciative noise. It was top of the range. Who would ever have thought that someone with his background would end up paying a few hundred for a bottle and being waited on as if he were royalty? Sussex Abbey had a quality of service to die for which was something Harry valued very highly. Even better, fancy running into a Kavani. That family were loaded. He took out his phone and pulled up a search.

'Listen to this. Kavani senior has an estimated net worth of ten billion. He has two sons, our Jared and Raj who's a bit older, and the company has doubled in value in the last five years. This has got wow factor.'

'Sounds cool,' Natasha said.

'I knew this Sussex place was going to be a biggie. The nicer the venue, the better the pickings. Jared is out of his depth in the business world yet he can't quite take his hand out of the honey jar can he? For all his pretty talk of making his own way as a writer, he's still got his nose in Daddy's cash trough. There's no way in hell a ghostwriter can afford to come to a place like this, nor live in a damn posh house in west London.'

'You think he still has financial ties to his dad?'

'Of course he has. With the tab they're running up for this place and with a house in Barnes, it's obvious. Even better, someone as naïve as Jared is going to be easy.'

It had been a very promising first evening. Harry started unbuttoning his shirt then stopped halfway and beckoned over his wife. 'Why don't you do this for me?'

'Of course. Let me take off my earrings first.'

Her mouth was so luscious. He imagined it brushing over his body. 'Okay but be quick about it.'

She wasn't. She went into the bathroom where he watched her first brushing her hair and then meticulously wiping off her make-up.

The cognac was almost finished by the time she joined him.

'That was truly splendid how you guessed their weak spot,' he said as he grabbed her wrist and yanked her towards him. On their way to the dining room it was Natasha who had whispered to him the little hint about fertility treatment.

'Ouch, you're hurting me. I told you I thought they had either gone through a previous miscarriage or they had serious fertility issues,' Natasha said. 'Which I guessed from the husband's massive overreaction to the wife's dizzy spell. It was way out of proportion to what actually happened. He was very frightened. Did you see how the paramedic kept having to repeat that the baby was fine? The guy was practically keeling over with stress which meant this pregnancy is a huge thing for them.'

'Clever girl.'

She was unbuttoning his shirt and then moved onto his trousers. 'How did you know which reason to pick?'

'I didn't know so I took a punt on fertility. If it had been previous miscarriage instead then I'd have known from their reaction and I'd have pivoted. Opening up our own vulnerabilities by pretending we were going through the same shit as them was a gambit. I was pretty confident it would work with those two. Jared is a big softie and Shannon is overflowing with emotion, maybe not always but she definitely is at the moment. They make it so much easier for us by being wrapped up in each other and not paying any attention to protecting themselves. Besides, as far as I see it, Jared doesn't have a suspicious cell in his body and though Shannon might, she's too gaga over the baby.'

'I wondered what made you change your mind about Samuel and Clarissa.'

'I recognised Jared from an article I read online about the Kavanis, and I guessed he must be the younger brother given the older one has a sterling reputation. Our Jared hasn't got any strategic sense and you can tell it from his face, his posture, everything about him screams *gullible*.'

'And then there are those calls his wife is so touchy about.'

Harry raised an eyebrow. 'I'm glad that little lady has a juicy secret or two. It could come in very handy.'

'Shannon's a pretty good liar but she's not good enough to fool me. Probably good enough to fool her husband though. From her reaction in the restroom, there's no way in hell those texts were from her sister.'

'You're sure?'

'Of course I am. No one feels guilty about texting their own sister, do they? She scrambled to hide the screen. You should have seen her reaction – it was absolutely textbook panic and guilt and shame all rolled into one. I only wish I'd actually been able to read something.'

He pulled her close and unzipped her dress and the material gave a little ripping sound as he pushed it from her shoulders.

'Not so fast, Harry, please. And be careful with this damn dress. You know how much I love it.'

He ignored her. 'Right. So she's got a secret. Let's find out what and maybe it's something we can work with.'

He was on top of her pinning her down. He trusted Natasha. She could always tell stuff about people and the guess about the miscarriage or fertility treatment was a great example. And now they had the possibility of leverage on the wife if they could find out more about the messages. This was getting exciting. He was going to enjoy playing with the Kavanis.

Natasha wasn't resisting but she had turned her face away so he pulled her chin back around. Natasha had been acting a bit strangely recently. He didn't know if it was because she was bored or restless? Natasha was very low maintenance but could it be she needed something different than usual? Maybe a bit of pampering, or variety in what they were doing?

Or was it more than that? He thought about that idea as he dragged his mouth over her body. He was pretty certain it had all started with her asking to do the nursing training. That whole episode had been a huge mistake. The idea of her doing stuff without him gave him a nasty feeling of losing control. Yet since then, she had been, well, *strange.*

He hoped the excitement of this job would make things go back to the way they had been. That she would settle down and be content to be at his side, like before. Because that was where she was supposed to be and that was where she would be staying.

Natasha was lying very still, not resisting although not into it either. He would soon see about that. Those pouty lips were too much for him to resist and he pushed her shoulders into the bed and planted a rough kiss, mashing himself into her.

Chapter Ten

Shannon

Shannon tilted her face to catch the morning sun. The air was still and quiet and the only sounds came from Jared's arms as he swam lengths of the pool. Her lounger was under the shade of a huge umbrella and the waiter came to place a cool drink by her side. This was the life, lying here sipping smoothies. What better way to let her stresses melt away? Her phone was buried at the bottom of her bag. She had blocked *his* number again. Mercifully it had been quiet all morning and she prayed it stayed that way.

A short while later, Jared dripped across the decking towards her. She admired him as he towelled the drops from his hair.

'How's the water?' she asked.

'It's a perfect temperature and crystal clear.' Jared pulled his lounger closer to hers. 'Oh look, here come Natasha and Harry. Shall we ask them to join us?'

She shaded her eyes with her hand. 'Of course. Hey you two, pull over a couple of loungers and let's get you started on the cocktails.'

Harry laughed. 'I can't wait. Don't tell me you're ahead of us already, Jared? What's yours, a mojito?'

'We're on soft drinks but now you've arrived Jared can start on something stronger,' Shannon said. 'Thanks to your good influence.'

It was fun to chat about nothing in particular and to share jokes and anecdotes. Harry and Natasha were easy company and Harry told a very amusing story about how he had once lost a bet with a friend and ended up sailing across the Atlantic with said friend. Apparently, there was a dead zone in the middle of the ocean where no radio communication was possible.

Both Harry and his friend had trained in first aid and emergency procedures in case they got into trouble. Nothing major had happened although a lot of silly things had and Harry made it sound very entertaining. The worst part, he said, was the sea sickness at the beginning and then the acclimatisation to being on land once it was all over.

'You wouldn't believe how the body adapts to the motion of the waves. When you get back on dry land you're so disoriented you can fall over and smash your face because you've become accustomed to constant motion. It takes days to recover and be able to walk in a straight line. That's why around-the-world sailors are always interviewed on board their boats once they've crossed the finish line, because they can't stand upright otherwise.'

The drinks flowed freely and Shannon didn't bother to count how many her husband had. The more the better, she thought. They needed to let go and have a laugh.

'Are you coming to the wine tasting this evening?' Natasha asked. 'The wine is from a local vineyard and, as I understand it, they've got a great reputation.'

'That sounds interesting,' Jared said. 'Yes, I'd like to go.'

'I might usually come along but it's not at all my thing at the moment,' Shannon said. 'It's bad enough watching everyone enjoy the cocktails. But don't let me stop you, darling, if you'd like to.'

'Okay.'

Natasha smiled. 'When I talked to Harry about it earlier he wasn't too enthusiastic either, were you?'

Harry ran a hand through his hair. 'Not really but I know you were, so tell you what why don't you go with Jared and I'll sit this one out and keep Shannon company?'

'If you like,' Natasha said.

Harry took a sip from his glass. 'Actually, Samuel and a couple of the others were talking about playing a hand or two of cards later. We were thinking of blackjack or perhaps poker. If you don't fancy the wine tasting, Shannon, might cards be your thing?'

Shannon hesitated. Her parents had been avid bridge players and they often enjoyed cards evenings and, more recently, she used to play blackjack with Rosie and her ex-husband. Jared had disapproved of it, because Rosie's ex liked to play for money and Jared objected even if only small amounts were involved. She glanced at her husband to judge his reaction.

'I do quite like bridge and blackjack,' she said.

'Then why don't we go for blackjack,' Harry said. 'What do you think?'

A slight frown creased Jared's brow although he didn't say anything. Instead he put his hands behind his head and closed his eyes. The expression on his face reminded her of the many times on this pregnancy quest when she had gone too far and Jared had somehow, against the odds, managed to stay calm and navigate her emotions.

Like once when she had screamed in the supermarket at the sight of a woman scolding her child and another customer had called the security guard. Or the months when she had insisted they walk home the long way even when it was pouring with rain, because she could not bear to go past the school at the end of the road and see all the happy mothers picking up their children.

Then there were the dark times after failed implantation treatments when she stayed in bed refusing to eat. Jared had been sick with worry but his kindness had given her the strength to put a first spoonful to her mouth. Her poor husband. He had been through hell.

Shannon smiled at Harry. 'I don't think I feel like it today but maybe we can keep each other company? What do you say to a stroll around the grounds? I hear there's a famous statue somewhere over by the maze.'

Later that day, when Jared had gone with Natasha to the wine tasting, Shannon changed into a cool evening dress. She met Harry downstairs and he looked very attractive in his blue silk shirt and pale trousers. The air outside was still hot and full of the scent of roses and lavender.

'You're very elegant this evening,' he said, as he offered her his arm.

She laughed. 'Aren't you the one for the compliments.'

'There's no harm in it, is there. Though I hope you're not hinting Jared is the jealous type?'

'Not at all.'

'I didn't think so, otherwise I wouldn't have suggested we pair up. I got the impression he's a very generous man.'

'He is.'

'Was it his idea to come to Sussex Abbey?'

'Yes. He booked it as a surprise to celebrate our good news.' She laughed. 'He even managed to talk them into giving us room nineteen.'

'Let me guess, you got married on the nineteenth?'

'No, but it's my lucky number.'

Harry raised an eyebrow. 'Nice. Yeah, that fits in with my idea of your husband. He comes across as a man who goes over and above. Let them enjoy themselves at the wine tasting.'

'I thought wine was your thing too?'

'Not tonight. I wanted the chance to talk to you in private, you know, about the treatments ahead of us. It's pretty terrifying, and that's just the bloke's point of view so goodness knows how Natasha is feeling. She keeps it all under wraps. I was hoping you could give me an honest run-through, just so I know how I can help Natasha deal with it.'

It was so touching how Harry talked.

'It's tough and it can be long. Come on, why don't we find our way to the maze and we can discuss it as we go.'

'Please don't put a positive spin on it. I need you to be honest with me.'

She squeezed his arm. 'Okay, that's a deal and although it's hard for the man, I really think it's worse for us women.'

Harry seemed to be hanging on her every word as she described her long journey through a range of fertility treatments. It was amazing how she didn't tear up as she talked, especially when she got to finding out about the various results and the difficult and dark days after each failure. It was another reminder of how the pregnancy had changed everything. Yes, it was another reminder how everything changed *for the better*, she told herself sternly.

'From beginning to end, Jared was my absolute rock. Without his support every step of the way I would never have made it.'

'I don't know if I'm up to the job but I hope I am. I hope I'm going to be good enough for her. I want to be as solid as I can for Natasha.'

'I'm sure you'll do fine. You seem like a good listener and that's really important.'

'It must have been like all your dreams come true when you found out the good news.'

'Oh yes. It was so much more than I could ever have imagined. You see we'd been spat out at the end of the line for fertility treatments which meant we were on our own. Adoption was the only option left to us.'

Harry dabbed at his eyes. 'Now you've got me started.'

What a softie he was. Shannon put her arm around him. 'Our pregnancy was a one-in-a-million chance. The doctors had no explanation and all they said was perhaps us taking the pressure off might have done the trick. I've read stories about how giving up on trying somehow made it happen, but I always thought they were just that – stories. You need to know most couples manage to conceive with treatment. Jared and I were the exception.'

'That's amazing. I can't tell you how much I appreciate you sharing this with me.'

They had reached the entrance to the maze and in front of them stood the statue of an angel. It had been carved by someone famous and they both gazed at it as the evening light reflected off the angel's wings.

Except Shannon wasn't seeing the angel. She was remembering the moment when she rushed out of the bathroom with the pregnancy stick in her hand. There had been fleeting confusion on Jared's face. Followed by astonishment. Then joy. She had been waving the stick and then he had picked her up and twirled her around and that's when he had cried and so had she.

Although they did it for different reasons.

Chapter Eleven

Jared

Jared always enjoyed a good wine tasting and it was often a nice opportunity to buy for his home stock. Tonight, the hotel was hosting a Sussex vineyard owner.

'It's special when it's a family business and even nicer that they're local,' Jared said.

Natasha nodded. They were with a small group gathered in a function room. The vineyard owner had already given a presentation on the history of his estate, part of which dated from the early 1930s and had originally been owned by the father of the English country garden, William Robinson.

'I love to hear about heritage, don't you?' Jared said, as he swirled a sample of wine in his glass. 'And the aroma of this one is gorgeous.'

'Hmm,' Natasha said, as she tried a mouthful. 'I think I can taste the history in it.'

'Don't tease me. I like to know where people come from. Their stories, their backgrounds, and why they do what they do. I find it interesting.'

'I know, I'm only joking. I warn you I really don't like that weird practice they have of spitting out the wine once you've tasted it. I've never got the hang of it. I don't think I'm going to do that.'

'It stops the alcohol rushing to your head.'

'Then what's the fun in that?'

Jared laughed. Natasha was really quite charming and she seemed younger than she did when she was around Harry, which brought out Jared's protective side. His phone buzzed and he pulled it out of his pocket, glanced at the screen and then pushed it back out of sight.

'Ooh, that took the smile off your face,' Natasha said.

'It's my brother. He keeps trying to contact me, which is really annoying. I don't have anything to say to him.'

Natasha raised an eyebrow. 'Why not?'

'That's not a story I want to bore you with.'

'I won't be bored. I think you're an interesting person and besides, like you said, family stories say a lot about people.'

He liked her quick wit.

Their host had moved on to another vintage and was pouring everyone a new sample. Jared took a mouthful and swirled it around.

'This one is good, I think you'll like it. It's more fruity than the last one.'

She nudged his elbow. 'Go on, tell me what happened with your brother. I'm a good listener.'

They were on their fifth sample of wine and the noise level in the room had increased a lot. People were loosening up. Jared placed his hand lightly on Natasha's waist and led her to a seating area at the side.

'You'd better get comfortable. It's a long story.'

He toyed with his glass as he told her how his father had always been a bully. That he assumed Jared would follow the rules as he had laid them down – work hard, get good grades and succeed, go into the family business, get married. According to his dad there was only one track in life and that's the one he had expected Jared to take. Raj was his father's favourite because he always agreed with everything their father said. It was Raj who had joined the family business and stayed whereas Jared had left. The worst thing about it was that

Jared had confided in his brother how he wanted to become a writer. Behind Jared's back, Raj had told their dad.

It ended up with a huge argument. His father had mocked all of Jared's dreams. Since then, he and his dad rarely spoke.

It had also taken a huge effort on Jared's part to forgive his brother, though he had finally managed it a few years ago when Raj's first child was born.

'My dad is so proud. He can't admit any failure and he sees me as a massive disappointment. In his eyes, I'm the useless son who's doing nothing with his life. As far as he is concerned, there's no value in writing.'

'But there have been plenty of famous writers and poets and plenty of famous Indian ones too.'

'Of course there have, but he doesn't translate that to me writing people's life stories. To him, I'm a huge embarrassment because he always boasted to his friends about his sons. You know the worst thing is, I know he's just waiting for me to admit he's right. He honestly thinks that one day I'll realise writing is a waste and I'll come crawling back and join him. It's maddening. He's so proud.'

'Don't take this the wrong way but are you sure the pride thing is confined to his side?'

'Oh no, that's very perceptive and I've been caught out again. Of course it isn't. It's one of the things Shannon's always saying to me. Though I hate to admit it, both of you are right.'

Natasha patted his arm.

'It's not all bad. In my parents' defence they've been very supportive of my marriage and that wasn't a given. They both adore my wife.'

'But you're still not going to take that call from your brother.'

'And have him spoil my holiday by doing my father's dirty work and checking up on me, or worse, trying to lure me back?

That's always Raj's sub agenda. No way. I don't want anything ruining this special time with my wife.'

'A perfect holiday with outside worries kept at bay,' Natasha said. 'That sounds delightful and I'll drink to that.'

He could smell her perfume. Natasha had slightly slurred her words and she was sitting a little too close to him, probably due to the wine. He didn't mind. What a sweet person she was.

He clinked her glass with his.

Chapter Twelve

Harry

After his walk to the statue with Shannon, and Natasha's wine tasting, Harry was surprised when Jared said he and Shannon would like a romantic dinner together. How disappointing. He had already succeeded in breaking through their defences and he had been expecting to be able to worm his way closer tonight.

They sat in a different part of the dining area to the other couple. Yet Harry had been clever and waited for the others to be seated first, so he could select a table from which he would have a direct line of sight to them.

Natasha was seated opposite him, looking ravishing in a dark blue off-the-shoulder dress, which helped a little to take the edge off his bad mood. She was playing her part beautifully, with her hand draped across the table and her fingers entwined with his.

On the other side of the room, Shannon was laughing. It was as if the woman had a glow about her. Was that really due to hormones?

Harry wondered what the woman had looked like a few months ago. Had the desperation shown on Shannon's face? How much would the Kavanis have been willing to pay to jump to the top of the queue and be offered a new-born baby? A huge amount, he was sure. Jared would certainly pay a similar sum to prevent anything *unfortunate* happening to his pregnant wife.

The waiter placed starters on the table and Harry picked at his with a fork. From the expression of adoration on Jared's face, it seemed as if the man was besotted. Harry gritted his teeth. He found the special connection between Shannon and Jared irritating.

It irked him because the connection between him and Natasha used to be as strong as theirs, as magnetic, as real. In fact, it had been better because he and Natasha had been glued together not only by chemistry but also by the exhilaration they shared in their work.

Natasha used to adore him and hang on his every word. He had been able to mould her like putty and train her to be his perfect partner, in love as well as in crime. And then it started to change.

He slugged back some wine. It was after the failed nursing training that Natasha's attitude started going downhill. She used to be all over him but not anymore. There was something off between them and he didn't understand what because he knew he still excited her. Money definitely excited her and the thrill of what they did was as intoxicating for her as it always had been. There was no need for her to want to do anything else or to be with anyone else because he was her universe.

That damn training. It made him angry how it had disrupted their perfect relationship. How had that stupid idea ever got into her head? He thought he'd stopped her interacting with pretty much anyone. He should never have indulged her but he had believed that if he allowed her to do the training and then it was a failure, it would bind her more tightly to him.

He remembered how she had gone on and on about wanting to be a nurse until he got so angry he finally gave in. It was against his better judgement, though of course, he had a plan in mind. His fear of losing control of her was why he made sure her nursing placement went wrong.

It had taken effort to find a key member of staff with a weakness. Those damned health care workers were so committed and nauseatingly ethical, and Harry had been forced to dig deep. It was only by perseverance that he discovered the lead nurse, Nurse Golding, had a brother with bad habits –stuff like heavy drinking and borrowing money he couldn't pay back. It had got out of control. In the past, the brother had a couple of convictions for petty theft and Golding was worried he might return to crime. Too bad for her the brother was in debt up to his neck with a loan shark.

Harry targeted Nurse Golding mercilessly and she had resisted his manipulation with all her strength, turning down offers of very large sums of money. Then Harry had the brilliant idea of buying the brother's debt and paying extra for the loan shark to break the brother's legs. That had been the moment the nurse cracked because Harry had graciously stepped in and offered to save her brother from further injury, in return for a small favour, of course. He remembered how much the nurse had cried when he told her what he wanted her to do – it had all been rather annoying.

Since Golding was a senior member of staff, she had enough influence to make things difficult for Natasha. Natasha was given the most difficult patients to deal with, she had responsibilities which she could not possibly fulfil on her own and she was left floundering so she made mistakes.

For Natasha, it was catastrophic. In fact, he was surprised how long she persevered, given how hard it must have been. After weeks of failure, she gave up, which suited him fine.

Yet since then she had been, *strange*. Distant, and much less interested in sex too.

He had to make this the best they had ever pulled off – nerve-tingling, daring, audacious. He was convinced it would win her back. And if it didn't? If it didn't, well, it was best not to think about what he might be driven to.

Chapter Thirteen

Natasha

The next morning Natasha awoke early. She lay quietly for a few minutes listening to Harry's breathing. When she slid from the bed, Harry grunted and for a horrible moment she thought he might wake up and make a grab for her. She really didn't want to go through that again. She kept still, her hand clutching the sheet and with one leg over the side of the bed. A few minutes later she was rewarded by his gentle snoring.

With a sigh of relief she slipped from under the covers. Likely Harry would stay deeply asleep for a while because he loved his lie-ins. She got dressed, did up her running shoes and left quietly.

It was a glorious morning. The day before she had chatted with the receptionist so Natasha knew where she was heading. In the gardens the air was cool and full of the scent of lavender. As she made her way across the lawn, birds were singing and the sprinklers were busy. She hummed to herself and greeted one of the gardeners. Taking the path through the rose garden she bent to one flower after the other to inhale their sweet scent. One day she wanted to have her own garden and her own little place, modest and pretty somewhere in the countryside with beds of roses and a lawn dotted with daisies.

She walked quickly, swinging her arms to loosen up her shoulders. The mornings were her special time to be alone and to have her own thoughts and dream her own dreams. She felt tired of their lifestyle. The problem was Harry, because he wasn't ready to give up yet. He was addicted to the chase and to playing the game and winning. She sighed and tied her hair into a ponytail. She had seen the way Jared gazed at Shannon, how devoted he was to his wife and the way he cared about her. If only she could have the same.

There were only two things Harry allowed her to do without him – one was exercise and the other was beauty treatments. It was one reason her morning run, free from Harry, was so important to her.

Dew from the sprinklers speckled her shoes. Her plan was to head towards the river which cut across part of the hotel grounds. It was a few minutes run away and it would be a great place to be solitary.

She followed the path and it didn't take her long to arrive. The river was blue-green and much wider than she had expected. She shuddered at the idea it was probably very deep. Luckily the path was not near to the edge and she set off at a steady pace.

Her shoes beat out a nice rhythm. She should know better than to complain about her husband. When she'd first met Harry she had been couch surfing and surviving by eating other people's leftovers. She had been facing a life of struggle and then she met Harry and he had picked *her*. He had trained her. He had fed her. He taught her fancy manners and sleight of hand tricks and how to deceive and lie. He said she had a natural talent and with his training she could go far. Now, all these years later and thanks to her husband, she could slip into someone's confidence without them ever suspecting a thing.

It was because of Harry she wore silk dresses and expensive lingerie, ate in posh restaurants and enjoyed menus prepared by famous chefs. She had to admit the food was one of the best parts. She loved to be served a plate of perfectly prepared steak which melted in your mouth and with a sauce to knock your socks off and a little dusting of goodness-knows-what around the edge of the plate which made it look like it was fit for a star.

Harry said one day she would be able to employ her own chef except that wasn't what she wanted. What she wanted was her cottage with roses in the garden and a cat curled up by the fireplace. She wanted a log fire in the winter and birds outside her window. She hadn't spoken to Harry about any of it and certainly not about the idea of having children because he was dead against them but that's what she wanted too.

What had first given her doubts about Harry and the life they were leading? It had been sparked by a chance remark made by her beautician. One day, she had told Natasha it was the anniversary of her breaking away from a controlling boyfriend to start her own beauty business, and that she had never looked back.

That little remark stuck in Natasha's mind and it grew and blossomed into the idea that one day she too might have a life of her own, free from Harry.

A while afterwards, she made enquiries about training to be a nurse. Becoming a nurse was a secret dream she had nurtured since being a little girl. It wasn't until a long time later she spoke to Harry about the idea. She had anticipated his reaction pretty accurately which was why it had taken her so long to screw up the courage to ask.

'Are you out of your tiny mind?' he had said, pacing the room and shaking his head in bewilderment. 'Nursing? You mean wiping people's arses and emptying bowls of piss all day?'

'That isn't what it's about. It's looking after people. Caring for them.'

Harry guffawed. 'Rubbish. Don't I give you enough? Haven't we got the absolutely goddam perfect life!'

'Of course, I just...'

He had grabbed the designer top she was wearing and the seams ripped as he pulled it off her. 'What's this then? And all the stuff I get for you, just rags and shit you can throw away?'

'No Harry, I didn't mean it like that.'

Harry's anger had been terrifying and it had taken all her skills to calm him. Yet Harry had coached her well and she persisted, dripping hints into conversation here and there, hoping it would wear him down.

It had taken many tantrums from Harry before he finally gave in. Still, he didn't need to worry, did he? Because although he had unbelievably come home one day and stood in their living room and agreed to her signing up, she had dropped out after less than a year. Why? Because she discovered she hadn't got what it took to be a nurse. It had been the most crushing defeat of her whole life.

The river turned a corner and a duck flew startled from the reeds. She settled happily into her pace. Harry was right – nursing had been a foolish dream. Her exam marks had been average but her training placement could only be described as a nightmare. The manager she was placed with had been against her from day one. Everything she did had turned out wrong. She made mistakes which she hadn't even realised were mistakes. She had been berated in front of her colleagues. Told she had put people at risk. Patients had refused to have her in their room. She received such terrible remarks she often fled to the toilets to cry. Until she had finally given up. The shame and disappointment had almost broken her.

She ran for a good half an hour before she turned around and by then the day was starting to heat up and she slowed to a jog. It wasn't until she was back close to the bend in the river when she spotted a figure up ahead.

It was a man sitting on a bench and he was staring out over the water. He was pale and slightly dishevelled. Though he was dressed in an expensive-looking shirt and linen trousers, she didn't think he was a hotel guest.

Her anxiety spiked because for a moment she thought it might be someone from her past. From the days before Harry, she had plenty of unpaid debts and unreturned favours. She had a good natural instinct and sometimes she felt watched, for instance when she went to the gym or visited the spa. She always told herself it was her paranoia and that all the unsavoury characters she had once known were long gone and she would never, she hoped, see any of them again. It didn't stop her arms breaking out in goosebumps whenever she had the feeling of being stalked.

Today, she shivered in the sunshine.

There was no alternative path to take so as she got closer she sped up. The footpath went in front of the bench and as she drew level with the man's face, a glance told her it was a stranger.

The man watched her go past and her skin prickled and she dared not meet his eye. She didn't know whether to be pleased or not that he didn't say a word, not even a good morning. The man was a little older than her, unshaven and with his dark hair awry. He seemed to be on edge and she didn't at all like the vibe he had about him. The type to be unpredictable, she thought. Once she had passed the bench, she went as fast as she could all the way back to the hotel.

Chapter Fourteen

Natasha

Natasha didn't slow until she had gone through the rose garden and raced up the steps to the decking area around the pool. Why did she feel so spooked? It wasn't like her to get upset easily. Her legs were shaky and she made herself walk up and down to stop the cramps and then she did her stretching and cool down routine. In the city, she wouldn't have given a guy like that a second glance. Yet out here, in the middle of nowhere, his wired-up intensity had been unnerving.

A lone swimmer was churning out the lengths and the steady slap of his strokes helped calm her. It wasn't until the man got out of the pool that she realised it was Jared.

'Hey, have you been for a run? You're an early bird.'

'You too.'

She glanced down the steps and checked across the gardens again just to make sure she wasn't being followed.

Jared's gaze mimicked hers and he scanned the grounds too. 'Is everything okay? You seem a bit... unsettled.'

'Oh, it's nothing.'

He pushed his hair out of his face. 'Are you sure?'

'I'm fine. Really. I went for a run and there was this guy and I got spooked except there was no need. It's just he had a bit of a weird vibe about him.'

Jared frowned. 'What happened?'

'Nothing. I mean he was sitting minding his own business and I'm sure I'm letting my imagination get the better of me. He was probably just some ordinary bloke.'

She tried to laugh it off except she was pretty sure Jared wasn't convinced.

'I don't like the sound of it. I knew something had got you worried.'

'Please don't tell anyone and definitely not Harry because he'll only go berserk and march down there, he's so overprotective. Please?'

It wouldn't be the first time Harry had accosted a total random stranger, always men, for looking at her the wrong way.

'If you say so, though maybe it might be best if you take a running partner with you next time.' He shrugged. 'Like me for instance.' He flexed his muscles and struck a body-builder pose. He did it to make her laugh although she had to admit he looked pretty good.

'I might take you up on the offer. Meanwhile I need some fruit juice, do you fancy some too?'

'Sure.'

Jared laid his towel on a lounger and she pulled a second one alongside.

'Let me go to my room to get changed and I'll be down in a jiffy,' she said.

A few minutes later and she was in her swimsuit on her lounger. She took a quick dip in the shallow end and then they ordered cool drinks and a huge plate of exotic fruits to share.

'This is the life,' Jared said, as he put his hands behind his head. 'Sun, pool, good company.'

She felt a flick of pleasure and she smiled. 'And great mangoes and pineapple.'

'Yeah, and that.'

'Would you mind putting sun cream on my back?'

'Sure.'

She towelled herself off and delved into her bag to take out her sun cream and her book. His hands were strong and smooth and she liked the feel of them on her skin.

'It was fun last night, the wine tasting, wasn't it?' she said. 'It's always nice to meet kindred spirits.'

'I enjoyed it too and so did Shannon. Is Harry still in bed?'

'He was when I went out, but he was gone when I just went back up. I guess he's working or maybe at breakfast. He's a bit of a night owl and I'm the one who likes early mornings.'

As they settled onto their loungers, Jared closed his eyes and she had a good chance to study him. He had a sultry, very kissable mouth. He struck her more of an introvert than an extrovert and someone who had deep feelings.

'I liked the stories you told about your clients. I think they're very lucky to have found you.'

He smiled and opened one eye. 'You think? I hope so.'

They chatted for a while and Jared told her another client story about a man who had set up his own luxury skincare company and he now sold bespoke hand and face creams to celebrities.

'And he had always been single and then he met the love of his life when he was personally delivering a special order to Oprah Winfrey.'

'You're kidding me.'

'I'm not. He totally fell for one of Oprah's research assistants and they got married and they spent a year travelling around the United States.'

'I adore stories like that with plenty of romance and a happy ending. You know one thing I was wondering about was how you met your wife.'

'That's an easy one to answer although not at all as interesting. As it happens I wanted to get some artwork done for my business, and when I walked into the design agency there Shannon was, sitting at the front desk.'

'She was the receptionist?'

'She was, in fact, she runs the office and acts as personal assistant to the director, actually he really trusts her and he and I are now good friends. Shannon says I was the best thing to walk through their door ever. She calls me her lucky charm.'

Natasha giggled. Wouldn't it be so nice to be someone's lucky charm? Especially Jared's.

'What about you and Harry?'

'We met at my friend's wedding. I was a bridesmaid and Harry was best man.'

'Sounds like a film.'

'I know but honestly I'm not making it up.'

She laughed and he did too.

'I'm sure you're a very good nurse. I don't think I told you but you were very reassuring the night we arrived. You seem like a natural to me.'

She shrugged. 'That's a very kind thing to say.'

There was a silence and she listened to the *slap* of the water against the side of the pool. What a nice person he was. What would he think if he knew she had failed the training? That she had been completely hopeless. That Harry was using it as a ruse.

She put on her sunglasses and rearranged her towel. Harry had seemed like such a great thing but compared to Jared she could see all Harry's faults laid bare. She could hardly admit to herself how sour it had gone.

She thought Jared was about to close his eyes when he suddenly sat up straight. 'I've had some horrible news.'

It was so unexpected, she wasn't sure she heard him right. 'I'm sorry?'

'I apologise. I know we're here to have a nice time and I don't want to drag you down with my worries.'

'Wait, what do you mean?' She leaned closer and put her hand on his arm. 'You know I'm a good listener. What's happened?'

'It's not important. Please forget I said it.'

'I don't believe you. Talking things through can really help and I promise you can trust me.'

'I know.' He wiped his hands on his legs. 'The thing is, actually I'm feeling a bit overwhelmed at the moment what with the baby, and you know, other stuff going on.'

Natasha waited.

'I've had some news about my father. It came as a complete shock but I found out he's not well.'

'I'm sorry to hear that. What kind of not well?'

'We don't know yet and he's going in for tests. You know I told you my brother has been trying to get hold of me and I've been ignoring him thinking it was about the same old thing of putting pressure on me to come back? I feel like a complete idiot because it wasn't about that at all. My mother called a few hours ago and she told me my dad hasn't felt good on and off for a while.'

'Ah.'

'I wish I'd known sooner. It's my own stupid fault for not speaking to Raj.'

'It's not like you knew why he was phoning. Don't be hard on yourself.'

'Shannon was in the shower when I took the call and I didn't tell her. We always tell each other everything but the thing is she's already super stressed about the pregnancy and I didn't want to put more pressure on her. She's been very fragile recently.'

'You want to protect her, I get that. But it sounds like keeping things from her doesn't feel right to you either?'

'Not at all. Do you think I'm doing the right thing?'

'That's a difficult one to answer. You know your wife best.'

'My family can be a real hassle. My mum said she had to persuade Dad to go and see a doctor and I know it's a pride thing where he can't admit to any weaknesses. My dad's old school which means he has to be strong. Invincible. Like I told you, it's caused a lot of problems between us.'

'When I listen to you talking about him, do you know what's coming across? You love him. Despite it all.'

Jared tipped his head to the side. 'It's funny to hear you say that. Yeah, I guess I do, though I often get caught up on how overpowering he is. He says he built the business for me and Raj. Then me turning my back on it is like me turning my back on him. He just doesn't understand it's not my thing.'

'Families can be a pain in the butt.'

'You're telling me. And now I can't help worrying that it's something serious. It must be bad otherwise he'd never accept help.'

She squeezed his arm again. 'Best to wait to find out what the doctors say. You don't know what it is or isn't. Did you tell him you're thinking about him?'

'You see that's just the thing, I didn't. I'd never say that kind of thing to my dad. First of all because he'd try to use it to manipulate me back into the office and second because we don't do emotions. If I'm honest it's one other reason I haven't told Shannon because I know for sure she would want me to get in touch straightaway.'

It gave her tingles of excitement that Jared had confided in her. It was exactly what she wanted.

'You're right, you are a good listener,' he said.

'Thank you, and I don't know if you're asking for advice, but if you are, I'd say take it one step at a time. First, wait for the test results so you know what he's dealing with.'

'Right.'

'Then you can decide when to tell Shannon and how to do it.'

74

Jared nodded. 'Thanks. I know I'm not thinking straight. It's good to talk it through.'

'When will you know the results?'

'By the end of the day.'

'I'm here if you need me, anytime, and I really mean that.'

If she played this right, it would be a great opportunity to get even closer.

Chapter Fifteen

Harry

It amused Harry how Natasha assumed he spent his mornings in bed. Actually, he awoke early, usually before she did. Keeping the image of being a lazy slob was convenient because it gave him many hours to carry out whatever business he wanted to without Natasha knowing what he was up to. She was used to coming back from her trip to the beauty salon or her run and gym session and still finding him in bed.

As soon as she left the room he opened his eyes, stretched, and got out of bed naked.

Natasha had arranged her belongings neatly in the closet. Time for a little check-up. First he checked her case, running his fingers along the lining and examining the seams to see if she had concealed any items inside.

Then he moved to her neatly arranged clothes, checking the pockets, feeling for hidden papers or small objects – keys, a spare phone card or a second mobile.

What did he expect to find?

Harry sat on the edge of the bed. He rolled his neck and his shoulders to loosen them up.

Since he met Natasha he had the habit of going through her belongings. For him, it was a question of self-preservation because basically he didn't trust anyone and never had. It was a lesson he had learned from his uncle - *always protect yourself.*

He checked Natasha's belongings whenever he felt the need to be sure she wasn't hiding anything from him. The same went for following her – he did it when he wanted to be *certain* about her, when he had to convince himself that she was telling him the truth about where she went and who she went there with.

He routinely stalked her to the gym and the beauty salon and to the very occasional date she had for coffee. Natasha didn't have any friends as such. Well, she didn't need any did she? He was the only important person in her life and he made sure she had all she could ever dream of – dresses, expensive jewellery, luxury holidays. What else could a girl want?

The problem was that recently the urge to check up on her had been getting out of proportion. Instead of once or twice a month, he wanted to do it every few days and each time, he found nothing. Why couldn't he just drop it?

Turning on the shower, he stepped under the hot jets. Keeping tabs on Natasha was a habit he couldn't kick because although he tried to dismiss it, he always remembered the advice drilled into him and that was – the person you are stupid enough to trust is always the one who will betray you. *Give it up, my man, there's nothing going on with Natasha.* Towelling himself dry, he tried to push his misgivings to the back of his mind.

When he came downstairs, he took his time scouting out the ground floor – the coffee lounge, the breakfast room, the library and the drawing room. After, he moved on to the spa and the conservatory. A few guests were up and about. He spotted Jared by the pool and he avoided him, instead going out to the garden via the spa. The evening before, Natasha had spoken about her plan to take a morning run along the river and he found a spot where he could observe the path and still be hidden.

She usually ran for an hour and he didn't have to wait long before she appeared. She was going fast which surprised him since on the way home her usual habit was to slow down. She looked great in her tiny shorts.

He scooted along the other side of the hedge so he could keep her in his sights. In all the times he stalked her, and there had been many, she never had any idea he was there.

He watched her go up to their room, return to the pool, and then he spied on her conversation with Jared and saw how she leaned towards the man and how Jared didn't rush putting on Natasha's sun cream for her. After, it looked like the two of them were having a real heart-to-heart. It made Harry's jealousy flare. *She's only working him,* he told himself. *That's what you asked her to do.*

Should he go there and break off their cosy chat? No, that would be stupid. Besides, they had already decided Shannon was his target this morning and Jared was Natasha's.

Harry ordered a coffee and sat in the lobby area, selecting a comfy chair where he could get a good view.

When Shannon came downstairs and walked towards the breakfast room she was dressed in a sarong ready for the pool and was texting as she went. He had the sudden crazy idea of trying to see her screen, of getting so close to her when she didn't even know he was there that he could touch her hair if he wanted to, and then he would peer over her shoulder to see the words. The idea of it excited him.

He had done similar to people before, for instance, in a crowded metro, or on a busy street. There was an art to it which involved not being seen as suspicious by anyone nearby who might raise a warning. And not ruffling the feathers of the target, so their instincts didn't cause them to look up or check around. He could do it, he knew he could, though a quiet hotel lobby would be a challenge. *Go on my man, you can do it.*

It was the sort of contest he used to have with his uncle where they had the game of setting each other stupid bets.

Harry made his way across the floor, smiling at the receptionist as she glanced his way. Another guest crossed his path and he nodded good-naturedly. It was important not to rush.

Shannon was so preoccupied she didn't realise when he came close behind her. He matched his pace to hers and then they turned a corner and headed to the breakfast room. Anyone glancing their way would have thought they were a couple. He shifted right up to her and would have been able to see the phone screen easily if only her fingers had been in a slightly different position. She smiled to herself and then a moment later she snapped the case shut and swung around with surprise as she noticed him at her shoulder.

'Hi Shannon, you were really absorbed there with your phone.'

'Oh sorry, I didn't see you. I was just texting my sister.'

She was relaxed, which made him think she was telling the truth, or at least, that the caller was someone she didn't feel the need to be furtive about.

He gave her one of his best disarming smiles. 'I was about to head to the pool. I think Natasha is already out there.'

'Jared too. He wanted to get his lengths in before it got busy.'

'Well my wife won't be any competition. She's a poor swimmer. Can't usually coax her away from the shallow end, so she'll be soaking up the sun. Shall we join them?'

'I think I need to eat something first. I'm going to grab breakfast.'

'Why don't I come with you?'

Shannon was an attractive woman though not his type. She was too... what was it, homely? Cosy? Too in love with her husband? She was the sort of woman to want several children not just one. He could imagine her turning into a homemaker who enjoyed afternoons in the park with the other mums and organising kids' parties. It made him shiver with horror.

He picked at a croissant while she worked her way through a plate of scrambled eggs.

'You're not hungry?' she asked.

'Their coffee is great and that's good enough for me.'

'Oh don't. The aroma of freshly ground coffee is driving me mad. It's strictly no caffeine for me from now on.'

'I won't tell anyone if you don't.'

She laughed. 'Absolutely not. It doesn't work like that when you're planning for a little one.'

She really was too good to be true. He forced a smile, hoping she wouldn't go off on a baby-adoration spiel. When the coffee came he made appreciative sounds and sipped it noisily, and was disappointed when he didn't get a reaction.

She was halfway through her plate of eggs when her phone buzzed. He sensed Shannon stiffen.

'Is that my mobile or yours?' he asked, as he patted his pockets and then pulled his out to check.

'It's mine and don't worry about it, I'm sure it's my sister again.'

'It doesn't bother me if you take it.'

As Shannon bit her lip, Harry smiled to himself. She really should learn not to do that when she was stressed.

'I'll call later. Rosie's hyped up about her soon-to-be-ex-husband. They're meant to be signing papers to do with the divorce and she always seems to be in and out of the lawyer's office these days. It will be a relief when it's all over.'

Her knife slipped and clattered to the floor and Harry summoned a waiter to replace it. It seemed to him Shannon was lying. She was very pale and suddenly jittery. He was sure she didn't believe this caller was her sister. When Shannon took a drink of water and accidentally splashed it down her front and then carried on talking about Rosie, hardly pausing for breath between sentences, he was even more certain he was right.

'Her marriage was so perfect and her husband was an absolute darling.' Shannon dabbed at her top with a serviette. 'Until one day he seemed to change overnight and Rosie told me she was astonished because he went from doting partner to hostile opponent and she could not understand why. He would not explain. The reason could only be another woman. Though I just can't see it with him, then again, you never know do you?'

As she went back to buttering her toast, her knife hand was shaking.

Shannon's phone buzzed again. This time she looked so flustered he wondered if she might faint.

'Maybe that's your sister again?'

'It must be.'

'She seems pretty insistent. Perhaps you should check?'

'No, I don't think I will.'

'Are you feeling all right?'

'I must have eaten too much or too quickly or something. I'm fine. I'd like to find Jared.'

He watched carefully as she pushed away the rest of her breakfast. Her breathing was rapid and she was clutching at her sarong. He offered his arm and she held on to him as they left the breakfast room. Who was Shannon's mystery caller? They must make it their priority to find out.

Chapter Sixteen

Natasha

From behind her sunglasses, Natasha's eyes were on Jared. He had shunned the shade and was baking in the sun, a small smile playing on his lips. She wondered what he was thinking about. Wouldn't it be nice to have someone like him as a partner?

Natasha was reading a novel, or pretending to, and she flicked to the next page. Not so long ago, she would not have considered herself ready for a man like Jared but things were changing – s*he* was changing. She was ready to settle down and she could give him everything he wanted, she was sure of it. The question was, how could she make it happen.

A while later, she watched as Harry and Shannon headed out onto the pool terrace. Harry was right up close to her as they came around the pool and Natasha noticed how Shannon didn't pull away.

Jared arranged another couple of sun loungers for Shannon and Harry.

'Where is everyone? I thought we'd be fighting for space,' Shannon said.

Shannon lay back and sighed. Her hair was swept up onto the top of her head and she looked chic, with a few stray strands hanging down to frame her face and the woman had a glow about her. Probably it was the pure joy of finally facing motherhood which gave her that look. Natasha swallowed down the lump of jealousy.

'Is that a good book, Natasha? I really must get into reading again,' Shannon said.

'Oh yes, it's a smasher.' She showed the cover. 'It's a beach romance. Did you sleep well?'

Shannon nodded. 'Great thanks.'

'Like a log,' Harry said.

'I wasn't asking you,' Natasha said with a laugh.

Harry came over to give her a kiss. 'Once Natasha has her head in a book I might as well not exist so it's a good job you and Jared are here to keep me company. She's a sucker for tears and drama as long as there's a happy ending, aren't you, darling.'

He dragged his lounger closer to Shannon's before he sat down, and Natasha got back to her novel as Harry and Shannon started chatting about their favourite movies. It took a while for Jared to settle but he soon had his eyes closed again and Natasha dragged her attention away from him to observe Shannon. The woman appeared ready for a day in the sun. The pregnancy showed a little and she was wearing a stylish bikini. Natasha had to admit Shannon had voluptuous curves.

Over the next few hours Shannon and Harry chatted whilst Harry worked his way through a second cocktail. The day got hotter and more people came to the pool. Harry was being a flirt, putting on the charm, and Natasha wished she could enjoy the sound of his voice but instead it grated and gave her a kind of empty, dead feeling.

It wasn't until Harry had finished his third cocktail that they were all startled by the sound of Shannon's phone vibrating. Shannon delved into her bag.

'It's not Rosie again, is it?' Jared said. 'Doesn't she know we're on holiday?'

There was a tiny note of annoyance in his voice which was interesting because it was the first sign of any discord between them.

'I don't mind if my sister contacts me and anyway it isn't Rosie, it's Donald.' Shannon turned to Harry. 'Donald is my boss.'

Jared sighed. 'Even worse. He should know better than to pester you when you're on maternity leave.'

'Donald isn't pestering me. He probably just lost a file or something and I said he could contact me any time. You know what he's like. He's a creative genius but can't organise his way out of a paper bag.'

'Right. And there's nobody else in the office who can help him? I find that hard to believe,' Jared said.

'You know how a lot of the older clients prefer dealing with me.' Shannon sat up and wrapped herself in her sarong. 'I'd better give him a call.'

Jared grunted and closed his eyes again as Shannon headed towards the conservatory. Though Harry put his hands behind his head and lay back, Natasha knew he would be itching to find out more. She waited a few seconds before she took off her sunglasses.

'Oh no. I don't want to move into the shade and I think I left my sun hat in the room. Would you be a darling and get it for me please?' she asked.

'Of course.'

It was the perfect excuse. Harry seemed pleased with her quick thinking and he showed it to her with a flash of his eyes. Then he went off to spy on Shannon.

Chapter Seventeen

Jared

After his morning swim, Jared towelled his hair dry. He and Natasha pretty much had the terrace to themselves. It was relaxing how the water lapped against the side of the pool. She was easy company. The idea of someone spooking her on her morning run annoyed him. Next time he must be sure to go with her. It felt natural to confide in her about his father and she had a very soft and receptive way of listening.

When Shannon arrived she looked so radiant it was difficult for him to take his eyes off her. He had been reading about pregnancy and the development of babies and he knew movements could be felt around twenty weeks. He couldn't wait. They had already listened to the tiny heartbeat, which had been a magical moment. Of course, it was early days, though the twenty-week date was firmly chiselled in his brain. He wondered if her belly was beginning to round a little or was it his imagination because that would be a bit early.

Though it was the middle of the morning, Jared ordered a cocktail when the others did, knowing it would go straight to his head. And why not? He was there to relax.

When Harry headed off after Natasha's sun hat, Jared lay very still. He made himself stay calm and think it through logically. It wasn't in his nature to be wary yet why, straight after Shannon's call, had Natasha sent Harry to find her sun hat when it was in her pool bag along with her sun cream? He had caught sight of it earlier and she must have seen it too because she had half pulled it out when she got her sun cream and her book.

It was a puzzle. Had he been mistaken about seeing it? Had the drinks gone to all their heads and she had forgotten it was in there? That didn't seem plausible because he was sure Harry and Natasha were seasoned drinkers. What other possible explanation could there be? Surely there couldn't be something much more odd at play but Jared couldn't help having a suspicion Harry could be going after Shannon and that Natasha had helped Harry do just that.

Jared knew his instincts were telling him to be careful, otherwise he would have told Natasha outright the sun hat was in her bag. Something had made him keep his mouth shut and that something could only be his Kavani reflexes.

He had been brought up surrounded by his father's sharp business mentality. Though Jared had chosen not to live by the family rules, part of him trusted his Kavani instincts.

No, don't be silly, don't think like Raj and Father. You wanted a different life. Not all people are dishonest and devious. He willed himself to let it go. Harry was no threat, he was simply a fun guy who had a bit of a flirtatious way about him though not in a lecherous sense. Besides, Shannon wouldn't be interested in a man like Harry. More than that, why would Harry's gorgeous wife be sending him after another woman? It didn't make any sense.

Being unnerved by the pregnancy and his wife almost fainting on him didn't help. Poolside she had been acting a bit strangely too, sort of distant and she was being unusually silent about Rosie's texts and now Donald was messaging her. Surely Donald would be more sensitive than to bother her when she was on holiday? Jared could understand Shannon didn't want to disturb their new friends by taking a call at the pool but was it really necessary to go inside? Just for a quick chat about work?

Then again, he wasn't being totally open with Shannon himself, was he? Usually, they told each other everything except he knew that if Shannon was aware his father was sick she would want him to call and to visit him and Jared wasn't ready for that. Also, the less stress Shannon had the better.

When Shannon had felt faint the previous evening it happened right after she got a text message. Rosie really should stop being so selfish and Donald too. They should know the baby was the only thing which mattered and Shannon needed a break.

'Would you like another drink?' Natasha whispered.

'That sounds like an idea but I think I'll go for something lighter. If I carry on like this I won't make it through the day.'

'I didn't know if you were deep in thought or asleep.'

He stretched his arms over his head. 'A bit of both. It's so nice to just lie here.'

Natasha smiled at him. She was rather lovely in her blue and green swimming costume and he couldn't help wondering how had an innocent girl like her ended up with a man like Harry. And she clearly adored her husband. There was nothing suspicious here. Jared took a sip of his drink and told himself off for being paranoid.

Chapter Eighteen

Shannon

Peaceful and with the faint smell of damp earth, the leafy conservatory was the perfect place to sit and try to work out what the hell to do. Shannon found a bench half hidden underneath a giant fern. She took deep breaths although it didn't stop the panic which was crawling its way up her throat. Her thoughts ran in circles.

The bench creaked as she shifted her weight and anxious sweat made her sarong stick to her. How could this be possible? Would she never get rid of him? The man would not leave her alone and his texts were getting worse.

I've got to see you. I can't live without you.

How could he possibly think they could still have a friendship? After what had happened, he must be out of his mind. But that was the thing wasn't it – he *was* out of his mind but she was the only one to realise it.

When Jared got up for an early morning workout, she had wanted to tell him, to fall into his arms and let out all the anguish and the pain. My god, how could she have been so stupid? She had trusted someone she believed to be a friend and he had betrayed her in the worst possible way.

The longer she left it the worse it was. *Tell Jared, he'll understand.* But would he? Though the real problem was she could not forgive herself for being so naïve.

She swiped at her phone's screen.

His text the evening before had been shocking.

I love you.

He was crazy and no wonder the shock of reading those words had made the blood rush from her head. It was enough to make anyone pass out. Thank goodness Jared hadn't seen it. She must find the courage to tell Jared what had happened but first she must deal with the messages. They had to stop. Otherwise she would be the one losing her mind. The threat to go to the police had been an empty one. After all, it would be the word of a seven-figure-income London businessman, against a receptionist. And she knew first-hand just how convincing he could be.

The greenhouse was like a tropical garden. Water dripped from somewhere close by and she counted the drops as a way to try to keep calm. She must be firm and clear so he knew she meant it. But she must be careful too, because he seemed to be losing all grasp on reality.

That they had a history and had known each other for several years must surely help her.

Her palms were slippery and she had to wipe them several times. The texts were bad enough and the last thing she wanted to do was speak to him but she had to give it one chance. She screwed up her courage.

He answered after the first ring.

'I knew you wouldn't be able to stay away from me,' he said. 'You were so passionate, so all over me. I knew it meant something.'

She felt light-headed again and wanted to throw up. 'I told you to stop bothering me. I don't want to hear from you.'

She could hear him take a drag on a cigarette before speaking again. 'That's not what you said when we were together.'

Her stomach clenched. *Oh God.* 'I never said anything.'

'Are you telling me you're not ready to leave him? Have you told your husband yet, or should I?'

A rush of horror surged from somewhere in her belly to her throat. 'You were a friend and you took advantage of me!'

'And *you knew* I was in love with you. Is that why you threw yourself at me? I've loved you for years and you've always known it. Prancing and teasing me behind that desk of yours. I knew what you were up to.'

She felt like screaming. No, no, no. He was deranged. 'Leave me alone.'

'I can't and I won't.'

She hung up. Pulling her sarong tight around her, she hugged her chest close to her knees.

How could he be so unhinged. When on the outside he seemed stable. It wasn't possible. He was mad. He had tricked her. She had awoken half naked in his bed and not known how she got there. The last thing she recalled was drinking with him in a bar. Stupid, so stupid of her. Why had she ever taken him up on that invitation. Because she had reached an all-time low in their quest for a baby? Because he was nice to her and she didn't suspect anything bad would happen? She had trusted him and she had poured her heart out to him and he had tricked her. The man must have drugged her.

When she woke up the next day she felt as if she had been knocked into by a bus. Her head and her body ached. She was disoriented and she could not concentrate, nor remember anything from the night before. He was no longer there and she had let herself out of his house and somehow found her way home.

She should have gone to the police. She should have told her husband straight away. And said what? That she had willingly gone out for a drink with a man who was not her husband? That she couldn't remember what happened afterwards? That she had awoken in a strange bed? That she had no memory of what had passed between them?

He later told her they had sex, but she had no recall of it. If it had happened, it had been against her will, that she knew for definite.

When the screen pinged again with a message she cried out. How could she survive more? The shame of it had almost destroyed her. Would she never be free of it?

She clutched her arms around herself and bent in two. Closing her eyes, she prayed for oblivion.

Chapter Nineteen

Harry

There was something intoxicating about having the nerve and the guts to creep up on someone. It made Harry feel as if power pulsed through his body and out his fingertips. He crossed the terrace and followed Shannon into the conservatory, keeping a good distance behind her.

He had a plausible explanation and a smile at the ready just in case she turned around, though she was so preoccupied he was pretty certain she would not. This didn't look like a woman going to call her boss about work. As he carefully closed the door of the conservatory, he ducked and scanned in all directions, peering down the little pathways. Good, they had it to themselves, which would make his job much easier.

His footsteps were quiet on the stone flagging as step by step he advanced along the central path. A leafy frond brushed his face.

Shannon was headed for the far end, which was full of ferns and hanging vines. *Perfect*, he thought, as he padded closer.

The air was humid and perspiration tickled his brow. Shannon had taken a seat hidden by a bunch of greenery and he took a few moments to choose the best place to hear her but not to be seen. In the nervous state she was in, he gauged she could be unpredictable and rush out, either back to the pool or into the hotel, perhaps in tears. If this happened, it would be better she didn't see him.

He selected a hiding spot away from the main exit path and tucked himself out of sight. There was plenty of foliage to hide behind. *This is child's play. Come on, Shannon, let's find out what you don't want your husband to know.*

As he crouched low, his heart beat fast with excitement. He had a partial view of her and could see the side of her face as she raised her hand to her ear.

'I told you to stop bothering me. I don't want to hear from you,' she said.

Harry breathed quietly, waiting for more.

Her voice was unsteady. 'I never said anything.' Then pleading as the conversation continued. 'You were a friend and you took advantage of me. You knew how desperate I was feeling.'

Bloody fantastic. This had *spurned lover who won't take no for an answer* written all over it.

'Leave me alone,' she said.

The pitch of her voice had gone frantic. Harry could hardly believe his luck.

At that moment, he heard the conservatory door. Peering from his hideout he spotted an elderly couple arm in arm as they headed his way. Time to make a speedy exit. He walked casually and slowly, keeping out of Shannon's eyeline and giving the couple a silent nod and a smile as he passed them by. Then he skipped through the door leading back to the hotel.

Yes, this is the damn jackpot. Harry almost felt like pissing himself. If he played this right, Shannon's secrets would give him enough ammunition to bleed Shannon and Jared Kavani dry.

Chapter Twenty

Jared

When Shannon came back to the pool, Jared knew there was something wrong. She was tugging at her sarong and pulling it around her and there was a strange look on her face. Her bag slipped from her hands, knocking the table and sending a glass over the side. Jared caught it just in time. His thoughts flew to Harry, who had not yet returned, and Jared severely regretted not going after Harry to find out what he might be up to.

'You don't look well. What's wrong?' Jared asked.

'Nothing.'

He frowned. 'Are you sure? You seem a bit... upset.'

She tied her hair up onto the top of her head though he couldn't help thinking she was doing it to avoid looking directly at him. 'No, I'm not, I'm fine.'

'Donald isn't putting pressure on you, is he?'

'You know he's not like that, what an odd thing to say.'

Jared put his hand on his wife's arm. 'Nothing weird happened, did it? I mean, everything really is all right?'

'What's got into you? Please don't imagine I'm going to be falling down all over the place. I'm fine. Nothing happened. The baby's fine. Just leave it, will you.'

'Right.'

He did not feel reassured. Something was off. Why didn't she want to tell him? If he was honest with himself, she had been odd for weeks, which was why he had thought Sussex

Abbey would be a good idea for them. Although he was used to Shannon's emotions and moods, it worried him. Then Harry came sauntering back carrying a floppy-brimmed hat.

What had taken the man so long? And how come he had returned a few moments after Shannon? *Stop it, stop it, there's nothing strange going on. And that hat, it's not like the one in Natasha's bag. She must have wanted a bigger one.*

'Thank you, darling,' Natasha said.

'How about another round of drinks?' Harry said, as he beckoned over the waiter.

More alcohol in the middle of the day? They were going to get plastered. Jared shot his wife another look except she was already busy with her sun cream.

'Yeah why not, we're on holiday aren't we?' Jared said. *And I need to calm down. If I carry on like this I'm going to be a nervous wreck by the time I'm a father.*

Though he tried to relax and he hoped the cocktails would help with that, he couldn't kick the feeling Shannon was not being straight with him. *Relax and enjoy the sun,* he told himself. *If there's anything to tell she'll tell you later.*

Shannon spent ages putting on sun cream and then she decided she was going in the pool. Surely the other way around would have made more sense, he thought, she really doesn't seem to be thinking straight. Though he didn't say anything.

Harry started talking about some boarding school friend of his whose great-great-grandfather had been a collector of orchids.

'The old guy was rewarded for his gifts to the Royal Gardens at Kew by a knighthood, can you imagine?' Harry said.

Jared nodded.

'Apparently he brought back over fifty different species of orchid, none of which were known at that time. Did you know the early explorers were so competitive they used to burn the rainforest to the ground around where they collected their samples, so no one could come along after them and get samples of the same plants?'

As Harry chatted on, Jared let his mind drift as he watched Shannon get into the pool. He must relax, wait for news of his father and not imagine the worst.

There were a few people taking it easy in the shallow area and Shannon headed for the deep end. Jared conjured images of him holding their baby. It had been so wonderful holding his brother's children soon after they were born – they had been so vulnerable, so precious. He wanted to look after the baby himself. He would stay at home and organise his writing around the baby's schedule which would mean Shannon would be free to go back to work when she was ready.

Yes, he would be a stay-at-home dad, what a fantastic idea. The thought made him smile. When the child was older, he would make sure to not impose his wishes and leave the way free for them to make their own choices. He would never put a stranglehold on his son or daughter.

He drifted off into his daydreams and was well installed imagining the future when he was jolted by a shout from Harry. Jared clutched at the arms of his lounger as Harry's lounger was shoved aside and crashed into the table. An older woman was shouting.

Someone was in trouble. Jared stood up. *Oh God.* His heart almost stopped when he recognised the hair and bikini colour of Shannon.

It was a nightmare in which his legs would not move fast enough. In which the distance between him and the water was impossibly far. Harry was a few steps ahead and he dived in and Jared followed. As he swum underwater, Shannon was up ahead flailing beneath the surface, her hair whipping around her face, bubbles streaming from her mouth. She was going down. Each stroke brought him closer but it was as if he would never reach her.

Harry got there first. He took Shannon under the arms and kicked for the surface and Shannon was clutching onto Harry so desperately that she dragged him down. It was something which happened often with drowning people because they were so panicked they could not think straight. Jared took over from him and the two of them got her to the surface. Then they got her to the pool side and dragged her out. There were many willing hands as people came to help.

The pool guard arrived and he massaged her lungs. Shannon retched. Her chest was heaving and she had water in her lungs and stomach. It was far too many minutes before she spewed out water. Then she coughed and struggled for air.

'Where the hell were you?' Harry demanded, turning towards the guard. 'She was drowning.'

'Sorry sir, I went to get extra towels. I was only gone for a second. Guests swim at their own risk, there's a sign.'

The young man was being defensive and it was true there was a sign.

'It's all right, yes, we understand. You're not to blame,' Jared said.

He was on his knees next to his wife and as soon as he could he put his arms around her. Shannon was a strong swimmer and she had not been drinking so how could she have got into trouble? He buried his face on her shoulder.

'I can't believe it and it all happened so fast,' she said. She clutched at her leg. 'It was cramp. The pain was excruciating. My leg went into spasm and it went up my back and it was so severe I went under. Then I panicked and that's when I went under again and took another lungful. Thank you so much, Harry. I don't know why I lost my head like that. It's not like me.'

'It's okay. Nothing bad was going to happen to you with me and Jared around,' Harry said.

It was true, Harry had been the one to react the fastest and got to her first.

'I don't know how I can thank you,' Jared said.

'Don't be silly,' Harry said. 'You were off in la-la land and I happened to have my eyes open, that's all.'

Natasha came up and she put a towel around Shannon's shoulders. 'We'd better get you checked over, just as a precaution.'

Harry slapped Jared on the back. 'Don't worry, I'll call an ambulance. You stay close to your wife.'

Jared's arms were shaking. A cramp? His wife had lost it because of a cramp and then almost drowned? How could that be possible. What had got her into such a state? What was going on? He didn't say anything more because he could feel himself trembling and he didn't trust himself to be able to keep his voice steady let alone not burst into tears.

Chapter Twenty-one

Natasha

When Harry shouted and ran towards the water, Natasha's book slipped from her fingers.

One glance at the pool told her Shannon was in trouble. Harry and Jared were soon in the water and ploughing their way towards her. The other guests were crowding around the pool.

She heard Harry's voice in her head, *Seize the chance when it comes because it might never come again*. Quietly, she got to her feet. With everybody else drawn to the pool side, wouldn't this be an ideal opportunity to see what she could find on Shannon's phone?

Shannon's bag was by her lounger. Bending down, she slipped her hand inside, all the while keeping part of her attention on the pool. She could feel the slippery plastic of a tube of sun lotion, a cool bottle of water, a silky top and then, ah hah, right at the bottom was the oblong of a phone case.

She pulled it out and turned it on. It was locked by a pattern of dots. Too easy. By angling it slightly to the light she could make out a greasy finger trail on the screen and she copied the pathway. Bingo. She was in.

They had pulled Shannon to the poolside where she lay in a heap. *Hurry up, Tasha, get in and out before the drama is over.*

She scanned Shannon's texts. *I love you. I have to see you.* It certainly wasn't her sister and it was obvious the person was a lover. Was it Donald, Shannon's boss? She checked. No, there were other texts from Donald and these ones were from someone else. Over by the pool, the lifeguard was astride Shannon and making her vomit.

Who was this person? She clicked on the icon and a little picture flashed up. He was dark haired, wearing an open neck white shirt and a dark jacket. The look on his face was sultry but it was the nick in his eyebrow which grabbed her attention. There was no mistaking that little characteristic. Well, well, what a surprise.

Some time later, after everyone had calmed down and Shannon had been seen by the paramedics, Shannon went to take a nap in her room. Natasha went with her.

'Let me do that.' Natasha took the hotel key from her friend's hand and opened the door for her. 'You've had an unpleasant experience and the sooner we get you lying down the better.'

They had left their husbands at the pool. Though Jared had wanted to go with Shannon to the room, Shannon had refused.

'I'm not an invalid. You and Harry have a few more drinks and chill out. I'm only going to have a rest and I don't want you to spoil your fun for me.'

Natasha had been clever. She waited until Shannon had left the decking and then she had gone after her, telling Jared she would quickly check on Shannon to make sure she was fine. Jared had been hurt by his wife's brush-off and then grateful for Natasha's offer.

'I've never had a cramp before,' Shannon said. 'It was really weird.'

'You played it down a lot to your husband.'

'Of course I did because he's such a worrier and I could tell I'd freaked him out. Actually, it was pretty frightening. I've had small cramps before after exercise or something, though never anything like that.'

'Your body is behaving differently than you're used to – the other evening you were light-headed and now you had a cramp. It's not unusual with pregnancy to have a few unexpected reactions and I know I keep telling you that in this heat you've got to be sure to keep properly hydrated. A cramp could be a sign you weren't.'

'I thought I was.'

'Look, I'm probably being overcautious, but how about if I stay until you've had your shower? Just in case.'

Shannon shrugged. 'If you want, though I feel fine now. Here, try one of these chocolates. They're gorgeous.'

Shannon passed a box of handmade chocolates shaped like flowers.

'Oh wow, these look great. We had some left in our room courtesy of the hotel but these ones seem different.'

'They're from one of Jared's ex-clients. Help yourself,' Shannon said as she headed for the shower.

As the water ran in the bathroom, Natasha carried on the chat through the open door.

'These smell like liquid heaven. Ooh, and they taste absolutely wonderful.'

'Jared wrote the autobiography of the man who makes them and afterwards the two of them became friends. Jared picks up a huge box at Christmas and one for my birthday and the guy sent those as a gift when he heard our good news.'

'That's so lucky.'

'Isn't it. You wouldn't believe the gifts Jared gets from people.'

Natasha took another and she thought how nice it would be if Jared's friend gave her chocolates, instead of Shannon. Wouldn't it be wonderful to have Jared as *her* doting husband?

And for her to be carrying his baby and staying in gorgeous hotels as his beloved wife?

Once the water was running in the shower, she put down the goodies and in a couple of steps she was at the wardrobe and sliding it open. Shannon had brought several gorgeous dresses. Natasha held one up against her and checked her reflection in the mirror. It wasn't exactly her style although it was still nice and must have cost a fortune. She checked the shelves, recognising the brands and the labels. Harry was right, the Kavanis would never be able to afford this lot on their own earnings.

By the time Shannon came out of the bathroom, Natasha was lounging on the bed. It was satisfying snooping yet she had something much better to work with.

'Wow, I'm exhausted. I think I'll lie down and watch a bit of television,' Shannon said. 'I'm pretty sure I'll fall asleep and then I can be in shape for this evening.'

Natasha reached for another chocolate. 'It's the emotions which are sucking the energy out of you, as well as the shock. It will do you good to have a long siesta. These are so yummy I'm going to have to order some for myself.'

'Take the box. I'm trying to cut back on sweet stuff.'

Natasha went to speak but Shannon cut her off.

'No, I mean it, please have them. You and Harry have been so solid and such good friends. I don't know how we'd have coped without you.'

'That's really nice of you. You make such a lovely couple.'

'Thanks. You and Harry do too. He's definitely great company and so funny and entertaining, as well as being a life-saver.'

'I'm really lucky and he's super-protective of me too which is sweet, though sometimes it can get a bit much.'

Shannon pulled back the bed covers. 'That doesn't sound so bad.'

'Oh you don't know the half of it and I definitely shouldn't tell him I was freaked out on my morning run. There was some guy hanging around by the river. He was really weird and I got a strange vibe from him. If I told Harry stuff like that he'd ban me or he'd go down there and find the guy.'

'A man hanging around by the river? I really wish us women could feel safe going out on our own but that's simply not true, is it. That sounds scary.'

'It was a bit. Actually, your husband offered to run with me tomorrow.'

Shannon was plumping the pillows. 'Good idea. You can never tell when there's going to be a creep turn up and Jared loves his morning exercise routine.'

'Well, I'd better let you have a rest.'

She watched as Shannon lay back and adjusted the covers. Shannon would not be so calm if she knew the man at the river was the same person as the one sending her messages. The one with a nick in his eyebrow. And that very soon Natasha would be speaking to that person herself.

'Thanks, Natasha. See you later.'

Natasha smiled. All she needed to do was come up with a plan to give Shannon a little nudge and send her tumbling out of the nest.

She hugged the chocolates to her chest. 'Sweet dreams.'

Chapter Twenty-two

Shannon

Shannon felt like screaming. The telephone call kept going around and around her mind. She had never wanted to hear his voice again. Never wanted to see him again. Had wanted to push it all away as if the nightmare never happened. *Help me, somebody please help me.* A faint scent drifted across the room. It was very like her mother's favourite perfume. She knew that was impossible. But she breathed it in and imagined her mother by her side and it soothed her enough to take the edge off the anguish.

Though she had played the whole pool episode down when she spoke to Jared, it all came back to her now as she lay in bed staring at the ceiling. She could feel the suck of the water pulling her down. It was even worse that she panicked just because of a stupid cramp. That was what had made it dangerous. It was the state she was in after the phone call which caused it. At the time, it had felt like a panic attack.

She shivered beneath the sheets as she thought back to the day of the pregnancy test. She had been locked in the bathroom, holding her breath like she had done a zillion times before. Back at the beginning of their quest for a baby, she tested herself each month using a home kit. Then once they were taken into the fertility program, she had had to bear years of the nurse at the clinic breaking the bad news. It was always the moment she dreaded. Even though it also held all her hopes and dreams.

Then she and Jared had to leave the fertility treadmill. All treatments had failed and their only chance was to wait for their names to creep their way up the adoption list.

That morning when everything changed she had been grasping the little pregnancy stick in her sweating hand knowing there was no point. Knowing there was no chance. Except there was always a tiny flame of hope.

She had been doing her best to stay balanced. To prepare herself for another defeat. Believing a miracle could happen was always the worst part because when that hope was dashed she couldn't help crumbling. It didn't matter how hard she tried to put a brave face on it, the despair always dragged her down. But anyway, that day was the decisive day.

The first blue line had come into view and she had stared at it. Water was dripping from the shower and it was as if time stood still. She was about to check how many minutes had gone by so she could slam the stick into the bin when another faint impression had begun to appear in the viewing window. It had been hazy at first. Then little by little it materialised into a second solid line. She had screamed.

Jared hadn't knocked on the door. He had learned that a little bit of grace time was required before he could rush in to deal with her emotions.

She had plonked onto the tiles, and that's when a cold wave of horror washed over her. She counted the days on her fingers and then had to crawl as fast as she could to the toilet to throw up. She was so used to the impossibility of becoming pregnant that she would never have imagined being raped could result in conception.

She tossed under the sheets and wiped the sweat from her face. She wanted to convince herself she knew for sure but the truth was, she didn't know if Jared was the father. The doctors said nothing was biologically wrong with either of them yet they were incompatible. What did that leave her with – years of trying with her husband versus the word of a madman who swore that something had happened between them and that it had been consensual.

Had he raped her that night? It was a question she had never wanted to know the answer to. The next day she had felt sore from head to foot and she was woozy and ill. She had gone home and taken a shower and then curled up in her own bed and pretended it had never happened. Whatever drugs he had given her stayed in her system and kept her disoriented and confused. If she didn't remember it then it didn't happen, that's what she told herself. Yet her body knew and she had denied it and pushed it to the darkest corner of her mind. It had been the only way to survive.

No. Jared had to be the father. Please God it had to be him. She had to believe that this baby which was so wanted, was theirs.

The anguish threatened to swallow her again and she clenched at the sheets.

If she told Jared the truth about what had happened to her, would he trust her? Why had she left it so long? She knew the answer – because she didn't remember details. And she didn't want to and she never wanted to. It was all a blank and she wanted it to stay a blank. If those memories ever returned, it would break her.

Her breathing had got ragged again and she fought to get it under control.

If Jared knew, would he leave her? Would their marriage survive? Would parenthood be enough to keep them together? She didn't know.

Her priority must be to get rid of Aleksey. Then she could plan how and when to tell Jared. *It's too late. You should have told*

Jared before, said a tiny voice in her head. *Now he'll never believe you.*

A few hours later, she took another cool shower and then headed back down to find her husband. It was late afternoon and the hotel was quiet and she only realised she had taken a wrong turn when instead of ending up at the staircase for the lobby she found herself in another part of the hotel, in the wing she presumed was over the spa.

Oh no, come on, get your act together. She would have to retrace her steps. She was about to head back when she spotted Harry coming out of one of the rooms at the far end of the corridor. That was odd because Harry and Natasha were along the corridor from her and Jared. Then, a woman appeared behind Harry and she flung her arms around Harry's neck.

Shannon slunk into a doorway. She had seen the redhead a few times downstairs and the woman was trying to pull Harry back inside with her, kissing him and running her hands all over him and Harry was loving it. Shannon shrank as far as she could against the wall, desperately hoping he would not see her.

Oh shit, you just saw something you shouldn't have. Get out of here before it's too late. Step by careful step she tiptoed to the corner and then ran until she was through a set of swing doors. She found an elevator and took it down to the lobby. There was no mistaking what she had seen. Harry was a cheater.

Guilt stabbed at her again. *Stop it. Going out with a work colleague for a drink doesn't make you guilty.* So then what did waking up naked in that person's bed make her? A victim? That Aleksey had caught her at a low ebb wasn't an excuse. She had known Aleksey professionally for years because he was one of Donald's first clients. Now Aleksey owned a million-dollar business and yes, she had been out to lunch with him a few times but she did that with plenty of Donald's clients.

107

She'd had no idea Aleksey was besotted with her. She'd had no idea he would drug her and force her back to his house and then…

How could she ever forgive herself? If Jared ever heard about it from Aleksey, which was what Aleksey had threatened, it would destroy Jared, and them, forever. There was no way around it. She had to find the courage. She must be the one to tell her husband and she must do it soon before it was too late.

Chapter Twenty-three

Jared

After the shocking incident at the pool, Jared wanted to have another quiet evening with his wife and so he politely told Harry that they would again be dining alone. It was the big gala the following evening, when everyone would be enjoying dinner and entertainment, so they would have plenty of time to have more fun with their new friends.

'No worries,' Harry said. 'I quite fancy a romantic evening myself.'

'Did Natasha tell you I'll be going for a run with her tomorrow morning? I hope that's okay?'

Natasha had already set it up with Jared.

'She didn't but of course it's all right, why wouldn't it be?' Harry said. 'I know I can trust you to look after her.'

'Of course I will. You can count on me.'

Shannon was quiet throughout their dinner together. She didn't want to talk about the event at the pool and Jared filled the silences by talking about Harry's plans for a new technology start-up. Apparently, Harry already had put together a top team and he would soon present the final phase of his business plan to his investors.

'It's a new venture in hydrogen batteries and his team have a prototype and they're ready to refine it and then go into production once they've got enough sponsorship.'

Shannon toyed with a strand of her hair. 'He's got his fingers in all sorts of pies, hasn't he. Harry's a real entrepreneur.'

'I guess.' Jared took a sip of wine. He still had not heard any news about his father's examination. The appointment with the specialist had been early that afternoon and his mother had promised she would call to let him know the results. The waiting was unnerving.

'How about we skip dessert and have an early night?' Shannon suggested. She was chewing at her lip which was a sure sign there was something serious she wanted to talk about.

'Sure, I've been getting the impression there's something on your mind?'

'Let's go upstairs and I'll tell you.'

She seemed so serious. As they left the dining area, he slipped his arm around her waist and she leant against him. He liked the feeling and he pulled her closer. It was a relief she was going to confide in him at last. *You see? All you had to do was wait. And once she's told you, you'd better fill her in about your father.*

'Natasha mentioned she's invited you for a run tomorrow.'

'Yes,' he said, as he pressed the button to call the lift. 'There was some guy she didn't like the look of hanging around when she went out today. When she got back this morning she looked pretty spooked, so I offered to go with her.'

They stepped inside the lift and Shannon smiled up at him. 'Are you going to be her knight in shining armour?'

'Not exactly,' he said then kissed her on the forehead. 'Anyway, I think a man with a cut in his eyebrow merits not going on her own, don't you? Even though I'm sure he got it in a tussle with his hamster or something, not from being a gangster.' Jared brought his hand up and ran a finger across his eyebrow.

The lift tinged as it arrived and he stepped out and then realised Shannon had not followed him. He turned round and she was staring straight ahead, immobile. Reaching out, he stopped the lift doors from closing and then took her arms to gently tug her towards him.

'Hey, what's up?'

'Nothing… I was just thinking about something else.'

He pulled her close and her body was stiff. If he didn't know better, he'd have thought she'd just had the fright of her life. She had gone very pale and was it his imagination or could he feel her trembling? What the hell was going on?

In their room, the first thing Jared did was phone down to order fresh supplies. Was Shannon feeling unwell again?

'I've asked them to bring fruit juice and water,' he said.

His wife gave a strange kind of laugh. 'Listen, Jared, I'm not dehydrated. There's something I need to tell you.'

He was tugging off his shoes, and he flung them in the corner and came to sit beside her on the bed. His heart was beating fast. Was her mouth quivering? Please don't let it be the pregnancy. Had something happened? Had there been bleeding and she hadn't wanted to tell him? He tried to take her hand but she pushed him away and that made him scared.

'It's all right, darling,' he said. 'Whatever it is just tell me. If it's the baby… whatever it is… I promise it'll be okay. I'm right here.'

'The baby's fine.'

That made him shaky with relief.

Then two things happened at the same time. One was room service knocking at the door. The other was Jared's phone ringing. One glance at the screen told him it was his mother.

'It looks like it's your mum,' Shannon said. 'Hadn't you better take it?'

Shannon knew that his parents rarely called. She slid off the bed and went to the door, while he fumbled with his phone.

111

'I better but you were going to tell me something important,' he said.

'It can wait.'

The connection went through and as soon as he heard the shake in his mother's voice he knew it must be bad news. He clutched at his mobile while she explained his father's diagnosis and then, as she carefully told him the treatment options, his mother started sobbing. Jared did his best to comfort her.

Shannon was sitting beside him with her hands folded in her lap and when he finished the call, she passed him a tissue and he wiped at his eyes.

'It's Dad. I didn't want to bother you with it but he's not been feeling well. My mum talked to me about it this morning.'

'I wish you'd told me.'

'He saw a specialist today and they told him it's cancer.'

'Oh darling, I'm so sorry.'

Jared felt his wife's arms around him as he broke down.

Chapter Twenty-four

Shannon

Shannon lay in bed staring into the dark. Jared had long since fallen asleep. She had been about to tell him what had happened with Aleksey when her husband had been dealt a terrible blow and it had stopped her. Poor Jared. As if his relationship with his father wasn't awful enough without cancer coming to put a knife in his guts.

Yet it was what Jared had told her about the man by the river that made it impossible for Shannon. It could only be Aleksey. *It might not be him*, she told herself, *you don't know for sure*. Except the description was too telling, after all, how many men had a nick in their eyebrow?

She was drenched in sweat. How could it be possible? How had he found her? She hadn't told anyone where she was going. It was the same as with his texts – the bastard never gave up. Even though she tried to stop him. Even when she changed her phone, he was able to pry her number from someone at work. Would she never be free of him?

Her breathing was ragged and she clutched at the sheets. It was horrible enough him hounding her by text and so much worse to think of him pacing the riverbank, just a few minutes away. What if he got to her? What if he spoke to Jared?

Panic tried to drag her down, its tentacles clawing their way up her throat.

Jared had been too distraught by the news about his father to notice her reaction. It had hit him hard. Estranged from his father and both of them too proud to find a compromise, this must surely make Jared see sense and make proper contact? But Jared had refused to cut short their stay. He wanted to continue their special vacation and he had specifically told her he would not let Natasha down and he would be going running with her as planned.

Her best move would be to tell Jared she wanted to leave Sussex Abbey and if she was going to prevent Jared from seeing Aleksey it would mean they would have to leave that night. That would simply be too weird. It was one in the morning. Or could she pull it off? She could use the pool incident or the pregnancy as an excuse. Was she overreacting? No. She never wanted to see him again.

What about the morning run? Maybe Aleksey would not be there. Natasha had seen him but it didn't mean he would be there every morning and even if he were, there was no reason for the three of them to talk. Yet the thought of Jared and Aleksey close to each other was enough to make Shannon feel sick. Especially with Jared in such a vulnerable state.

Come on, think of a way out. Maybe she should alert security at the hotel. They must be used to protecting the privacy of their clients including, apparently, royalty and Hollywood stars, so why not show them a photograph of Aleksey? She could say she went for a walk and he tried to follow her. *No, no that's stupid you can't do that because Jared would find out.* Though Jared wasn't someone who provoked conflict she couldn't rule out him wanting to confront the man.

She *must* come up with an idea. They had to leave as soon as she could manage it. Meanwhile, she must prevent Jared from bumping into Aleksey on this damn morning run with Natasha.

A while later, Shannon slipped out of bed and got dressed. She had a plan. Natasha had told her Harry was a regular in the bar and liked to stay until the early hours, whereas Natasha preferred to be in bed by midnight.

It was surprising how many people were drinking downstairs. Harry was holding forth, grouped at a table with two men she did not recognise. Harry stood and pulled out a chair for her.

She swept her hair off her face. 'I couldn't sleep.'

'I can never get off early,' Harry said. 'I think it's because my brain won't stop working.'

The other two left politely, and Shannon had Harry to herself.

'Jared doing okay?' Harry asked.

'Actually no. He got some bad news. Family stuff.'

Harry raised an eyebrow though she decided not to play ball. It was for Jared to talk about his father if he wanted to, not her.

'It's complicated and listen, I hope I didn't interrupt your evening. You seemed engrossed in conversation with those two.'

'No worries. We were about to start a card game if you're interested, in fact they're becoming my regular buddies.'

Before Harry got restless and wanted to start his game, she had better come out with it. What would be the best tactic? Could she use the redhead and Harry's liaison as a lever? Might he react badly? Would it be better to try to appeal to his good nature?

The waiter brought her a drink and she sat staring at Harry, tapping her nails on her glass. Unlike most people, Harry seemed to have a great deal of patience. He was relaxed and he didn't pressure her into conversation. It was as if he was waiting for her to open up to him. Was he the sort of person who was used to people coming to him with secrets? Could she trust him?

'I'm wondering if you might be able to do me a favour.'

His blue eyes were quite piercing though they didn't give much away. 'If I can, of course I will.'

'Jared told me he's going for a run with Natasha in the morning and, well, I don't want him to.'

'Now you've got me intrigued. Why wouldn't you want your husband to go running with my wife?'

'To be honest it's a bit of a delicate situation and not at all what you might think.'

'Try me.'

'Jared's had some bad family news and it's made him very emotional.'

'Okay. So are you telling me he wants to pull out?'

'No, he doesn't want to do that because he doesn't want to disappoint Natasha.'

'But you think he should?'

'I'm not jealous or anything.' She leaned forward. 'The thing is there's a man who's been hanging around down by the river and that's why Jared wants to go with Natasha, to keep her safe.'

'And why exactly don't you want him to?'

'Because I know who that man is.'

Harry took his time thinking that over. 'I'm not sure what you're getting at. Can you be a bit more specific, I mean, why would I want Natasha to go on her own when she can have a bloody good bodyguard if Jared goes with her? I don't like getting up early so your husband is the ideal person.'

'That man is not here to make trouble for Natasha. He's here to make trouble for me.'

'What?' Harry stared at her. 'Let me get this straight, this guy is here to make trouble *for you*? About what?'

'I can't tell you but all I can say is he's dangerous.'

'I see. Dangerous.' Harry took his time mulling that over. 'And why would you want to stop Jared crossing his path? Do they know each other?'

'No and I want to keep it that way.'

'Ah.' Harry was nodding and she wondered what he was thinking so she spoke quickly.

'It's work. He's a client and he's not happy with the designs my boss put together. He's a high-profile person with plenty of connections and he wants to complain and make a stink other clients will get to hear about. I get on well with him and asked him not to take any action. In our business, reputation is everything. I asked him to speak one on one with Donald to try to sort it out first. Since then he's been bugging me.'

'You mean following you on vacation and loitering close by? That's a bit extreme isn't it? Are you sure this guy doesn't have a screw loose?'

'Well, that's what I mean when I say he could be dangerous. Jared has had bad news and I don't want our time here ruined by some creep who's got a grudge. I don't want Jared meeting this man. Period. Please, could you ask Natasha not to go?'

It sounded ludicrous even to her own ears and there was no way Harry would buy such a silly story, let alone help her out.

He sat back and regarded her, waving a hand to keep away one of his card-playing buddies who was asking him to join them.

'It looks like you're needed,' she said. 'Listen, forget I even asked. It was stupid of me.'

Harry put a hand on her arm. 'No, it wasn't. I like you, Shannon, and you and Jared are a really great couple. How about I persuade Natasha to give up on her morning run for the rest of our stay? Would that help you out?'

Were her ears playing tricks? What person in their right mind would have believed that ridiculous story she'd just trotted out? Certainly not Harry.

He gave her a smile which didn't reach his eyes. Had he always smiled that way, and she simply hadn't noticed?

Harry nodded. 'Like I said, I can sort that out for you, no problem. So don't you worry about it.'

'That's really kind.'

'Don't mention it and hey, since we're talking of favours, me and the guys are missing a fourth so how about you join us?'

What she would have preferred to do was go back upstairs and curl up in bed with Jared but that seemed ungrateful and ungracious. 'I suppose I could.'

He winked at her as he swept up their glasses and she couldn't help wondering if she had been really clever hoodwinking Harry, or if she had just been really stupid to put herself in his debt.

Chapter Twenty-five

Harry

By the time Harry got back to his room it was gone four in the morning. Shannon had ended up with quite a big win while he had lost money at the card table, yet he was in a good mood because it was all part of his strategy.

He shook Natasha. Though she took a while to blink the drowsiness from her eyes, she did her best to concentrate on what he was saying and didn't complain about him waking her up. What a good girl she was. He told her his plan, laying it out step by step.

At the end, she nodded. 'Okay, if you say so.'

'The first stage is I want you to work on this Aleksey guy. Get him to trust you and then I say we should get Shannon and Aleksey together. What do you say? What I want is some juicy evidence of the two of them having fun.'

'You think that's the best way forward?'

Harry ripped off his shirt. 'Aleksey is Shannon's lover, I'm sure of it, and she doesn't want Jared to find out. Once I've got concrete proof, I'll have the little minx right where I want her.'

Natasha blinked. 'I suppose.'

He could see she wasn't totally convinced by his idea, perhaps because it was going to be up to her to persuade Aleksey to cooperate. Though if those messages of Aleksey's were anything to go by, he sounded pretty desperate so it shouldn't be too hard.

'Meet him tomorrow and put the idea to him. See how he reacts,' Harry said.

'What if he's not there?'

'I'm betting he will be.'

'This is a huge leap. Why should he have confidence in me?'

'Everyone trusts you, darling. Just make something up and anyway, Aleksey will believe every word which comes out of your pretty little mouth. Talking of which, why don't you bring those luscious lips over here.'

He pulled her on top of him and gave her a long kiss. Though she squirmed, he knew she wanted it as much as he did though when he went to push off her lingerie, she twisted from his grip and scooted into the bathroom.

'Hey, don't be too long in there, I'm waiting. And don't sweat about Aleksey. You can handle him. Then we can move to the next stage with the Kavanis.'

Chapter Twenty-six

Natasha

Natasha tied her shoelaces and left the bedroom quietly. In the early hours, Harry had asked the hotel reception to inform Jared she had changed her mind and would not be going running. She had sent Jared a text also. She hoped he had received at least one of the messages and would not be annoyed with her.

She made sure to avoid the pool area in case Jared was having an early-morning swim. Or maybe he was working out in the gym. Either way, she intended to avoid him until later in the day and then make her excuses.

There was a slim chance he had decided to go for a run anyway and so what if he had? She was good at improvisation and if she saw him by the river she could make up a plausible explanation. It might even be useful for him to meet Aleksey, though Harry certainly wouldn't approve.

She passed a fountain, with drops lightly pattering from the mouths of dolphins down into a pool. Behind were the ornamental hedges clipped into the shape of animals. What an amusing thing to ask a gardener to do. She had read it was a tradition from Sussex Abbey's heyday when the lord and lady of the manor invited their guests for hunting weekends and entertained royalty with banquets. Perhaps having hedges snipped into the shape of foxes and birds tweaked their sense of humour.

Harry had been asleep when she left. He had been so selfish waking her up at four when he returned from the bar, and it was typical of him – demanding that she listen and then demanding sex. Still, there was no point in making an issue of it because Harry would only react badly.

She glanced behind a few times to make sure no one was following, then she headed out of the gardens and down to the river.

It was nice along the riverbank, though the run was not as pleasant as before because her mind was turning over how she might open up a conversation with Aleksey. When she passed the bench and it was empty, her stomach lurched. Harry would be furious if she didn't manage to speak to the man, even if it wasn't her fault.

She stopped and took a seat. Aleksey might turn up, though just because he was out early the other day didn't mean he would do the same every day. Damn it, the man was desperate to see Shannon. He seemed to have some kind of obsession with the woman and had tracked Shannon down, surely he would still be lurking close by?

Might he try to enter the hotel? Or the gardens? She didn't think so. There were cameras everywhere and security was tight. If he had made an attempt to get in then security guards would have intercepted him. Actually, the only fool-proof way would be through the front door as a guest. However, that would incur Shannon's rage. From the messages she read on Shannon's phone, it seemed to her he wanted Shannon to want him and to invite him herself.

He was unlikely to give up and go home, no, he would be holed up somewhere whilst longing and frustration frittered away his nerves. If he wasn't staying at the hotel then where might he be? Wouldn't a desperate Aleksey stay as close as possible to Shannon? Pulling out her phone she did a search. The nearest village was a few minutes away. Interestingly, there was a footpath leading from the village to the river and maybe that was why he had found his way to the bench. The internet told her the village had a pub called the Horse and Hounds and they did bed and breakfast so it was worth checking it out. She set off at a brisk pace.

The village was a few houses scattered along a main road and the pub was the only landmark. She always liked British pubs. Maybe one day when she had her cottage, she would have a friendly pub down the road where she could have lunch, with a landlord who knew her name and greeted her like a local.

The Horse and Hounds had flowering baskets hanging at the entrance and a blackboard propped on the pavement listing their menu. Since the door was closed, she presumed they would not be opening until lunchtime.

She wandered around to the back where she found a garden. Bingo. Her luck was in. There, sitting in the garden with his back to the sun, was Aleksey. *Well done, you.* She had been fortunate, though in reality she would have been prepared to drive around half of Sussex until she tracked him down.

He was drinking coffee and he was unshaven, like the day before. There was no one else in sight, though the back door to the pub was open. She walked softly to the edge of the lawn, took a few deep breaths then gave a quick cry of pain and grabbed at a railing. As Aleksey turned, she gave another gasp and doubled in two.

'Are you all right?' Aleksey said. He was already halfway across the grass, hurrying in her direction.

'Oh gosh, I've gone and pulled something, strained a muscle maybe.'

'Can I help? Do you need to sit down?'

'Please.' She made as if to perch on the bottom railing of the fence, which was very awkward.

'You can't sit there. Come to a chair. My name's Aleksey and here, why don't you lean on my shoulder.'

'That's so kind. I'm Natasha and I've got to say I feel like a complete idiot. I think I might have aggravated an old injury.'

'You sports people, you're your own worst enemy.'

He helped her slide through the railings and then hobble to the nearest table. His pale shirt was linen, which was classy, and he wore a very nice spicy cologne. Yet her sixth sense was giving her goosebumps. There was something about him which was simply *off*. Was it a creepy look at the back of his eyes? Or something hidden in the tone of his voice?

'Let's see if I can get the waitress to find us some ice or would a heat pack be better?'

She winced as she sat down. 'Ice would be fantastic, thank you so much.'

She had smelled alcohol on his breath, faint but unmistakable. He must have had a glass of spirits that morning. He had the same edgy feeling she had sensed at the riverside, though he was probably toning it down for her benefit. She wondered what exactly the liaison was between a man like this and Shannon.

It didn't take long for an ice pack to be organised and she soon had her foot up on a chair and was chatting to Aleksey about the time she had inflamed her Achilles tendon and had ended up having to take a week off work. He was very sympathetic and smiled good-naturedly at her story. He had a vague recollection of seeing her before and she told him she was staying at Sussex Abbey. That's when his interest in her started to pick up. Aleksey rubbed his hand over his chin, the stubble grating.

'Oh yes you were on a run yesterday, weren't you? I've seen the place. It looks very nice.'

Of course you've seen it. You've probably been watching.

'It is.' She smiled. 'And what are you doing around here, if you don't mind me asking? Are you on vacation?'

'Sort of, you know, taking a break from it all.'

There was definitely something slightly disturbing about the man. Who cared? She was here for a job and that was all that mattered.

He started talking about his work and it turned out Aleksey was an architect. He had a passion for it and he had grown from being a sole trader to running a top-end business which worked on most of the major developments in London and the south-east. She got the impression he was passionate about a lot of things.

'What about you?' he asked.

'I'm lying low for a while, actually I'm trying to get over my boyfriend or rather my ex-boyfriend breaking up with me and I'm failing miserably.'

'And another broken-hearted damsel falls by the wayside.'

'Yeah. It sucks. I'm not very good at being on my own and with all the couples swanning around at Sussex Abbey I'm wondering if it's really the right place for me. That probably sounds pathetic.'

'No it doesn't. Being alone is hard, especially if there's someone you want to be with. Believe me I know what I'm talking about.'

She adjusted the ice pack. 'Sorry to drag you down with my problems.'

'Don't think like that because you're not. You've got to stay strong. Things will turn around.'

'I'm not so sure. Most of my friends are married and the ones who aren't are in serious relationships. All I can do is have failure after failure though I'm certain you've got much better things to do than listen to me moaning on about my life.'

'Actually I haven't. Tell you what, why don't you join me for breakfast and afterwards I'll drop you back at your hotel?

Go on, it's a lovely morning and I was only going to be spending it alone.'

She tossed back her hair and gave it a good few seconds before accepting his offer with a smile.

They ordered a full English breakfast of bacon, sausages and eggs and had a nice time talking about nothing of any importance. He was a little younger than Shannon and she wondered how the two of them had met. With his rugged features and the intensity he had about him, she could see how Aleksey could win someone over, but what had he seen in Shannon? A married woman who was terribly in love with her husband and wanted to get pregnant? How well did he know Shannon? But then there was no logic or reason behind love nor obsession, was there? She knew that herself from her relationship with Harry.

Once breakfast was finished, she toyed with the idea of inviting Aleksey back for a drinks by the pool. While it would have been nice to see the fireworks when he walked in with her, she knew Harry's idea was the better one.

'That was a wonderful breakfast and you're right, it's no good letting it churn around and around in my head. He's gone and I've got to get over it.'

Aleksey wagged a finger at her. 'That's not exactly what I said, though I'm glad you're feeling a bit better. Shall I give you a lift?'

'Please but only on one condition.'

She leant on his shoulder as she stood up.

'And what's that?'

'There's a gala tonight at the hotel and I'd really like to go, except not on my own.' She flicked back her hair. 'I was wondering, if you haven't got plans maybe you might like to join me. I mean as a favour.'

Aleksey ran a hand over his stubble. 'I'd really like to help you. Only I don't know if that would be a good idea.'

Here she was offering him a way in on a plate which must be so tempting. How would he be able to resist?

'It will be a really nice evening with dancing and a band and a lovely dinner and I've got to tell you their chef is wonderful.'

'I'm sure. The thing is my own life is complicated enough at the moment. There's a woman I can't stop thinking about.'

'Oh?'

'She's playing hard to get but I know she feels the same way about me.'

'Then the gala can be a distraction until you get things sorted out. No strings, I absolutely promise and you'd be doing me a big favour. Please say yes and I really do mean as a friend. If you don't I'll just spend the whole evening in my room, watching some stupid movie and knowing I'm missing out.'

Aleksey stared into the distance.

'Please?' She waited, giving her ankle a little massage, until Aleksey looked at her.

'Oh all right, why not? I've got to admit I've been wanting to see the inside of that place.'

Yes I bet you have.

'That's wonderful. We're going to have a great time.'

Chapter Twenty-seven

Shannon

Shannon was worried about Jared. He had got out of bed late and then spent most of the day mooching around their room. He did a bit of work on his laptop but didn't have breakfast nor lunch.

Though he wanted her to think he was handling the news about his father well, she knew this was untrue. Jared was deeply upset. The situation was made even more complicated because her father-in-law was not answering Jared's calls. Each time Jared phoned he was either resting or not feeling well enough to talk.

Every time her husband put down the phone after speaking to his mother, he seemed more worried and even quieter. The obvious thing to do would be to leave Sussex Abbey and go and visit her father-in-law but Jared was not ready. He was adamant they should not cut their vacation short.

Shannon kept Jared company, sitting on the huge sofa in their room and staring out the window at the gardens of the hotel. All she could think about was how much she hated Aleksey.

As soon as Jared had made peace with his father, she promised herself she would tell him about Aleksey. She must find the courage to do it and put her faith in how much she loved Jared and how much she believed he loved her.

Chapter Twenty-eight

Natasha

Later, Natasha found Harry and Jared by the pool. Both were working their way through the cocktails, especially Harry who had several empty glasses by his side. He gave her a few direct looks and she knew he wanted her to give him a subtle indication about how it had gone with Aleksey. She gave nothing away, not even one little hint. She enjoyed making him wait. Jared told her Shannon was spending some time in the spa and Natasha decided to join her.

The spa had Nordic styling with grey slates all over and pine loungers. Everything was pristine with just the slightest scent of pine tinging the air. The indoor pool had beautiful blue-green tiles which made it look tropical. Dipping in a toe, she found the temperature pleasant.

Shannon was in the jacuzzi.

'I hope I'm not disturbing you,' Natasha said as she discarded her robe.

Shannon half opened her eyes. 'Goodness, I was day-dreaming and of course you're not. I've had the place to myself and it would be nice to have some company. Where have you been?'

'I did an early morning tour of the gardens and then I had coffee with Clarissa.'

'The older woman who always wears pearls? I haven't spoken to her or her husband.'

'I like her, she reminds me of someone I used to know and she's a bit worried about her husband. She told me he's got some health concerns and I hope I was able to put her worries to rest.'

'How nice to be able to comfort people. I think it suits you.'

'You do?' Natasha stepped into the jacuzzi and settled down opposite Shannon. Bubbles fizzed and burst around her. 'This is the life. I love spas.'

'Me too, though I'm sure if I stay in here too long Jared is going to come and check up on me.'

'Hmm, how long have you been in here?'

Shannon laughed. 'Only a few minutes.'

'As long as you don't overdo it you should be fine so don't worry about it. Harry told me you had a lucky streak at the cards last night. Seems like you cleared him and his new mates out of a few thousand.'

'I don't know how it happened, I mean I used to play with my sister and her husband although I was never that good, and don't start Jared on that one either because he hates it.'

Natasha took a drink from her bottle. 'He doesn't like you playing cards?'

'It's the whole gambling idea even if it's between friends. When I told him about my winnings he almost burst a blood vessel. When Rosie and her ex used to come to play at our house he would sit it out and fuss with the cooking and drinks instead of joining in even though we only did friendly games.'

'Really? I got the impression he was more open-minded than that.'

'Generally he is, though Jared just found out his father is ill so he's a bit sensitive at the moment. Anyway, let's talk about tonight's gala. Have you decided what you're going to wear?'

They moved from the jacuzzi to the shallow steps of the pool and spent the next hour or so chatting about their wardrobes and deciding for each other what might be the best choices. Natasha kept thinking about the nasty surprise Shannon had coming at the gala. The idea of it was exciting. Natasha smiled to herself. She could hardly wait.

Chapter Twenty-nine

Jared

Jared never liked wearing dinner jackets. He only agreed to put one on that night because Shannon had suckered him into it by telling him how handsome he looked in one.

He had not yet managed to speak to his father but his mother had promised that his father would call him back and that was supposed to be happening soon. Jared could not help thinking it was typical of the man to go for the power play and keep his son waiting. How could he possibly relax or enjoy himself until that conversation was over? He was only at the gala to please his wife. The last thing he wanted to do was spoil their special time away.

He ran a finger inside his collar to loosen it a bit. Shannon had gone to inspect the wonderful array of finger snacks. Harry was by his side and Jared wondered how Harry managed to look so comfortable and at ease.

'Don't these collars annoy you?' he asked.

'Not really and look at this lot – Britain's finest at leisure,' Harry said as they surveyed the ballroom.

True, it was an impressive sight if you liked flamboyant dresses, glittery jewellery and the flaunting of wealth like there was no tomorrow, none of which Jared particularly enjoyed and especially not that night because he had spent the afternoon talking to his brother, which had been stressful.

'Right,' he said, as he took a sip from his glass.

'You all right, Jared? You seem a bit on edge,' Harry said.

'It's this damn suit, I think it's getting tight or maybe it's too damn hot in here.'

Harry patted him on the shoulder and Jared resisted the urge to tell Harry that he did not appreciate him playing cards with Shannon.

Shannon returned carrying a full plate of canapes. 'These are so delicious you've got to try them.'

Harry helped himself. 'Don't mind if I do, thank you.'

'There's going to be a swing band and the waiter told me they're really good,' Shannon said. 'Has Natasha still not come down?'

Harry took another snack. 'I'm sure she'll be joining us soon. When I left she was putting on the final touches and was taking so long about it I got impatient. Actually, Jared, maybe this might be the right time to ask for your advice because I've got a financial presentation to make to my backers and I'd appreciate your input on a couple of points.'

'Sure, I'm a bit distracted so let's find a few quiet moments a little later. It'll be nice to get my brain working rather than being swamped by the usual rubbish chit-chat at these events.'

'Jared!' Shannon said.

He shrugged. 'You know it's true. I'm only here because you begged me to come.'

'Because I thought it might do us good to have a change of air and have a nice time with our new friends. Soon I'll be so big and round I'll probably waddle, so a dance before that happens will be nice.'

Harry gave him a wink. 'The things we do for the women we love.'

Harry seemed to be in a particularly buoyant mood. As if he had received some great news, perhaps about his new venture? And why shouldn't the man be happy? Just because

Jared was depressed didn't mean other people couldn't enjoy themselves.

As his wife dragged on his arm, Jared kissed her, downed half his champagne, and sighed.

Harry laughed. 'Here's to a good evening. Something tells me it's going to be a lot of fun.'

Chapter Thirty

Shannon

Shannon was on her second plate of canapes when she spotted Natasha over by the band. They had just started playing and it was difficult to see properly through the crowd of guests clustered around the stage. She was pleased to see Natasha had chosen a turquoise dress, which was a very good colour for her.

Shannon left Jared and was making her way across the room when Natasha leaned a little to the side to speak to someone standing right by her. Shannon stopped suddenly, causing a man behind to spill his drink as he avoided bumping into her. Her breath caught in her throat.

She peered through the people gathered around the stage. Who was Natasha talking to? *No, it couldn't be.* She could only see the back of the man's head yet the fear mounted, crawling its way up from her stomach. Was she hallucinating? *Calm down,* she told herself, *you're imagining things.*

A waitress came alongside and enquired if she was okay and that's when Shannon caught a clearer view of the man Natasha was talking to.

'Oh my god.' Her legs went weak and she wondered if she might collapse.

'I'm sorry, ma'am – is something wrong?' the waitress asked.

Shannon clutched at her throat. 'It can't be.'

The waitress was beckoning over one of her colleagues and Shannon quickly made her excuses. 'I'm fine. Really, I'm fine.'

She had to get out of there. She hurried as fast as she could back to Harry. 'Where's Jared gone?'

'I'm not sure. Maybe he's taking a phone call?'

She leant against the wall. There were black dots dancing in front of her eyes. Oh God, she had to escape, and she had to take Jared with her. How the hell could this be the moment Jared had managed to speak to his dad!

She wafted a hand in the direction of the band. 'Natasha's with some strange man. Do you know him?'

'Are you feeling all right? You look a bit…'

'I'm fine. Do you know him?'

Harry was giving her an odd look and no wonder because she was barely holding it together. 'I can't see too well from here, er, do you want me to find Jared for you?'

'No! Just tell me who Natasha's talking to.'

'Sorry I've no idea. If you like, shall we go and say hello and find out?'

She shook her head.

'Or I could go and ask him if you want.'

'It's the man from the river.' She blurted it out and then regretted it.

Harry ran a hand through his curls. 'I'm not sure what you're talking about, what man from the river?'

'You know – the one I told you about! The one I don't want to meet.'

'Ah okay, you mean the person you don't want your husband to bump in to because of some kind of weird thing going on at work?'

She nodded, searching around feverishly in case Jared was on his way back. From the look on Harry's face she was certain he didn't believe a word of her story.

'I think I get the problem. Well, there's no reason Jared will see this guy, I mean there are plenty of people here so I think you're probably safe.'

Harry must know there was more to this than she was telling him but she didn't care.

'Not if he's speaking to Natasha! What if he comes over here with her? He must have snuck in so he can get to me. Like I told you I'm in a very awkward situation and he absolutely must not talk to my husband.'

'I can see that might be a bit awkward. Don't worry, perhaps I can help.'

She clutched at his arm. 'How? Can you get rid of him?'

'I can do my best and if it's important to you he disappears then I'll make it my business to persuade him to do exactly that.' Harry put down his glass. 'You can rely on me. Let me see what I can do and please don't stress. I'm sure I can sort it out and Jared will never be any the wiser.'

While Harry was gone, Shannon felt the sweat trickling down her back. She clutched at her glass. The sensible thing to do would be to leave the ballroom, except she could not make herself do it because she had to be certain Harry got rid of Aleksey. Might it be better if she spoke to Aleksey herself and asked him to leave? No, not ask, *told him* to leave.

She dreaded Jared returning. Aleksey had to go. And what the hell was he doing talking to Natasha? How dare he sneak in here and get close to her friends. What if he was using them to get to her? What if he told them lies about her? But Harry was too clever for that and he would get rid of Aleksey, he had assured her he would.

Damn Aleksey. He had her backed into a corner with his lies, and the horrible things which came out of his mouth about what she had done with him, willingly, as he told it. She should have screamed at him it was rape. She should have gone to the police. If only she could go back in time and do everything differently. But it was too late for that.

When Harry came back, she was shaking so hard her drink trembled in the glass. Harry took it from her.

'Did you tell him to leave?' she hissed in his ear.

'I tried. He promised he would, although first he wants to speak to you privately.'

No! She shook her head so hard one of her earrings got caught in her hair.

'Your jewellery's got tangled up. Here, let me sort that out.' He reached out a gentle hand and teased the earring free. 'Listen, if you want him to leave, then as far as I can see it, speaking to him is the only way. I'll keep Jared busy while you meet him say, in five minutes time, in the garden. After that, if he doesn't play ball, I'll kick him out.'

Words failed her and her knees felt weak. 'This can't be happening.'

Harry put a comforting hand on her shoulder. 'I don't think it'll be as bad as you imagine.'

What? Speaking to the person who raped you when you were unconscious wasn't going to be bad? A man who was crazy enough to tell you he loved you? Who believed you felt the same way about him? That your boss and probably everyone else who knew him, believed to be a pillar of the community, respectful, successful and honest?

Harry gave her a little squeeze. 'He seemed quite reasonable to me and other than making a scene it's probably your best bet if you really want him to piss off.'

She gave the tiniest of nods. After all, what other choice did she have?

As she walked out of the doors and into the garden, it was as if her body did not belong to her but was some kind of puppet propelled by her own willpower. The sound of the band faded into the distance.

Aleksey was drunk. In fact, he was a wreck. He stood half propped against a low wall with his shirt awry. As she got closer, she could smell the stink of alcohol on his breath.

'How dare you come here.' She had meant her voice to come out strong except to her own ears it was more like a whisper.

He shrugged and then swayed. 'I couldn't stay away. I had to see you.'

'Don't you understand? I don't want to have anything to do with you! I don't want to see you. I don't want to speak to you.'

'That's not what you said to me before. You couldn't get enough of me.'

'Shut up! You're lying.'

'Just have a drink with me.'

He lurched forward to grab her but she side-stepped. 'You're drunk.'

'That's a lie. I had a couple to calm my nerves, what do you expect. Is your husband here?' Aleksey made a noise which was half a snort, half a laugh. 'Why didn't you tell me you were pregnant?'

Her blood went cold. How could he have found out?

'Donald told me you'd left, only he wouldn't tell me why, even though I kept pestering him. I'm happy for you I really am. I know how much you wanted it.'

Yes, she had asked Donald to keep the pregnancy secret from Aleksey, even though Aleksey was one of Donald's best clients and a friend. So how had he found out? Surely Natasha had not told him?

Aleksey raised his glass as if to make a toast. 'Why don't I go and talk to that nice husband of yours and ask him how many weeks ago it happened, do you think he'd appreciate it?'

'Don't you dare go anywhere near Jared. Like I said you're drunk and you need to leave.'

'Oh so you're making threats now, are you?'

It was difficult to judge his state of mind though she was certain there would be no reasoning with him. How could you reason with someone who was deranged?

'At least have a drink with me,' Aleksey said.

'Only if you go away and never come back.'

He stared at her and his champagne glass tipped and the contents dribbled onto the ground. 'You told me you loved me.'

'No! I never said that. You made it up. You drugged me and then you raped me.'

'I did not!'

There was a flash of anger in his eyes. Aleksey was a man of fire and drive, not the type to give up. How would she ever get rid of him?

She took a few deep breaths and sat next to him on the wall. She stared up at the stars and then reached for her glass which she had brought with her outside. 'One drink. And Jared stays out of this.'

'You're a beautiful woman, Shannon.'

She took her time putting the glass to her lips. Then she handed it to Aleksey and he took a sip.

She counted the seconds and it didn't take long. In fact, as she knew only too well, any tiny trace was enough to set him off.

Aleksey put one hand to his throat and then he dropped the glass and it shattered on the ground. 'Nuts,' he said.

She had been eating canapes all evening and her favourite ones had been covered in sesame seeds. Her saliva and lips would be tainted with it. With a nut allergy as bad as Aleksey's, the slightest trace would set him off. That was why, on any work lunch she arranged for him, there had to be no nuts.

She knew his mouth and throat would already be swelling because he had explained his allergy to her. His blood vessels would dilate, causing his blood pressure to plummet. His throat and airways would swell so catastrophically he would very quickly not be able to draw breath. Without a shot of epinephrine, he would be dead within minutes.

When Aleksey's hand went to his back pocket for his epi-pen, she lunged and grabbed it. There was a brief tussle which she won because his breathing was already laboured.

Holding the epi-pen ready to inject the life-saving drug, she stared straight into his face. 'You will go away and you will leave me alone. I never want to see you again.'

She grabbed his shoulders. His eyes were already wide and staring.

'Did you drug me?' she said.

Aleksey shook his head.

'You raped me! That night, you drugged me didn't you? Say it!'

'You... wanted... it.'

'No! You forced me! You gave me something to knock me out and you raped me!'

A sudden rage overtook her. Raising her arm, she flung the epi-pen into the night. Aleksey sank to his knees.

'Help... me.'

He was on the ground and she stared at him.

'How does it feel to be helpless? To be at someone's mercy!'

His body went into spasm and she leaned close.

'Say it! Say you raped me. Admit it.'

He was making gurgling noises and there was froth at the corners of his mouth. She suddenly realised how far she had gone. Falling on her hands and knees she searched for the small device which would save his life. Where had she thrown it?

Which direction? Onto the grass? Into the bushes? She couldn't remember.

In the pitch black her hands contacted small stones and grass and prickly leaves. It couldn't be far away. She crawled and scrambled in all directions sweeping and patting the ground while Aleksey made more horrible noises. What had she done!

A few seconds later, Shannon came to her senses. She would never find it in the dark. He did not deserve it but he needed an ambulance and fast.

Chapter Thirty-one

Harry

Harry had been standing in the garden watching and listening. He was in the shadows with his back to the doors into the hotel. Natasha stood silently by his side.

As Shannon rushed to get help, Harry intercepted her and took her by the shoulders.

'Call an ambulance,' Shannon said.

'Hey, calm down.'

'Call an ambulance!' Shannon screamed. 'He's dying.' She gestured over her shoulder into the dark and Harry could just about make out a form lying on the ground.

He knew exactly who it was and what had happened and he intended to play this to his advantage. 'Who's dying? What the hell's going on?'

'Allergies, the man out there has nut allergies and he needs help.'

'Right, I'm on it.'

Taking out his mobile phone, Harry jabbed at the screen.

'We need an ambulance at Sussex Abbey. There's been an accident, no not an accident, we think a man is having an allergic reaction and he's collapsed, uh-huh, uh-huh, yes, my name is Harry Forrester.'

When Harry hung up he turned to Shannon. 'They're on their way.'

'We've got to find his epi-pen. He, er, he lost it. He dropped it and we've got to find it.'

She was struggling not to panic and Harry put his arm around her to support her.

'Take it easy, Shannon, help is on the way,' he said. 'I think you'd better sit down. Natasha, go and see if you can help that poor guy.'

Harry led Shannon to a bench and as Natasha ran towards Aleksey he quickly shifted behind Shannon, picked up a rock from the ground and slammed it into the side of her head.

'Natasha! Help me out here, she's fainted,' he called.

'I need to help this man, he isn't going to last long,' Natasha called back.

'No, Shannon needs you. What about the baby?'

'Oh God.' Natasha came running back and she knelt to check Shannon over. 'She's breathing. She must have hit herself pretty hard when she passed out because there's blood but she'll be okay. We've got to find Aleksey's medication. He'll die without it.'

She tried to move back towards Aleksey but Harry took her arm and held her firmly. 'Let me handle this. We're going to get Shannon inside and I don't want anyone else coming out here. Do you understand?'

'Did you hear what I said? He's going to die without his epi-pen. The more people searching the more likely we'll find it. We need to get people to help.'

'No we don't. Because we're not going to search for his fucking medicine.'

Natasha tried to pull away. 'Let go of my arm.'

He gripped her more tightly. 'Listen to me and do exactly what I tell you. We're going to get Shannon inside and you're going to make sure nobody comes into the garden. Do you understand?'

'You're hurting me. What about Aleksey? He's going to asphyxiate.'

'Leave him to me.'

'He'll die if we don't help him!'

'And?'

Natasha stared at him. 'You don't mean that.'

The band had momentarily stopped playing and he could hear Natasha's rapid breathing. There was no defiance in her eyes, simply disbelief and horror. He waited a few moments for the truth to sink in. When he let go of her arm, she stood motionless.

'That's it, get yourself under control,' Harry said. 'It sounds like the man's a rapist anyway, so why should you care? Don't mention him to anyone. Have you got that clear?'

For a moment, he wondered if Natasha would turn against him. His hold over her had been slipping but just how far had it gone?

'Grab her legs and let's get her away from here,' he said.

He wasn't sure, but perhaps Natasha was crying. He caressed her face and kissed her. 'Trust me. I know what I'm doing.'

She picked up Shannon's legs and they carried the unconscious woman into the hotel. They deposited Shannon in a hallway as far from the garden as he could manage in the short time he had. Harry left Natasha with Shannon then he rushed back outside. Aleksey was squirming on the ground and Harry ignored the man and sat on a nearby wall. He needed to work out a plan.

A few moments later though, Natasha reappeared and she went straight to Aleksey's side.

'What the hell are you doing? I told you to stay with her,' Harry said.

'Jared's called an ambulance. I thought you should know.'

'Shit. I hope you kept your mouth shut about this guy?'

145

'Of course I did. Did you find the epi-pen?'

'I told you I wasn't going to look for it.'

'I didn't believe you.' Natasha knelt by Aleksey's side. 'I can do heart compressions and artificial respiration. I can try to keep him going.'

'You're not listening to me.' Harry bunched his fists and stood over her. Now was not the time for Natasha to defy him. 'Don't touch his damn chest and don't try to save him just stay with him until it's over. You were here watching with me the whole time so you know as well as I do that Shannon threw his epi-pen away. She's the one responsible for this. Her prints must be all over it and all over the champagne glass. The rim is going to be tainted with nuts because I'm pretty sure she knew about his allergy and she kicked it off deliberately.'

'No!'

'You know it's true.'

He felt certain Shannon had deliberately tainted the champagne glass using her own mouth. He had seen what she had been eating that evening and he had sampled the canapes himself and if he were the one who had wanted to kick off someone's allergic reaction he would have either kissed them, fed them a forbidden substance, or as Shannon had cleverly done, tainted a drink.

He had wondered why she had taken so long sipping from the glass before she passed it to Aleksey and now he knew – she had been making sure to get a good coverage. How smart of her. Then she had offered it to Aleksey. Shannon had known he had a serious allergy and she had set it off on purpose.

'We saw her do it,' Harry said.

'You don't know that. It could have been a mistake.'

'Like hell it was. He was either a spurned lover or what she said about him raping her is true, and I don't care which it is. She deliberately grabbed his medication from him and threw it as far away as she could. You saw it as clearly as I did so I don't see how that could have been a mistake.'

'Harry, we can't let a man die.'

'Why not? Is he even still alive?'

Natasha felt Aleksey's chest and listened for a heartbeat. 'Barely. There's still a chance though – why the hell isn't the ambulance here yet?'

'Like I said, don't bother trying to save him,' Harry said.

'What about the paramedics? When they arrive, if he's dead they'll want to know who he is and what he's doing here. They'll involve the police and then the link to Shannon might come out and suspicions might turn to her. There are cameras here. What good is it to us if Shannon gets arrested?'

'Don't worry about the surveillance cameras. There's only one trained on this door and I changed its angle earlier. Which means nobody else knows about their cosy little chat. She won't be arrested and there will be no police.' Harry waved his phone at her. 'I didn't make the call for an ambulance I simply pretended to.'

He tapped the side of his head. 'Brains, you see. Which means no one is on the way. Not for him. Which means I'll be the one in charge of the evidence against her and in charge of disposing of our friend here.'

Natasha had her hands on Aleksey. 'That's crazy! We can't do this. It's a man's life.'

'Shut up and do what I tell you. We're not the ones to kill him are we, she was.'

Natasha shook her head. 'I never signed up for murder.'

'Neither did I but it's one hell of a ride, isn't it? It's all right, babes, let me take care of it.'

What he really needed to do was locate the epi-pen and stash it away for future use and then he would dispose of the body and Shannon would be forever at his mercy.

'I can't.'

'I told you before about getting sentimental! Pull yourself together. You already told me he's pretty much gone so just stay with the poor bastard until the end.'

Natasha was hiding her face and in the dark it was impossible to make out what she was thinking. It didn't matter, she had obeyed him once that night and now there was no turning back.

Harry turned away from his wife. He had more important things to do, like find the epi-pen. How long would it take for Aleksey to breathe his last? Not too long, he hoped. Meanwhile, he must work out how to dispose of the body.

Chapter Thirty-two

Shannon

Shannon lay on the floor. The carpet beneath her smelled fresh with the faint aroma of cleaning fluids. The band was still playing somewhere far away and the *thunk thunk* of her own heart was loud in her ears. Jared was by her side and he was talking to her and it was as if she were underwater and all the sounds were muffled and distorted and her husband's face kept going in and out of focus.

Her head hurt so badly. What had happened? In a rush she remembered about Aleksey. Oh God.

She wanted to tell Jared everything which had happened – the rape, the phone stalking, the allergic reaction – everything. Yet she was incapable of speech and she would think back to this moment many times, with regret.

'The paramedics are on the way,' Jared said. 'You got a nasty bash on the head when you fell. Thank goodness Natasha found you.'

Shannon closed her eyes. Thank goodness yes, and the paramedics were on their way. The bastard didn't deserve it and she had wished him dead so many times. But they would help Aleksey.

She must have passed out again because the next thing she knew the paramedics were there and Jared was crying.

For a moment, she could not remember where she was or why and then it all came back to her.

'It's all right, sir, let me look after her. She's your wife, is that correct? If you would go with my colleague, please,' the paramedic said to Jared.

The paramedic put a blood pressure cuff on her arm. 'I'm going to give you a check over. It looks like you had a fall and your husband has told me you're pregnant. Can you tell me how you're feeling?'

'Terrible.'

'Do you remember what happened?'

'Where is he?' Shannon asked.

'Do you mean your husband? He's right behind me talking to my colleague,' the paramedic said. 'Can you tell me what happened?'

'Is he all right?'

'Don't worry, your husband is fine. You're the one we're concentrating on right now. I'm going to just give you a little prick on your finger to test your blood sugar.'

Natasha came close. 'I'm a friend. Is she going to be okay?'

'We're making sure about that, miss. If you wouldn't mind giving us some space and being patient.'

'Is he okay?' Shannon said. 'Did he make it?'

'Harry's gone to the car and he says everything is fine and he'll fill you in soon,' Natasha said.

'I don't understand.'

'If you wouldn't mind stepping back please, miss, so that I can carry out my examination,' the paramedic said to Natasha.

Shannon's head was swimming and she tried to reassure herself. If the paramedics were here that must mean they were also helping Aleksey. They would have taken him to hospital.

Jared had been led a short distance away and she could see he had a blood pressure cuff on his arm too. As she tried to sit up, the paramedic helped her and gave her a drink of water.

'So your friend Natasha told me she came to find you and discovered you on the floor. She thinks you fainted on your way back to the ballroom.'

Wait a minute that wasn't right. She didn't remember falling. She remembered feeling lightheaded in the garden and Harry helping her to sit down on the bench. How had she managed to get inside? Or was she getting mixed up?

'I don't really remember.'

'Let me check with my colleague and write up my notes,' the paramedic said kindly. 'You've had a nasty bash on the head so I'd like you to come in for observation overnight.'

'Oh no, please. I'd rather stay here,' she said, and she closed her eyes. Walking back into the hotel was a complete blank. How had she managed it? She didn't care. Though she hated Aleksey with every cell in her body, all she wanted was for someone to assure her he had been taken to hospital and she certainly didn't want to be in the same hospital as him.

'The man,' she said. 'How is he?'

The paramedic was a little distance away and he was writing on a chart. 'Which man do you mean?'

At that moment she spotted Harry. He was in a hurry to get to her and he was in shirt sleeves and seemed out of breath.

'How are you, Shannon?' he said. 'Everything is fine.' Harry nodded good-naturedly to the paramedic. 'I think she means me. I'm a good friend and it was my wife who called for help. How is she doing?'

'Not bad,' the paramedic said.

'Is Aleksey all right?' she asked Harry.

Harry bent close. 'Don't say his name out loud,' he whispered.

'What? Why? Have they taken him?'

Harry gave her such a dark look it sent a terrible chill up her spine. Her throat went dry and her head throbbed so hard she wanted to close her eyes.

151

'We don't have much time, so listen carefully,' Harry said, his voice still low. He glanced towards Jared then locked eyes with Shannon. 'This is going to be difficult for you to hear right now but I know you're the one who threw away his medication because I saw you do it. Aleksey took it out of his pocket and you snatched it from him and threw it into the bushes.'

Her head swam and she felt sick. 'It was an accident,' she whispered.

'Of course it was.'

'I didn't mean to do it.'

Harry nodded. 'I know and you have to understand that doesn't look very good for you.'

Her hands were shaking and she clasped them together. 'What do you mean?'

'It was too late. Natasha did everything she could and we couldn't find his medication in time.'

No, no it couldn't be true. 'It was an accident, I didn't mean to…'

'Shh.'

'You don't mean he's…'

As Harry nodded, his face and his blond curls swam out of focus.

'I don't understand. What about the paramedics they must have been able to–'

'No one could save him. I told you. It was too late.'

Aleksey was dead?

'Be quiet, Shannon, and listen. We don't have much time and we need to get your story straight.'

'I don't have a story. It's my fault.'

'Listen, I know how badly these things can go and I can protect you but only if you do exactly what I tell you. Now, do you want me to make this go away? Shannon, we're running out of time. Do you want me to help you or not?'

She bit her lip hard and tasted blood. Oh my god. Aleksey had died? She was a murderer? 'Where are the police?'

Harry glanced behind his shoulder and smiled at the paramedic and then leant forward to give Shannon a kiss on the cheek. 'If you do exactly as I say there won't be any police,' he said in her ear.

No police? How could that be? If Aleksey was dead, they would be coming for her. She was the one responsible.

'Do you want me to help you or not?' Harry hissed.

She stared at him.

'It's a simple yes or no,' he said.

As if it did it of its own accord, her head nodded.

'I'm sorry, I can't hear you,' Harry said.

'Yes,' she whispered. 'Please can you help me.'

'Then all you need to do is keep your mouth shut. You never mention him and you act like nothing happened. Let me handle the rest.'

Chapter Thirty-three

Harry

Harry felt on top form the following morning. Still, he decided to lounge in bed for a while and then he joined Natasha at the pool. The water was a wonderful blue and the sun felt good on his skin. He wondered how Shannon was feeling. Most likely she was being crucified by her own conscience. He had seen it many times before – the good person who, on the spur of the moment and overcome by emotions, does something stupid and irrevocable.

Taking a sip from his cocktail he smiled to himself. Shannon would get what she deserved, he would see to that. Meanwhile he also had Natasha to deal with because she had been giving him the silent treatment since last night.

'Are you still in a bad mood?' he asked.

Natasha turned a page of her book and ignored him.

'It's very tedious and you know I can hold out much longer than you. Please tell me you're not going to keep this up all day?'

She pressed her lips together and he gave it a rest. True, it had been asking a lot to expect her to watch a man die and do nothing. Too bad. She would come around.

Harry took a dip and when he came out of the water he was pleased to see Jared pulling up a lounger.

'Hi Harry, it looks like this will be my last morning at the pool.'

Grabbing a towel, Harry squeezed water out of his hair. 'How so?'

'Shannon's not feeling well and wants to go home.'

'Sorry to hear that,' Natasha said.

'She wants to check in with our obstetrician and make sure everything's okay and I need to visit my family and see my father.'

Harry threw his towel on the ground. He beckoned the waiter over to order more drinks. 'Then we'd better make it a morning to remember.'

He made sure to keep a smile on his face though his anger had stirred. The cunning minx. He had disposed of a body in the river and had taken a great deal of risk on her behalf. Did she think she could escape so easily?

Harry had to wait quite a long time before Jared got into the pool to cool off.

'Keep him here,' he told Natasha quietly, and he was pleased she nodded in response. See? She could never keep the cold treatment going very long.

He sauntered to the first floor and knocked at Shannon's door. 'Special delivery,' he called.

'Oh it's you,' Shannon said, as she opened the door.

'That's not very polite. Aren't you going to invite me in?'

She looked a ghastly colour and her hair was a mess. When she plonked onto the sofa her gaze was vacant. Perhaps she was in shock which meant he would have to be delicate with her.

'How are you doing today, Shannon? I guess it's going to take a while for things to get back to normal and I wanted to check in and make sure you're okay.'

'Get back to normal, are you mad?'

'Now, now, let's not be melodramatic.'

'How could I possibly be okay? A man died. I feel terrible.'

155

'There's no need to. If you want my advice the best thing is to move on and put it behind you.'

'I've made a decision, I'm going to contact the police.'

'You're not thinking straight. First, from what I heard you say, the guy might have deserved what he got. Second, you'd be throwing your own life away, not to mention the life of your unborn child. Plus, you'd be dragging me down with you. I'm the one who got rid of the body, remember? We'd both be going to prison, not just you, and I can't let you do that.'

'Shit.'

'You're upset and I understand. Like I said to you yesterday, let me handle this.'

When she started sobbing, Harry crossed his arms. 'For goodness sake stop. He's gone. What's done is done and like I said I would, I've made all of this go away for you.'

'I don't understand. How could it happen? How could he die? It was just an accident!'

'I know it was. We tried we really did and there was nothing we could do.'

'You really mean he asphyxiated?'

'Yes, he died before the ambulance arrived. I'm sorry.'

'So where is he?'

'I suppose you didn't sleep much imagining them joining the dots together and coming to knock on your door? I'm sorry about that but Jared wouldn't let me anywhere near you last night so I couldn't explain things properly.'

She looked so terrible he almost felt sorry for her.

'Shannon, you did a good job following my instructions and keeping quiet. You don't need to worry because no one breathed a word about Aleksey. I took care of it.'

'How? He was lying there in the garden. It's not possible.'

'Oh it is.'

'You mean you... you buried him?'

He laughed. 'In such a short space of time that would not have worked. You've been watching too many films. Of course I didn't bury him. I dumped him in the river.'

'No no no, we need to go to the police.'

'You didn't want me to dispose of the body then? You want the police to find it and to come questioning the guests? What are you planning to do – confess? You want the link between you and Aleksey to come out?'

'I don't care if it does.'

'What about the epi-pen? What are the police going to find? An epi-pen that hasn't been used although it's got your fingerprints all over it?'

'What?'

'Oh yes, I saw everything you did. I saw you throw his medication away and then stand there watching him choke. I heard you screaming at him.'

She clutched at her knees.

'Don't worry. We can keep that a secret between the two of us. I know you feel bad so please try not to dwell on it. Think about the baby and don't do anything stupid. I told you I could make this go away for you and that's exactly what I've done.'

'This is wrong. He was evil and deranged but it was a man's life.' She put her head in her hands.

'Hey it's all right.'

'No it isn't – how can you say that? This is a nightmare.'

'I imagine it is but rest assured because you're safe. That river has a strong current. He's going to be miles downstream and if we're lucky, out to sea, before he ever comes to light.'

Shannon groaned.

He nodded in a good-natured way. 'Your husband says the pool at your place has been repaired and I've got to admit I quite fancy the sound of it so here's what I'm thinking – how about you invite us to come and stay with you for a few days.

Jared said you're heading home today. We can be your houseguests.'

When she didn't answer, he nudged her shoulder. 'What do you say?'

'Why are you acting like this is normal? We just killed a man.'

'Correction – *you* killed him. I did you a big favour tidying up the evidence and let's be clear about that. You owe me and what I want as a thank-you is for you to invite us to stay.'

'You've got your own place with grounds and a gardener and Natasha told me it's huge with a view over the park. Why the hell come to London?'

'Because I want to.' He smoothed a hand through his curls. Surely she wasn't going to make this unpleasant when it could be fun and easy. 'And that's all the reason you need. I want you to talk to Jared and make it happen, period. Am I being clear?'

'And what if *I* don't want to.'

'Shannon, Shannon, you've got to understand how this works and I think you do. I did you a favour and now you do one for me. What's so hard about that?'

She pulled her robe around her and a mutinous look flashed across her face. Don't say she still had some fight left in her? This was going to be amusing.

'I saw you with that rather attractive redhead, what's her name? You were coming out of her room and she had her arms around your neck and the two of you were kissing.'

He almost laughed out loud. So Shannon had more guts in her than he had given her credit for and she was trying to use this against him? No chance. Shannon was no match for him – she was weak, inexperienced and at a terrible disadvantage.

'If you're thinking of using that as a lever against me, think again,' he said, his voice hard. 'Natasha knows about my adventures and she ignores them so I'll give you one chance and one only – it's houseguests, and nothing less.'

'I'm the one who killed him. I'm the one responsible.'

'Yes you are but we won't talk about things like that out loud. Though since we're alone I want you to rest assured no one will ever know what happened. If his body turns up at some point believe me likely they'll view it as a tragic accident.'

She had gone such a terrible colour he wanted to get out before she threw up.

'Now pull yourself together, my dear. We've all got our packing to do, haven't we.'

He sauntered to the door. As he closed it behind him, the gold numbering caught his eye. He smirked. Funny how she had told him nineteen was special. It really wasn't turning out to be lucky for her at all.

Chapter Thirty-four

Shannon

When Harry left the room, Shannon broke down. She flung herself onto the bed. The nightmare she had tried so hard to put behind her had become even worse. This time *she was* the guilty one. She had taken a man's life and though she had wished him suffering or dead so many times, she would never in a million years have wanted it to happen by her own hand. *Oh God, please help me.*

There was no one she could confide in. Not Jared, who she had never told about Aleksey, and not her sister either. Still, hearing her sister's voice would be a comfort. She dialled the number.

'Hi,' Rosie said. 'I thought you were out of touch for a while? Aren't you still on holiday?'

'We're going home,' Shannon said.

There was a small silence and she could hear Rosie sitting up and taking notice.

'Hey, you sound funny. Is everything all right?'

No, a man raped me and I never told you. 'I'm feeling a bit tired.'

'You sound very down. Have you been crying?'

He's been harassing me ever since. He's deluded. Thinks he's in love with me. 'A bit. I don't know why.'

'I knew it. What's wrong?'

He told me it was my fault. That I wanted it. He was a liar. 'I don't know. I just wanted to hear the sound of your voice.'

'Sweetie, what's going on? Is the pregnancy okay?'

Last night, I killed him.

She stifled a sob. If she didn't pull herself together Rosie would be coming straight over to check on her. 'It's going fine. I don't know why I feel teary when I should be happy.'

'You and Jared have been through a lot but it's behind you now.'

'You're right and hey, I've got to go. Don't worry about me. I'll speak to you soon.'

She hung up, flung herself onto the bed, and cried.

Chapter Thirty-five

Jared

Jared unlocked the front door of their house and ushered their guests inside. 'Welcome,' he said.

'Three floors in the fashionable neighbourhood of Barnes, aren't you the lucky couple,' Harry said.

Natasha twirled in the entrance. 'Ooh, so much light and space I love it. And what's that scent? Sandalwood? That's my favourite.'

Being a pleasant host came easily to him, though Jared could not understand why Shannon had asked them to stay. He had wanted her to go to the hospital overnight and she had refused. She had been so pale and shaky since the gala. And she knew how much they liked their quiet time.

Harry and Natasha had been good company at the hotel yet he would never describe them as close friends. He had voiced his objections and he had then given in since she told him she already made the offer and she would find it very reassuring to have a nurse close by. When Shannon had put a protective hand over her belly, Jared had caved. He didn't at all feel confident he would be able to manage if there was another crisis.

'Okay, though only for a few days and you go to see the doctor first thing tomorrow,' he had said.

Shannon had kissed him. 'Don't worry I already have an appointment and thank you for being such a sweetie. What would I do without you?'

They took them on a tour, starting at the top floor with its master bedroom, cinema room and wonderful panorama over the River Thames, then the second floor with the split-level lounge diner and Jared's office. Natasha oohed at the view, and the styling, and the decoration and it was true, they had been very lucky with the house thanks to his parents.

On their combined salaries, they would never have been able to afford it and it was Jared's parents who had loaned them the money. His mother had insisted they accept and she had said that having a nice place was important to *reduce stress*. By which she had meant, help with them trying for a baby. It had been very generous.

'This is your suite on the ground floor,' Shannon said. 'It's cosy and private and you can go straight through to our basement pool from here. I hope you like it. And our pool's been fixed, so we can chill out.'

'I can't believe you've got your own private spa,' Natasha said. 'It sounds perfect.' She turned to her husband. 'We're going to have to get one too, aren't we, darling?'

Harry laughed. 'Of course. Shannon, this looks very comfortable and we really appreciate your hospitality.'

'We really do and it will be nice to get to know you better. Where are you going to put the nursery?' Natasha asked.

'We've just started converting the cinema room on the top floor. I'd like to have the nursery right next to our bedroom,' Shannon said as she linked her arm with Jared's.

Jared couldn't help sensing she was tense and he wished they could have been alone with the space to care for each other rather than look after guests.

Harry clapped his hands. 'I tell you what, why don't you let us fix supper for tonight?'

'I didn't know you enjoyed working in the kitchen,' Jared said. 'Really there's no need, we can order in or I can throw something together.'

'I'm not exactly chef of the year but I do a mean lasagne and I spotted a supermarket on the way over so I can pop out and get what I need,' Harry said.

It was a very generous offer. 'Great, that sounds wonderful. I'll deal with the wine.'

'You all go and do your own thing and leave it to me,' Harry said.

Jared slipped his arm around Shannon. Perhaps this wasn't going to be so bad after all.

A few hours later, Jared went to the kitchen and found Natasha alone, chopping up vegetables.

'Is Harry out shopping?' he asked.

'He's having a lie down and I was restless so I decided to get a start on the dinner.'

That was a surprise. Harry had given the impression he would be the one preparing supper, not Natasha.

'Right. Shannon is having a nap too.'

'She needs to get plenty of rest and...'

'... stay hydrated.' Jared finished the sentence for her and they both laughed. 'It's very comforting having you here.'

'Is it? It's kind of you to say so. What Shannon needs at the moment is reassurance more than anything else. There's nothing medically wrong with her. It's emotions and deep feelings and perfectly expected for the journey the two of you have been through.'

Was it his imagination or had Natasha been crying? Her eyes were a bit red though maybe she had been cutting onions?

'Can I give you a hand?' he asked. 'I don't feel too much like resting either.'

'If you like. Would you mind chopping these?' She pushed some celery and garlic towards him and sniffed.

A quick scan of the worktop told him the onions had not yet been done and he was just wondering if he should ask her what was wrong when she started crying for real. A woman in distress was always his weak spot.

'I'm sorry this is really silly of me and it was so kind of Shannon to invite us. She told me how she would appreciate having me on hand.'

'We both do.'

'I never told you but I was so disappointed I never actually got to have a job being a nurse. All I wanted was to look after people and I did my training and then Harry acted like an idiot. You probably won't believe me but he was an obstacle to me signing up in the first place. Then he kept telling me what a waste of time it would be and that I'd never like it. When I graduated, he made it clear that he never wanted me to actually find a job. It was weak of me I know, but I went along with his wishes.'

Jared put his arm around her shoulders. 'That must have been tough. It sounds like you really had your heart set on it.'

'It was kind of my dream.'

She sobbed on his shoulder and he let her.

'It's hard when the people we love don't support us.'

'Totally miserable and it spoils everything and looking after Shannon has somehow brought it all up again.'

He gave her a little squeeze. 'Maybe Harry didn't understand how much it meant to you?'

'Oh I'm sure he did. He was selfish and he was worried about me becoming too independent. He doesn't do it on purpose, but I've come to understand that he likes to control me.'

165

It wasn't at all the image he had got of Harry and Natasha's relationship. Yet who could really know what went on behind closed doors?

'It's not the same but I had the experience of my own father trying to control me and it almost ruined my life. He had his idea of who I should be and what I should do. The path he wanted me to follow was in his mind right from the time I was born. As I grew up and as my own ideas moved away from his, he reacted by putting as much pressure on me as he could. I hated him for it.'

She dabbed at her eyes. 'Harry is a great guy but the thing is, the only way to do things is *his way*.'

He sighed. 'Maybe you need to tell Harry how you feel. I firmly believe our only hope for changing what doesn't work in our relationships is to talk to the people we love. We have to do our bit and tell them what's wrong. We have to explain to them how it makes us feel.'

'Is that tactic working with your father?'

He pulled a rueful face. 'Actually no, or not yet though I'm still trying.'

'I wish you a lot of luck with it.'

'Thanks, I'll need it. With Dad's illness it's an odd thing to say because of course I wish it wasn't happening, although maybe it gives us more possibility of working things out. We had a civil phone conversation and that hasn't happened in years.'

'I'm not sure I've got as much chance with Harry.'

'Sure you have. If you love each other, anything is possible.'

'You're such a nice person and full of positive vibes.'

She leaned into him. He waited for her to move away and instead she turned her face up to his and he felt the warmth of her breath on his neck. Then she rose onto her toes and planted a kiss on his mouth. Jared was so surprised he didn't react and Natasha quickly pulled away.

The kitchen door closed behind her as he touched the tears she had left on his lips.

Chapter Thirty-six

Shannon

The last thing Shannon wanted to do was spend a cosy evening with Harry yet she was obliged to do exactly that. It would be too strange to ask them to stay and then not get out of bed and it would not at all be fair on her husband.

Any moment, she expected there to be a banging on the front door and that it would be the police coming to arrest her. Half of her wanted it to happen and the other half wanted to pretend this was all a bad dream that would go away in the morning.

She scoured the internet for reports of a body being found near Sussex Abbey. How long would it take for it to surface? Or, like Harry said, would it find its way all the way to the coast? Her imagination played out the scenario in her mind – the four of them would be halfway through dinner and she would be sitting at the table. There would be a thumping at the door and when the police put cuffs on her Jared would be horrified and she would hang her head in shame.

She had several times picked up her phone to call the police. Each time she pushed two numbers on the keypad – nine and then another nine. Then she stopped herself from pushing the third. She lacked the courage. To her horror, part of her believed he deserved it. She didn't care about what would happen to Harry and she wasn't even sure she cared about what happened to her, but the thought of her baby being born in prison turned her resolve to jelly.

To her surprise, Harry delivered on his promise and a pleasant scent of lasagne soon wafted from the kitchen. When she made her way downstairs, there was a huge bowl of salad on the table, and garlic bread. A raspberry dessert sat in the fridge, which Natasha said she had concocted from fruit and sponge and cream.

'These two have been hard at work,' Jared said.

'Thank you, it looks fabulous,' Shannon said, as she sat on the sofa next to her husband.

The three of them were already started on glasses of wine, which she eyed enviously. How wonderful it would be to down a few glasses and blot everything out.

'Wait until you taste it first before you give us any praise,' Harry said. 'I've got to be honest and tell you Natasha did most of the work. Unfortunately, I was tied up by a difficult call with one of my investors. He's pulled out at the last minute despite all the assurances he gave that he's one hundred percent behind my new venture. It's really maddening. Now I've got to sort out the mess he's dumped me in. I so hate it when people let me down.'

Jared popped the cork on a second bottle of wine. 'It sounded like you had all the investors you needed lined up and ready to go.'

'That's what I thought. If I don't sort it out pronto the whole project is going to go south. I could lose a year or more and give my competitors space to get the jump on me. And that absolutely cannot happen.'

'Yikes. This is why I never liked business. It's too cutthroat. Here, taste this and let me know what you think.'

Harry swirled the wine in his glass and sniffed it, then took a sip. 'Very nice. You know what, you would make an ideal sleeping investor.'

'Me? No way.'

'Think about it, all you need to do is invest and then sit back and collect the profit while I put in the hard graft.'

'Sorry, venture capital is so not my thing. Besides, we don't have that kind of cash.'

Shannon had a horrible sinking feeling as she snuggled next to her husband. What the hell had she got herself into relying on a man like Harry? 'Jared's right, though I hope you find someone soon to fill the gap.'

Harry didn't comment and he did not meet her eye either which she took as a bad sign. They chatted through dinner and she did her best to chime in though her heart was numb. She was relieved there was no more talk of money and she hoped Harry would let it pass.

It wasn't until a while later that Harry cornered her in the kitchen.

'I expected you to be a lot more supportive of me earlier.'

She was taking bowls out of the cupboard for dessert and at the annoyance in his voice she almost dropped them. 'I don't know what you mean.'

'Then let me spell it out. Don't look so worried I'm not going to be unreasonable because we're friends, aren't we.'

She sidled away from him and found herself with her back against the sink.

'What I want,' Harry said, 'is for you to persuade Jared to back my project.'

'He would never agree to it. He hates that kind of thing.'

Harry smiled and it sent a shiver up her back. 'That's not my problem it's yours. After all, you wouldn't like your husband to find out about Aleksey would you?'

The sink pressed into the small of her back and she swallowed as she tried to collect her thoughts.

'Don't play all innocent with me, you know what the deal is.'

'How much are you talking about?'

'Half a million.'

'What! Are you crazy?'

'Keep your voice down. That's a drop in the ocean for the Kavanis and you know it. Now all you have to do is get Jared's cooperation and I have a feeling you'll find a way.'

Harry sauntered out and she had to put the bowls down for fear they would slip from her fingers. She felt sick. Oh God, she could have confessed to Jared about going to the bar with Aleksey but she could never tell him about the murder. The only option she had was to go to the police and confess everything – that it had been an accident, that she had searched for the epinephrine and not been able to find it, that Harry had prevented her from calling for help and then she had collapsed and when she came around everything was a muddle. Yet she had not phoned an ambulance herself had she? She had not alerted anyone that a man was dying or dead in the garden. It would be her word against Harry's. Her mouth went dry and she heaved.

Harry came back into the kitchen carrying a pile of plates. 'Oh, and just in case you're thinking of doing the dirty on me.' He put down the plates and delved into his pocket, bringing out a small plastic bag which he waved in the air. She put her hand over her mouth.

'That's right – I eventually found the epi-pen. Unused of course and with your fingerprints on it. If you think you can go to the authorities then I'd consider this little piece of evidence very carefully if I were you, because the only conclusion the police can come to is that *you* withheld it from the poor man. Oh and I almost forgot.'

Tapping at his phone, he walked up to her and held out the screen.

171

'There's also this little video I took of you throwing away his life-saving medication. I mean the lighting isn't too good though I think with technology so advanced these days the police will be able to make out what happened. Here take a look – he takes a sip from the glass you gave him and then he clutches his throat. Then he reaches into his pocket, and look, there you are grabbing something from him and flinging it away.' Harry smiled.

'Oh and I like this next bit where you scream at him about being raped.' He shrugged. 'The police aren't stupid. Will they believe you? Did you make a report about him assaulting you? Were you examined by a doctor? No, I don't think so. And will it even matter, because you're the one who's the murderer.'

She felt sure she would black out and she clutched the sink behind her.

'Of course, they'll want to know who took this video but I know plenty of techie experts who can sort that out for me and hide the identity. Maybe my techie friend could make it look like this came from Jared's phone. Then your husband would be implicated too, perhaps as an accomplice?'

'Yes, I made a mistake but I believed you had called an ambulance. You told me you would help him and then you left him to die. You lied to me. And why did I pass out? Did you have something to do with that?'

He wagged his finger in her face and tutted. 'Now, now, let's not tell lies. Then of course there are all the questions any investigation would raise about the nature of your relationship with Aleksey in the first place. I wonder what Jared would make of that. It's quite simple. All I want is a little financial backing.'

He sauntered out and the door swished shut behind him. Harry was right – she had not filed a report about the rape and she had not seen a doctor, which meant there was no evidence. Besides, killing a man weeks later was not a legitimate defence even if rape had been proven. No, she was a stone-cold killer. Shannon threw up in the sink.

Chapter Thirty-seven

Jared

The next morning, Jared went with Shannon for her check-up with the obstetrician. The doctor was very reassuring and told them that Shannon's blood pressure was good and the baby's movements all seemed normal. Then they went for an ultrasound and when he saw the scan he could hardly believe it. The tiny heart was beating fast and the sonographer turned the screen so they could have a better view. He swallowed the lump in his throat.

Shannon was smiling. 'Is everything as it should be?' she asked the sonographer.

'Everything is normal for this stage of the baby's development and you have nothing to worry about. I've taken measurements and I won't be recommending further screening for Down's syndrome because I haven't detected any anomalies. So based on these measurements I'll be noting the due date to be the second of March.'

'That's a bit earlier than we thought,' Jared said.

'It's an estimate based on the baby's dimensions and often there's a bit of discrepancy between the mother's date and the one I put on the records. This one which is based on actual sizes is usually the most accurate.'

Jared nodded. It was a huge relief to know everything looked normal, especially after Shannon's recent fainting episode. They had talked about this to the obstetrician who had been very attentive but not especially concerned. She had said they would be monitoring Shannon carefully as the pregnancy progressed.

'If you've no other questions I'll print off a copy for you,' the sonographer said, and she left the room.

Shannon swung her legs off the couch and her eyes were shining. 'Isn't it exciting?'

'Seeing the baby on the screen is, you know, beyond words.'

'We're really going to be parents at last. Doesn't it make you look at things in a different way?'

He nodded. It certainly did.

Shannon grabbed a pad of tissue and wiped the gel for the scan off her belly. 'And you know I've been thinking about our future and our baby's future and money and stuff, and how maybe it might be a good idea to go in with Harry.'

He wasn't sure he had heard her right. 'Huh?'

'I mean it could be a great opportunity if we back his idea, don't you think? Like he said, it's a sleeping investment so we don't actually have to do anything and as Harry's business grows so would our investment. By the time the baby is older, it could be his or her college fund.'

It was so out of character for Shannon it took a few seconds to take in what she was saying.

'It's not *when* Harry's business grows, it's *if* it grows. We don't know if it's going to be a success.'

'He's very confident and it sounds as if he's got a good track record.'

'The other big problem is we would need to stump up half a million and that's money we don't have.'

'Couldn't you borrow it from your family? This would be an investment for the baby. For our baby's future. I know they've been very generous with us, they would lend it for their grandchild, wouldn't they?'

'I don't think it's wise and I don't know enough about Harry or his results.'

'But we do know he's already set up and sold two businesses and made a fortune. This could be our chance.'

In his view it was their chance to lose one hell of a lot of money. What on earth possessed Shannon to even consider the idea?

'Please say you'll think about it.'

'If you like.'

'I mean it. Talk to Harry and see if we can come to an arrangement. If you don't want to do it for me, do it for our baby.'

The sonographer came back in and handed the picture of the scan to Shannon. Jared stared at it. He had been planning to cut the tie with his father's bank, except now that didn't seem possible.

'Okay,' he said. 'I'll think about it.'

After the visit, they went home. Jared helped Shannon settle comfortably in bed with the ceiling fan on full speed. It was another terribly hot day and he brought a jug of iced water to the bedside.

It was not going to be an easy afternoon because he was going to see his father. When he headed out, Natasha was downstairs watching television. Shannon had wished him luck and Natasha did too.

It ripped at his heart to see his mother tearful about his father. Jared gave her a hug and she hung on to him and she was so small he could see over the top of her head. When they talked about the pregnancy, she was so delighted and she cried again, from happiness, she assured him.

The house was quiet. He and his brother had been brought up sharing a bedroom in a grotty part of south London. Now his parents had a huge house in the expensive borough of Richmond upon Thames, not to mention a villa in Italy and an apartment in New York.

Despite its grandeur, the house was still homely. It was filled with the knickknacks his mother liked to collect from her travels. There were plenty of elephant carvings and wall tapestries from India, as well as souvenirs from Malaysia which was one of his mother's favourite places to visit. Just like his own house, the place smelled faintly of sandalwood, which always reminded him of pleasant childhood memories.

He would have liked nothing better than to sit and talk in the kitchen and eat the homemade sweet snacks his mother had prepared. Instead, he contented himself with telling her about the ultrasound visit as she organised a tray to take through to his father.

'I'm so happy for you and so is your father. A baby will make all the difference to your lives. Why don't the two of you come over to dinner soon?'

'Let's take it one step at a time, we both know Dad and I have a lot to work out first.'

'He's been looking forward to seeing you.'

Jared doubted it.

'Your father is going to be starting a round of chemotherapy next week. He was worried he might not be feeling well enough to have a proper talk if you didn't come before then. He's hardly been sleeping, except don't let him know I told you that.'

Jared felt sorry for her being caught between the two of them and always trying to make the peace. It was the last thing she needed to be using her energy on.

'Don't worry, Mum, I'm not going to be stirring him up.'

He carried the tray through. All his life he had been called the bad son. The one who caused conflict and disappointment, and try as he might, he had never been able to get rid of the label his father had given him. And it had been true, hadn't it? He had been the one to stay away, not even knowing his father was unwell. Now he had to find a way to make that right.

His father was at his desk. Along the side of the room was a huge picture window with a view onto Richmond Park. Horses, deer, soldiers in training – you could see a whole world through that window and he knew his father loved to sit and watch.

There was no sign of illness in his father, except perhaps a slight slowness to his movements. Or was that simply in Jared's imagination? Fuelled by his fears? His mother sat quietly while Jared stumbled his way through how sorry he and Shannon were. Then he told his father about the ultrasound visit and about Shannon giving up work for the time being.

His father stroked his white beard and chewed at cumin seeds, popping a few in his mouth at regular intervals as he listened. Then it was his father's turn to talk and he told Jared about the treatment he would be having, and about how he had been feeling unwell for a while and how he had always mistrusted doctors which was why he hadn't wanted help sooner. Jared discovered it had been Raj who finally persuaded his father to get help and Jared instantly felt a rush of gratitude towards his brother.

'It's the early stages so they're hopeful they've caught it in time. They tell me there's a very good chance the treatment will be successful. We'll know more later on when they redo the scans so there's no need for you to sit there looking glum. Especially when you've got such a wonderful time ahead of you. A first baby is always so exciting.'

'Right.'

'Let's not dwell on the negative. I want to put all that behind us, so tell me, how's your writing career going?'

Jared's stomach tensed ready for the criticism. 'Not bad. I'm finalising a project and I've another one lined up.'

'Good prospects?' His father rubbed his thumb against his forefingers, meaning "have they got money to spend?"

'Yes.'

'I was talking to Amir the other day. He mentioned to me he's interested in creating his autobiography. He wants photos and a hardback version, you know like those coffee table books, so he can pass it onto his grandchildren. He wants them to remember the family story. He wondered if you might be able to help him.'

Amir was one of his father's oldest friends. He had started out at the same time as Jared's father with one tiny takeaway and he and his wife doing the work. Amir and his wife now owned a chain of restaurants and were multimillionaires.

As far as Jared knew, his profession as a ghostwriter had never been talked about to any of his father's friends because his father considered it an unworthy profession. Something to be embarrassed about. He had come here ready to hold out the olive branch and here his father was doing a much better job of it than him.

'Yes of course, I didn't even know Amir knew what I did.'

'Well he does now and don't tell me you haven't got something troubling you because I can see it written on your face. You haven't at all got the look of a happy, expectant father. I thought it might be this wretched cancer thing on your mind except now I'm not so sure.'

Wow, his father had not lost any of his powers of perception. Jared squirmed, though like usual in front of his father, there was little point in trying to cover it up. 'It's complicated.'

His father took another pinch of seeds. 'I bet it is, so spit it out then. I haven't got all day.'

His mother poured cups of tea. She gave Jared a smile of encouragement as he launched into a retelling of Shannon's odd behaviour after the ultrasound visit and her request that he back Harry's business to the tune of half a million pounds. His father listened carefully.

'If you want me to lend you that kind of money so you can lose it, the answer is no.'

'I think this could be a great opportunity. I know the man and he's had impressive business success in the past.'

'Are you sure you've checked him out properly?'

'Don't worry, that's what I'm going to do.'

He intended to find out everything he could, not only about Harry's track record but also about the man himself.

'Shannon has the idea of investing in Harry for the baby's future and maybe she's right.'

His father sighed. 'I'll make the funds available. But if this project goes down the toilet it's a debt you'll have to repay. We've had our disagreements, but you need to know I've always trusted your judgement which is one of the reasons you were such a great loss.'

'Thanks, Dad.'

His mind went to the sun hat incident and to Natasha's little comments about Harry. Was there something he was missing? And what had made Shannon so interested in Harry's proposal, had Harry been talking to her behind Jared's back? Jared aimed to find out if Harry really was as squeaky clean as his image suggested.

Chapter Thirty-eight

Shannon

Shannon's world was falling apart. She couldn't eat, she couldn't sleep. Her mind felt like a sieve, and she couldn't think straight. The only thing keeping her focused on survival was the baby.

Jared and Harry were out. For the first time since the incident, she and Natasha were alone and she must take the chance to speak in private. The thought of it made her weak with anxiety. She had spent every moment trying to shut out the nightmare and now she would have to revisit it. Talk about Aleksey. But she had to try. Natasha would surely be on her side?

When Harry left, Shannon had heard Natasha say she was going to the jacuzzi. Steps led to the basement spa and she padded down them in her bikini and bathrobe, clutching a towel to her chest.

A faint smell of chlorine wafted towards her as she pushed open the glass door. Natasha wasn't in the jacuzzi, she was sitting on the steps in the shallow end of the pool. Natasha glanced up but there was no smile on her face and she didn't greet Shannon. Shannon's stomach knotted.

Throwing her things onto a lounger, she stepped into the water. Natasha was a nice person and had already proven herself to be a good friend. Surely she would be supportive and they could come up with a plan?

'Where's Harry?' Shannon asked, as she sat down.

'Out.'

'That's what I thought. I want to know what happened.'

Natasha stared straight ahead and did not answer.

'Did you hear what I said?'

'I can't discuss the gala. He's told me not to talk to you about it.'

'Are you being serious? I want to know. I want to know your version. Why did I pass out? All he needed was one shot of drugs and Aleksey would be alive today!'

'Except you deprived him of that.' Natasha was reclining back against the steps and she let her arms float in the water. 'There's nothing more to tell.'

Why was the woman so relaxed? What was wrong with her?

'Yes there is, damn it. How did I come to be passed out in a corridor? Did Harry have a part in that?'

'If he did, then I did too.'

'You let Aleksey die. How can you live with yourself?'

'I don't think about it, that's how, and the best thing for you to do is follow my example. Try to forget it.'

'How the hell do you imagine I could?'

Natasha made a noise as if she were exasperated. 'Because he raped you, maybe? If what you were shouting at him is true then something bad happened between you didn't it? So didn't he deserve what he got? Didn't he have it coming? I wouldn't feel so sorry for him if I were you.'

'I don't feel sorry for him but I know it wasn't right. I can't prove he raped me. I woke up at Aleksey's place half naked and I can't remember a thing except being at a bar with him. I don't even know what happened.'

'But your body knows.'

'Yes! Which is why I think he must have drugged me.'

'Then you were dumb to not go to the police.'

Yes, she had been dumb and stupid to stumble home and step straight in the shower so that by the time she could think straight it was too late to go to a doctor, let alone the police. And stupid to not tell her husband. And then there was the pregnancy result and it was too late.

'Listen, Natasha, I've been thinking, you and I could go to the police. You were there with Harry and you saw what happened. We could tell them the truth.'

'For goodness sake shut up. Are you that naive? Nobody is going to believe us. And what in God's name would possess me to do such a ridiculous thing when Harry is the one holding all the cards? I'd end up being arrested as an accessory to murder. I don't want to go down with him. No thanks.'

'Harry wants money and he's blackmailing me. You've got to help.'

Natasha sat up suddenly. 'You don't get it, do you?'

As usual, Natasha was wearing a swimming costume. She turned, slid off both shoulder straps and started rolling down the top.

'What are you doing?'

Once she had pushed it all the way down to her hips, she moved to the higher step and leaned forward. The bruises at the base of Natasha's back were ugly and ranged in colour from yellow to purple.

'Now do you understand?'

'Oh my god. I had no idea. Are you telling me Harry did that to you?'

'Always out of sight and where people won't see or suspect, he's clever like that. Why do you think I don't wear bikinis? There's nothing I can do to help you, I can't even help myself.'

The words Natasha spoke and the bruises seemed to speak for themselves, yet for the first time, Shannon hesitated. Natasha had never given the vibe of an abused wife. She seemed happy and carefree and very attached to Harry. Was this woman really at his mercy?

Shannon folded her arms across her chest. She had a sudden, chilling thought. Harry was so slick and nasty in his demands, what if this wasn't the first time he had extorted money from his "friends".

Natasha pulled her costume on. 'Don't try to fight back, Shannon, just live with it like I do and cooperate with Harry and it won't turn out so bad. What I've learned is, it's best to go along with him and then he can be super friendly and even quite nice. You definitely don't want to get on his bad side and the worst would be if you try to go against him. Harry always wins.'

Chapter Thirty-nine

Natasha

Natasha tied her shoelaces. She had to get a break from this craziness. A morning run was the only way. Closing the front door softly behind her, she breathed a sigh of relief. Harry was acting like a mad man. She now knew she could never, ever rely on him again.

Although it was early, the pavements were surprisingly busy. Barnes was a wealthy neighbourhood with a charming mixture of old and modern. It had the air of being a village rather than part of one of the largest capital cities in the world. She passed historic houses dating from the eighteenth century, a duck pond, and cobbled streets. Business owners were getting an early start and the scent of fresh bread wafted from a bakery.

She started jogging at a steady pace but as soon as she finished her warmup time and began picking up the pace, she struggled to control her breathing. It was as if she had a band tied around her chest and her breath came in short gasps. The day was not yet hot and it wasn't her body causing the problem, no, she knew the reason – it was her conscience. At last it had caught up with her. Ever since that night at Sussex Abbey, she had been haunted by the sound of Aleksey struggling to suck in air.

She slowed down. She had been prepared to go along with Harry and carry out his sick plan. Who had Harry turned her in to? Her dream was to care for people not murder them in cold blood.

There was no doubt in her mind that Harry was mad. A few days ago she would never have believed him capable of such evil but it was Harry who had commanded her to stay by Aleksey's side and watch him die.

Afterwards, she had been forced to help Harry load the body into the back of their car. Harry had been hyped as hell and he kept laughing. Then he had taken poor Aleksey down to the river. He showed no remorse, no regret. All he was interested in was the Kavani money and he had his claws into Shannon.

Another runner greeted her and she gave a nod back. She wanted out and she was not stupid enough to believe Harry would let her go willingly.

She had one thing going in her favour and that was the kiss she had shared with Jared. If Shannon were out of the way, in time, he could be hers.

She stopped running and pulled out her phone. Bringing up a map of the underground, she studied it for a few moments. She needed to remind herself she was a better person than Harry. That he could not drag her down with him. Time to make a quick visit.

Twenty minutes later, she arrived at an entrance to the underground. She joined people going to work, taking the steps down and then boarding a train to a different district of London. She felt her usual paranoia and kept checking around to try to spot anyone who might be tailing her but there seemed to be no one.

At the other end, she came out on Kensington High Street. She headed quickly along the streets, navigating her way to a row of fashionable mews houses. She checked the address. This was the place. Natasha stopped at a red door and rang the bell.

Chapter Forty

Jared

Jared was on his way to The Savoy hotel in Westminster. It was his usual place to meet his client Lilith for afternoon tea. She told him she loved the genteel atmosphere. She liked to sit in the glass-domed atrium while a pianist played beautiful music. Also, to be practical, it wasn't the sort of venue her fashion fans went to, so she could enjoy it without being mobbed by them. Lilith was sitting at her favourite table.

Jared kissed her on the cheek.

'Did you have a great time on vacation?' Lilith asked.

'It was a good recommendation, thanks. Sussex Abbey was nice.'

'Nice? Is that the best thing you've got to say about it? I was expecting more like – it was majestic, with sweeping views over the gardens and marble fountains and opulent rooms reminiscent of a palace.' Lilith waved her manicured hands in the air. 'I adore that hotel almost as much as I adore The Savoy. One day I'm going to hire it for one of my photoshoots.'

'Sounds like an idea. Are you sure they do that kind of thing?'

'Darling, everyone does that kind of thing if the price is right even snobby joints like Sussex Abbey. But you didn't invite me here to talk about your holiday, did you?' She scrutinised him, tapping her nails against her cup. 'Does this mean the final version of my book is ready? You haven't sent me the manuscript yet and I've been waiting. Mind you, I'm not complaining because it will be so hard to let you go.'

She reached across the table and stroked the back of his hand. He didn't pull away. Rather, he patted hers gently with his other hand.

'Oh my god, you're wearing that musky cologne again,' she said.

'You know that I'm not available. We've had a great working relationship and I like and respect you.'

'It's all right you don't need to say more, I know there's always been a 'but' in there. So handsome but so damned professional. Don't worry I've got the message.'

A waiter came with Jared's tea.

Lilith sighed. 'You can't blame a girl for trying. So if you're not here to flirt, which I really wish you were, and my damn book isn't finished yet, then I guess I'm here for that little favour you asked of me?'

He cleared his throat. 'I'm sorry and I feel a bit awkward about it. I know it sounded a strange request when I spoke to you on the phone. The thing is I wouldn't come to you unless it was important and I wouldn't ask if I didn't trust you.'

She arched an eyebrow. 'I don't know whether to be flattered or concerned but you know I'd help you in any way. It's always difficult to dig out information but I made it my priority and I've looked into it for you.'

'Thanks, and I didn't want to take advantage either.'

'You're not. Unless I want you to.'

He smiled and so did Lilith. They fell silent as a waiter brought them a plate of cakes.

'Oh my, these look delicious,' Lilith said.

Jared took a scone and smothered it in strawberry jam and cream. Lilith was a world-famous fashion influencer with a social media following of millions. She had started her business from her bedroom at age fourteen, on a council estate riddled with crime. Her brothers had been involved in criminal activities and they still were. Drugs, trafficking, stolen goods – she wasn't proud of them although she did love her brothers. He knew she kept in touch. He had contacted Lilith because what he needed was for her to use her networks to find out if Harry had criminal connections.

'You told me you met these people at Sussex Abbey and now they're staying with you?'

'Yes. There's something which doesn't feel right and Shannon's been acting strangely. The problem is they both seem very nice and there's nothing concrete to put my finger on. Maybe I'm being suspicious for no reason and what with the pregnancy and everything I've been finding it difficult to keep a perspective on things. Harry Forrester, the one I talked to you about, has made me a business proposition and Shannon wants me to invest.'

'Uh huh. Half a million up front is a lot for one investor. He must have a big deal going on to ask for that kind of cash.'

'He has and why shouldn't the guy ask? He has other people onboard. He's an entrepreneur who's used to taking risks and coming out on top. It could simply be how he operates, couldn't it? I know it all sounds bizarre.'

'I don't care,' Lilith said. 'I like bizarre.'

'Lilith, this is serious.'

She pursed her lips. 'I know, I just can't help feeling disappointed that you're not trying to get me into bed.'

Jared smiled. 'So did you find anything out?'

'I made sure my brothers knew how important it was to me. Harry Forrester isn't known by any of their connections. It's possible he moves in different circles but my younger brother has contacts with high-end fencing operations, you know, jewellery, art work and collector's pieces and so on, and he's got connections in Europe and the States. That name hasn't come up anywhere on the radar.'

'Right.'

'You've got to ask yourself, what was he doing at Sussex Abbey? Either he's a genuine guy who was on holiday or, it's possible he was there to thieve from the rich. It's the most likely scenario if he doesn't have the legitimate income to afford to stay there. If that were the case he would have to pass those stolen goods on somehow.'

'I suppose so.'

Lilith nodded. 'I know so. But there was one small detail my brother found and I didn't at all like the sound of it. It seems a few years ago Harry Forrester was questioned by the police in connection to some rich guy who had killed himself. It seems this guy, who had inherited wealth, lost most of his fortune over a couple of years. He gambled it away. Then he did himself in.'

'Did the police think anyone else was involved?'

'Nope but even so I don't like the connection to Forrester.'

'It could be a coincidence. Though Harry is a card player.'

'Is he now.' Lilith bit into an éclair topped with pink icing. 'That doesn't sound like a coincidence to me.'

'True. It's odd when you put the two things together.'

'Did you thoroughly check his business credentials?'

'I did. The Kavani lawyers looked into it and Harry came out without a blemish. They didn't find any red flags.'

'And yet here we are talking about him and coming up with questions.'

'I feel it's not rational. I've nothing concrete against the poor guy. In fact, he's very likeable.'

Lilith licked her fingers. 'If you really think there's something strange going on and he's got into your life, then you're playing a dangerous game. You should get him out straight away. I don't want to see you burned.'

Jared offered Lilith another cake. Was it possible that charming, easy-going Harry had another side to him? One which he kept hidden and which was much less nice? Possibly even dangerous?

Chapter Forty-one

Harry

Everything was going Harry's way, so why did he feel unsettled? He knew why. It was because of Natasha. She was acting aloof and cold and was keeping him distant. She was snubbing him in the bedroom and hardly glancing his way the rest of the time. It was as if the connection between them had been cut and that made him feel out of control. Enraged. It was why sex was becoming so rough because he couldn't hold himself back. Shit.

Natasha had gone off again on her bloody morning run. He paced the bedroom. Once Jared coughed up the money, he had planned to be out of here but now he had a better idea. Why not up the stakes and demand much more? Wouldn't that be a thrill ride Natasha would find impossible to resist? How could she say no to five million bloody pounds handed to them on a plate?

He ran his hands through his hair. The more he thought about it, the more he got hooked on the idea of snapping Shannon like a twig. Destroying her fucking perfect relationship with her fucking perfect husband. Those two were making him sick. He and Natasha were so much better than them.

Yes, pushing this job to the limit would bring Natasha back to him and then he and Natasha would ride laughing into the sunset.

Chapter Forty-two

Shannon

Rosie texted Shannon again that morning. *How are you doing? Yesterday, you sounded so down and sad. I was worried about you.*

I was just being silly. I feel better today, Shannon lied.

Mum would be happy about the baby. Try to concentrate on that and keep positive.

With both her parents passed on and her mother's birthday coming up soon, Rosie must be imagining she felt down because of the anniversary. It was so much worse because she always told her sister everything.

All she did now was lie.

Did the baby sense the horror and guilt which swirled around her belly? Would the negative feelings affect its development? Though she tried to tell herself she was being irrational, the thought of it twisted her insides into knots.

I'm worried the baby might sense something is wrong, she texted.

You mean with Mum's birthday coming up?

Yes.

I don't think so. What's going on with you? You don't seem yourself.

I guess it's hormones.

The baby will know its grandparents are sending love.

That made her reach for the tissue box.

'What's up, Shannon?'

She jumped, sending the tissue box skidding from the bed onto the floor. Harry laughed and picked it up as he walked straight into her bedroom as if he owned the place.

'I wondered where you were hiding. I really hope you haven't been trying to avoid me.'

'I've been busy and I don't feel well.'

'Oh dear, we're not having another wobbly moment, are we? You really mustn't and you know what? Why don't I make supper for us again tonight, wouldn't that be nice of me?'

'You're supposed to knock first, not waltz in.'

'I'm thinking homemade pizza and a rice salad with anchovies and sun-dried tomatoes, what do you think?'

She shrugged.

Harry tutted. 'Let's not be tetchy. Here I am trying to be nice, though I've heard pregnant women can go right off the rails with their feelings and all. Natasha tells me you might get food cravings and your legs might swell. Sounds like a horrible process to me.'

He sat down next to her on the bed and she shrank away, her skin crawling.

'I'm not feeling well.'

'Of course you're not and I want you to know I understand and I've got a wonderful little idea to cheer you up.'

With his blue eyes and blond curls, Harry had a perfect angelic face. No wrinkles. No signs of a bad conscience or sleepless nights. How could he carry on as if nothing had happened? She examined his face. How could such a nasty person be hiding underneath?

'Would you like to hear my idea?' He nudged her shoulder. 'Well here it is – you know how much you and I like playing cards and you already told me your sister is a player too, right? So I'm thinking we organise a game for tomorrow night. We can order in food and get plenty of booze and off we go.'

She wrapped her arms around her chest. 'No.'

His smile twitched and she caught a glint in his eyes. 'Now, now, Shannon, the correct answer is yes. Surely you can't be against a nice evening with friends? It will take your mind off, you know, *things*. Besides, I'm dying to meet Rosie. You've told us so much about her and I know she's been going through a difficult patch. Come on and be a sport and let's have some fun.'

Why on earth would he want to meet Rosie? And even if he did, she could not allow her sister to be dragged into this. She jutted out her chin. 'Rosie's busy tomorrow.'

'How do you know before you've even asked? Now don't spoil it, ask her. I'm sure you can be persuasive.'

She could think of nothing worse than a cards evening with Harry and Rosie. No, there was one thing worse and that would be holding it the following night. The day before their mother's birthday. She closed her eyes and prayed for the nightmare to go away. But when she opened them again, he was still there.

Jared had prepared a tray of fruit and snacks for her and Harry was busy helping himself and licking his fingers and then putting them back in the food. It turned her stomach.

'Jared would never agree to it. He doesn't like me playing cards.'

Harry shrugged. 'I know I can rely on you to talk him round. Now, what about this sister of yours, have you got some photos you can show me?'

Grabbing her phone out of her hand, he swiped his finger across the pattern of dots to unlock it.

'What? Don't look so surprised. How do you think I knew there was history between you and Aleksey? How do you think he got to that gala in the first place? It was from this little gem which you have the bad habit of leaving around. Let's see, photos. Oh dear, is this her, the one with the scruffy haircut?

Goodness, she needs to sort that out. I'd have imagined her to be much better looking. Still, looks and polish have nothing to do with her playing ability. Is she any good?'

Oh my god. Harry had his part in Aleksey being there that night.

'How dare you.'

Harry put his arm around her shoulders. 'You know very well why I dare so please answer my question about your sister. Is Rosie any good at cards?'

'She's not bad,' Shannon muttered.

'Speak up. Did she learn from your parents like you did?'

'Yes, we played as a family. Listen, Harry, okay I can organise something though not for tomorrow night and Rosie's very unlikely to be free, so how about in a few days?'

He wagged his finger. 'Tomorrow night is when I want it and tomorrow night is when you'll organise it for. Before I go, why don't you tell me a bit more about your parents, you know, so I've got some background and I can kick off some nice conversation with Rosie and make her feel at home.'

'She will feel at home because this is where I live.'

'Your parents, Shannon. Tell me about them.'

She tried to tie back her hair but gave up because her hands were shaking too much.

'I'm sure you'd like me to leave and the sooner you start talking the sooner that will happen.'

He threw a handful of dried fruits into his mouth and then flopped back on the bed with his hands behind his head.

Shannon swallowed. No, not her family and definitely not Rosie. Why all these questions? He was a monster but there was no way she would break down in front of him again. What was he up to? She had a horrible presentiment that Harry was manoeuvring to burrow deeper into her life. Why would he do that when he already had so much damning information against her?

196

Taking a drink of water, she told him about her parents, who had both been teachers. Her father had died of cancer and her mother had died in her sleep a few years afterwards, from heart failure.

'How awful for you. It must bring back such bad memories with Jared's father going through the same ordeal as your dad.'

The way Harry said it made it clear he didn't give a damn.

What was he up to?

He was staring at the ceiling. If he closed his eyes, could she suffocate him with a pillow? Push it over his face and hold it there until he stopped struggling? Who was she fooling, she didn't have the strength, though now she knew that she wished she had.

She took another drink of water. Wait, that wasn't the way. To beat Harry she would have to be cleverer than him. She didn't know how yet, but she swore on the life of her unborn child that she would keep Harry Forrester away from her sister *and* get the better of him.

Chapter Forty-three

Jared

It was generous how Harry had again volunteered to prepare supper. Jared appreciated it, though he did not appreciate the idea of inviting Rosie for cards the following evening. Shannon knew he didn't like those kinds of events. She had dropped that one on him when he came back from his meeting with Lilith and he had not had the heart to protest. He didn't play bridge and he didn't like blackjack and Shannon knew he only put up with her and Rosie's card evenings because of the fond memories it held for them of their parents.

He drummed his fingers on his desk. He was sorting through emails and Shannon was lying down with the bedroom door closed. She was doing a lot of that recently. He had overheard her spending a lot of time on the phone, though she ended the calls whenever he came in. He had caught the tone and they sounded professional rather than personal. What was she up to? It fed into his feeling that something was very wrong.

Was she hiding something from him? Though he had taken her in his arms and practically begged her to confide in him, she had assured him everything was fine and she was simply worried about the pregnancy. He felt sure it was more than that. Whatever it was, they could fix it, as long as they worked it out together. He had told her exactly that and it had no effect, which had been disheartening. Why had she stopped talking to him? Didn't she trust him anymore?

Shannon had again mentioned how she wanted them to invest in Harry. When she said it, Jared immediately told her he wanted Harry and Natasha to leave. Shannon's response had frightened him. She had begged him tearfully to let them stay, saying she didn't feel she could cope without Natasha in the house.

The only thing which calmed Shannon down was him promising they could stay.

Jared scanned the lawyer's report again. Harry Forrester had never been bankrupt. He was not listed as a director of any limited company but that didn't mean anything because Harry had explained how his previous endeavours had been partnerships, which did not need to be registered. The problem was, Jared had no concrete information which he could use to explain to Shannon he didn't want to go ahead. Given her reaction to him wanting their guests out, he didn't dare bring up the subject.

He rubbed his hands over his face. God, it was impossible to think properly with Shannon acting so strangely.

He read through Harry's business plan one more time. It seemed solid and professional, as did Harry when he spoke about his strategies.

A while after, he made his way downstairs. Shannon was sitting next to Natasha on the sofa and Harry was reclining in Jared's usual chair. Harry already had a glass of wine in his hand and he put it down and jumped up.

'I didn't mean to take your place, my friend.'

'You're not, so for goodness sake make yourself at home.'

Though it looked as if Harry already had, since a bottle of red and one of white were opened. In one glance, Jared realised they were two of his best bottles. Ones which he had been saving for a special occasion. For sure, Harry had realised their worth.

Jared bit back a remark and poured himself a red. Harry taking liberties irked him a lot. But why shouldn't the guy? Jared hadn't made it clear any of the bottles in the store were out of bounds. He went to look out the window.

'Your pizza smells good,' Shannon said.

'Thank you,' Harry said. 'I hope it tastes good too.'

Was it Jared's imagination, or did she sound nervous? Like she wanted to keep everyone happy. Had she sensed his annoyance over the wine?

'I'd better go and check on it, and you're a darling for saying so,' Harry said. He leant across and patted Shannon's knee. Then he went to the kitchen.

Jared frowned. *He's only being friendly*, he told himself. Yet he hadn't liked the way Harry acted so familiar, and it wasn't really her knee he touched was it, more like her thigh. He took a gulp of his drink. The bottle had cost a few hundred pounds and he couldn't even enjoy it because he was so stirred up by misgivings. *Yes, misgivings with no substance*, he reminded himself. *Remember, Harry and Natasha have helped us out several times.*

Half a million of his family's money – for him and for Shannon it was a ridiculous amount to gamble with. But for his father, it was not so serious.

On the outside, Harry's behaviour was as charming as ever yet the man was making Jared grit his teeth. However, what he was sure of, was that if he offered the investment, Harry's guard would be down and if there was something bad going on that was when it might come out.

The man might make a mistake and if he did, Jared would be ready. As far as he was concerned, there were no limits on what he would do to protect his wife and his unborn child.

200

Chapter Forty-four

Harry

Harry laughed to himself. Jared had taken him aside and had solemnly said that he agreed to invest in the business venture. What a loser. The man didn't have a suspicious bone in his body and little did Jared know this was just the beginning because this time he was going all out. This would be the jackpot for him and Natasha. Half a million was peanuts to the Kavanis, but five million sounded about right.

The next step was to get Rosie under his control. It would give him an extra pressure point if he needed it, and then he could squeeze Shannon until she popped.

He took another sip of wine. This red really was pretty good. He had found the bottle stashed at the back of Jared's wine store and he had immediately recognised it as being an expensive vintage. Jared had not passed any comment on Harry helping himself to it, which cemented his view that the man was a pushover.

Harry raised his glass. 'Here's to our success.'

He surveyed the three of them. Natasha was giving him an adoring gaze. Shannon was smiling although it was perhaps a little strained. That was to be expected but at least she was making an effort. Meanwhile, Jared had one hand in his pocket and he was standing relaxed over by the window, ready to enjoy an evening with friends.

'Who's for a slice of pizza?' Harry said.

My god, he was a master and they were putty in his hands.

Chapter Forty-five

Shannon

Following Jared's decision to back Harry, Shannon had expected to feel relieved. Instead she felt stressed to the point of feverishness. What had she got them into? Why hadn't she been courageous and told Jared the truth? Or taken the brave decision to go to the police?

She spent as much time as possible online researching Harry and Natasha. She wanted information about their lives. She wanted to find out as much as she could and then she might have a chance of discovering leverage. Harry was so polished and devoid of morality. What if she was not the first person he had blackmailed?

Natasha had accepted her Facebook friend request and Shannon had been trawling through Natasha's news feed. She had found photographs of their wedding and of them arm in arm at various events. It seemed Harry was a motor racing enthusiast and there were pictures of him posing with men whom she presumed were famous drivers. She had also found pictures of Natasha in nursing uniform.

There had been nothing which didn't fit in with their image of a well-connected couple. To identify the people in the pictures she had enlisted the help of a company specialising in facial recognition software, whose owner happened to be one of Donald's clients. He had been happy to help her.

The anxiety was affecting her physically, making it hard to eat. She was in a downwards spiral as she stressed about the wellbeing of the baby. She had to force food into her mouth, squeezing her eyes shut as she swallowed. She must eat protein, and she must eat fruit and vegetables or her child would suffer. Its health could be affected or her own blood pressure could mount and jeopardise the entire pregnancy.

She also had a balance problem, and often had to steady herself on the wall. She didn't dare tell Jared for fear he would ban her from going to the spa. Her bed was one escape and the pool was another and she could not bear the idea of being deprived of either.

Natasha had told her that the wobbles were likely caused by the adjustments her body was making to the pregnancy and to stress. Of course, they both knew the true cause of the strain. Natasha recommended maximum rest.

'Don't worry,' Natasha said. 'It will all be over soon.'

'I don't believe you.'

'You should. Once Harry gets what he wants, he'll move on.'

That afternoon Shannon went to the pool, and cooled off on the steps with her legs in the water. Jared came to the spa too, to keep an eye on her, she felt sure, though she hardly spoke to him and kept closing her eyes to stop him talking to her.

Jared kept asking her to trust him. He must wonder why she was acting strangely. Why she was so silent and closed off from him. She did trust him. Yet she knew how honest he was and how much integrity he had and no way would he ever be able to accept what she had done. She could not cry about it, all she felt was numb as she struggled to free herself from Harry's iron claws. Was Harry wanted by the police or was she the only one to suffer at his hands? Was Natasha innocent or was the woman Harry's accomplice? They were questions she was determined to find answers to.

That evening when Rosie arrived, Shannon flung her arms around her sister's neck and hung on. Rosie hugged her and stroked her hair.

'Hey come on now, these are happy days not sad ones,' Rosie said gently.

Oh God, just like Jared, Rosie thought she was upset about their mother's birthday. If her mother and father knew what she had done, they would be turning in their graves.

'I know, and I've missed you,' she said, and it came out muffled against her sister's shoulder.

She caught Jared exchanging a worried look with Rosie.

'Lovely to see you,' Jared said, and he kissed his sister-in-law.

'You too, and like I said to Shannon there's got to be no talk tonight about Mum, and none about my damn divorce either. Before you ask, it's almost finished. I'm so totally sick of it I just want it over as quickly as possible so I can move on. No sad stuff tonight please, just drinks and laughs and fun.'

'Right. Well, come through and we'll introduce you to our friends,' Jared said.

Rosie looked very nice in a short flowery dress.

'You look great. Is that new?' Shannon asked.

'I bought it on my way home from signing the settlement, as a celebration for getting rid of that asshole.'

'It suits you,' Shannon said.

It was so comforting to have Rosie there that for a moment Shannon imagined the world might go back to normal. Then they reached the lounge and she heard Harry's voice and her spirits plummeted.

'Is this the lovely sister I've been hearing so much about?' Harry said.

Jared introduced Harry and Natasha, and Harry was just as disarming as he had been when they first met at Sussex Abbey, raining charm and good humour onto Rosie and enchanting her with his sparkly eyes.

It wasn't long before Rosie was acting like a flower that had been starved of sunlight. She laughed along with Harry's jokes and delighted in his comments. Oh God, please don't say that Rosie – cynical, hard-headed Rosie who had had enough of men and wanted to wipe her dirty shoes all over them – was going to be caught like a fly in Harry's web. Shannon could not bear it.

They had ordered in takeaway from their local Greek restaurant – houmous, tzatziki and falafel and deep-fried haloumi cheese. It was one of her favourites yet she put food in her mouth and did not taste a thing.

At one point, to Shannon's horror, Harry leant towards Rosie and wiped a splash of houmous off her cheek with his finger. It happened when Natasha had gone to the bathroom. Shannon's heart leapt into her throat. She prayed Rosie would swipe his hand away or make a barbed comment, but when she giggled, Shannon felt like gagging.

When Natasha returned to the table, Harry acted as if nothing had happened. He kept topping up everyone's glass, including Rosie's. Was it because she was the only sober one that she noticed what was so wrong about him? It had never been so obvious to her as it was that night.

After dinner, they settled to play blackjack. Jared didn't join in despite being pressured and cajoled by Harry. Shannon admired her husband for sticking to his resolve.

During the cards, she couldn't help thinking that Harry's attention kept focusing on Rosie. She wanted to scream at him to stop, except he wasn't doing anything wrong, was he? Giving compliments wasn't bad. Being attentive and passing wine and smiling wasn't evil. Yet she could not help seeing a sinister undercurrent in everything he did.

She was last in every single round and she didn't care. She watched for her opportunity to speak to Rosie in private and as soon as she got a chance, she followed her sister to the bathroom.

'Are you sure you're okay?' Rosie asked. 'You're all jumpy and spikey with Jared.'

She rubbed a hand over her forehead. 'I can't help it.'

Rosie made sympathetic noises. 'Hormones, I guess? Emotions? How about after we visit Mum and Dad's grave tomorrow, then we go somewhere for lunch?'

They had agreed to a ritual of laying flowers a couple of times a year together. On her mother's birthday and on her father's.

'I can't do lunch, I'm sorry. I've got too much on and I have to take care of our guests.'

'Of course you do and they are so nice, I mean you're really lucky to have met them.'

'I need to talk to you about Harry.'

They were standing outside the bathroom and she dragged Rosie along the corridor and into Jared's study.

Once the door was closed, she took a deep breath. 'He's dangerous.'

'What are you talking about?'

'I wanted to tell you before except I wasn't sure if maybe I was going a bit crazy. After seeing how he's acting around you, I know I was right to be suspicious. He's up to something.'

'Up to something? Seriously? He's your friend isn't he and you invited him to your house. That doesn't make sense.'

'You're flirting with him.'

'No, I'm not.'

'You need to stay away from him.'

'So what if I'm having a nice time, isn't that what you invited me here for? I mean it's a bit odd he's so charming when his wife's right there but don't you want me to be happy? It's been ages since a man treated me with respect and why shouldn't I enjoy it.'

'You don't understand!'

'Then explain it to me because you're really sounding odd here. Harry is kind and considerate. He's funny and smart and I can't see anything I don't like, so accusing your own guest is a bit irrational isn't it?'

Shannon started trembling.

'You're shaking.' Rosie put her arm around Shannon. 'Has he done something? Please don't tell me he's made a pass at you?'

'Of course not.'

'Then what's going on? If you don't like him then say it. Me and Jared can kick them out if that's what you want.'

If that happened Harry would go berserk and goodness knows what he would do to punish her. With the power he had over her, he could do anything he wanted, couldn't he?

'No! I want them to stay.'

'Then why are you acting so strangely? I don't get it.'

'Do you trust me?'

'Of course I do.'

'There's stuff I can't explain right now, not even to you, but you've got to help me. I need to get information about Harry and if you could play along with him that might work except it's got to be an act. He can't suspect that you're digging on my behalf and I can't risk you falling under his control.'

'Jesus, what the hell's happened?'

'I can't tell you. Not yet.'

Rosie pulled her into a hug. 'Are you sure?'

I killed a man and Harry knows it. He'll break me if I don't do what he says. 'I can't get a grip.'

208

Rosie stroked Shannon's hair. 'Sweetie, you're all over the place.'

I don't want my baby to be born in prison and taken away from me. I'm so ashamed but I can't tell anyone. 'I know I'm being horrible to Jared but I can't seem to stop myself. It's Harry, he's to blame. Will you help me?'

'Of course I bloody well will, you're my sister. As long as you promise to explain it all to me. No, I don't mean now, I mean someday, when you're ready.'

Shannon nodded. 'I promise.'

'We're going to get through this anniversary together. I'm going to look after you. Then all you've got to look forward to is you and Jared and your wonderful baby. Tell me what you need me to do.'

Chapter Forty-six

Natasha

For the cards evening, Natasha chose a short red dress with frills and lace. The dress Rosie wore looked frumpy in comparison, and as for Shannon, she was a mess. Though she wore a nice skirt and a silky top, Shannon's make-up was a disaster area, giving her panda eyes. Clearly Shannon's mind was elsewhere. Perhaps the woman was on the verge of a breakdown.

Watching Harry work on Rosie was amusing. She had to admit it was slightly sad how easily Rosie fell for it. Natasha almost felt sorry for the woman making a fool of herself like that, when Harry was simply jerking her chain.

Up until now, she had always thought of Harry's looks and his charisma as a gift. A gift which gave him a great advantage in conning people. Now she wondered if perhaps it had been a curse. After all, if Harry had been born with plain looks, might it have forced him to earn an honest living? Might he never have made a success of worming his way into people's lives? The same could have been said for Harry's mentor, his uncle, who had matching angelic curls and blue eyes.

She enjoyed her wine. It was wonderful quality. Likely Harry had selected one of Jared's best and without bothering to ask permission either. It was Harry's way. He gave people a lot of attention and praise and at the same time he stepped on their toes. Usually, they were so dazzled by him that they dismissed their own misgivings and that gave Harry the opportunity to wriggle his way closer.

Natasha understood Harry's game. He had his sights firmly set on the Kavani bank balance and Rosie was a means of putting more emotional pressure on Shannon. He should not overdo it. If he put more strain on Shannon and it ended up with her losing the baby, the whole show would be off.

For the time being, they were still the pampered guests with posh toiletries in their ensuite bathroom, a gorgeous double walk-in shower and a king-sized bed and round-the-clock access to a private spa.

They had a very nice dinner and then Harry started off the cards. She let herself get pleasantly drunk and daydreamed about sneaking off to the pool with Jared. There was a sauna there too. Wouldn't it be wonderful to sit there with him, her skin glowing, and to allow the moment to overtake them? *That won't work*, she told herself, *he wouldn't want to go so fast, he's too loyal to Shannon*. No, she must work on him very slowly so that when this was over he would naturally be drawn towards her.

It wasn't until later in the evening that she had a chance to follow Jared to the kitchen. He stored the wine in a cool room at the back and when he went inside, she followed him.

'Oh hi, Natasha. Can I get you something?' Jared asked.

Ever the gentleman. She flushed with pleasure and flicked back her hair.

'Some ice cream would be nice.'

'Of course. There's some in the freezer. Just give me a moment.'

It was dim in the store and quite cramped and she wondered if he was looking at her body. She hoped so.

'I've been meaning to talk to you about how things are going with your father. I know you met with him. Has there been an update on his treatment?'

'It's very kind of you to ask, actually he had his first chemotherapy today. Mum said it took the strength right out of him and she had difficulty getting him home afterwards. She could hardly get him up the stairs to bed.'

'Oh dear. That's not unusual and it doesn't mean it's a bad sign. Chemo affects everyone differently. He'll need to get plenty of rest. I don't know if it will be practical, but you might like to think about putting a bed downstairs. Just temporarily.'

'That's a good idea.'

'You might find he gets used to the treatments or the hospital might adjust his dosage so he can manage better. Be sure your parents talk to the nurses each time to keep them updated about how it's going.'

'Yes, I'll remember to tell them, thank you. Mum said he had his infusion in a room with other people who were having the same treatment. I think it must have been really hard for both of them.'

'It's strange at first. Don't worry, people get used to it very quickly. I've heard stories of a lot of support and friendships happening in chemo rooms. More seasoned patients like to help the newcomers.'

Jared pushed back his hair. 'It's reassuring talking to you about it. I'm going to see if I can help Mum out with the driving back and forth. As soon as I feel I can leave Shannon on her own.'

'That will be nice for them and it will help your mother to save her strength. She needs to look after herself too. You know I'm here, so I can keep an eye on Shannon if you need me to.'

'You're really kind. I haven't wanted to talk to Shannon too much about it. She's got a lot on her mind.'

Natasha nodded. 'She mentioned the upcoming anniversary. She's not doing too well, is she? I mean psychologically.'

'Not really. She didn't even ask how Dad's treatment went today. I think she forgot about it.'

'Oh, I'm sorry.'

'I'm worried there's something serious bothering her. She's just not behaving normally and she's shutting herself off. When we had the pregnancy news she was so bright and happy. And I mean it's been so up and down the last few years I sort of got used to it, but this seems different.'

In two steps Natasha was standing close to him. She breathed in the scent of his cologne, hmm, it was a nice one. Jared put down a bottle of wine. His expression was unfathomable.

'Hormone levels play a big part in how we feel,' she said, 'both physically and emotionally and they play a big part in pregnancy.'

'We've been through such a rough time and I thought it was behind us. Shannon had such longing for a child. At times she was depressed and I remember her mother's birthday last year was a particularly bleak period. I didn't expect it to happen this time around what with the baby news.'

She reached out to touch his arm. 'Anniversaries are difficult to cope with. She might need time. Things will go back to normal soon, I'm sure they will.'

Jared seemed close to tears. 'I'm trying to understand and give her the space she needs and I'm trying not to burden her too much with news about Dad. I'm sorry to overload you with my problems.'

'You're not. If I'm being honest it's nice to have someone to talk to. I mean, have you seen how Harry is acting this evening? It can be so humiliating when he flirts like that right in front of me.'

'I think he's just being nice to Rosie.'

She dabbed at her eyes. 'We both know it's a bit more than that.'

'Please don't cry,' he said. 'You're making me go teary.'

There was a silence and she gently reached to encircle him with her arms. When she hugged him close, he didn't pull away.

'Remember,' she said. 'You're not alone. I'm here for you.'

Chapter Forty-seven

Harry

Harry flopped onto the bed. As far as he was concerned it had been a successful evening and everybody had fun, especially him.

Rosie had been impressed by him. Shannon had towed the line and been quiet and obedient. Jared had been the perfect host, not even batting an eyelid at Harry helping himself to the most expensive wine in the house. Well, Jared could hardly complain, the wine had been used to celebrate, hadn't it? Because Harry could feel in his guts he was about to close this mammoth deal and there was nothing and no one standing in his way.

He pointed at Natasha. 'Take my shoes off for me, will you?'

Natasha was removing her earrings and she turned her back to him. 'Can't you do that yourself?'

He didn't like it. Her tone was neutral but he could not see her face. She must be teasing him. One thing was for sure – she could not possibly be serious.

'If I wanted to do it myself I wouldn't be asking, would I?'

He kept his tone light and as she moved towards him, he gave her a smile to sweeten the deal. Her reluctance was annoying. It wasn't so long ago that his wife would have dropped everything and come running to attend to his every need.

The sooner things got back to normal between them the better. Which meant getting the booty and getting out as a matter of urgency. Once he had her on her own it would be much easier to control her.

'Five million smackeroos, isn't that amazing? Pour me a drink, babes.'

She passed him a glass of bourbon and he took a swig. The night the man died had taken its toll on her. He understood that. Soon they would be able to forget all about it.

Had Aleksey's death affected him? Not really. Collateral damage, that's how he thought of it – an unfortunate necessity for the sake of business. In his mind they were opportunists and Natasha had to get that into her pretty little head. He could understand it was difficult to come to terms with, but there was only so far his patience could stretch.

If he was being honest with himself, he wasn't certain *collateral damage* was the only source of the problem between them. Natasha had been acting much more distant since Sussex Abbey and although she had given up on the silent treatment he couldn't help feeling she might have *turned*.

The idea of it gave him a nasty muscle spasm in his neck. *Turning* was a terminology his uncle used to describe when associates, who had previously been your loyal partners, secretly and manipulatively began to act against you.

Did she think he had been too preoccupied with Rosie to notice her leaving the room to follow Jared? They had been away for rather a long time. Finding one bottle of wine and some ice cream should not have needed half an hour. It had taken a while for Jared to meet his eye too, which was a sure-fire way of indicating something significant had happened between Jared and Natasha. It had made Harry hot with jealousy.

Like a pro, Natasha had given nothing away. Yet during the second half of the evening he could sense a change in her.

She had seemed almost, well, happier. Yes, the sooner they got out of there the better.

'My shoulders are absolutely killing me,' he said. 'Be a darling and give me a massage.'

He let her take off his shirt for him and then he dropped his shorts to the floor and told her to strip. She did, and he was soon staring up at her beautiful body while she rubbed oil into him. Yet he could not totally relax because it was as if there was a strange undercurrent in her which he could not put his finger on.

Later, Harry flopped on his side and pretended to sink quickly into sleep. Angry thoughts kept him awake. She belonged to him. Till death us do part – she had stood there and sworn herself to him and if she no longer wanted to be by his side he would rather see her dead. And that was the damn truth.

Chapter Forty-eight

Shannon

Shannon wore a black dress and matching shoes. Jared had tried to persuade her to select something more colourful but she had refused. This was how she felt. Bleak.

Jared had bought a lovely bouquet of white and yellow roses, her mother's favourites.

'Are these good enough?' he asked.

'Yes thanks,' she said, her voice monotone.

She was going downhill and she knew it. During their quest for a baby, she had been seeing a psychologist and it was only a matter of time before Jared suggested she have another consultation. He was probably waiting for the right moment to propose it. Maybe he would talk about it tomorrow or the day after, once the flower laying was out of the way, she supposed. But it wouldn't help, would it? Because she could tell no one the truth about why she was so down, not even a therapist.

She was running out of time. Rosie was spending the morning with Harry but would it be enough for her to find out anything of value?

Shannon had several names of wealthy people who had been pictured in shots with Harry and she was working her way down the list, digging into their backgrounds and searching through news snippets. So far, she had found no dirt on Harry and no connection to bankruptcy nor police investigations. Her next move would be to phone these people or even to visit them but she was already on her knees. How could she manage it before she cracked up?

She and Jared were the first to arrive at the cemetery and she knelt before the plaque bearing the names of her parents. They had organised the meeting for two o'clock and it wasn't like Rosie to be late. Jared had not dressed in black, and Shannon stared at his shoes and the hems of his pale trousers as he stood close to her.

'I can see Rosie coming along the path,' Jared said. 'She's got somebody with her. Did she say her ex-husband was coming?'

'No. Why would she bring *him*?'

'I can't see properly, she's behind the trees but it looks like him. Oh no, wait, it's not. It's Harry.'

She clutched at the grass. She and Rosie had agreed this was how it should play out but she had not expected such a strong physical reaction to the fact that he would now sully this morning of remembrance.

'Hi Jared, hi Shannon,' Harry called out cheerily. 'I thought I'd offer your sister a lift, given she's on her own and all, and that this is a sensitive day.'

'*We* could have given Rosie a lift if she needed it,' Shannon said. 'I don't want you here. This is just for family.'

Jared patted his wife's shoulder. 'It's all right, darling.'

'Come on, Shannon, don't be like that,' Rosie said. 'Harry's welcome and he's been such a dear. He picked me up and he took me to buy flowers. Then we had to wait ages in the traffic on our way here. He's been an angel.'

Harry was smiling at her. It was one of those horrible smiles of his which didn't meet his eyes. 'I can go if I'm causing upset. Just say the word, Shannon, and I'll leave. I can wait for Rosie by the gate.'

A frisson of fear raced up her spine. And he might what? Tell Rosie what happened at Sussex Abbey? Shannon was powerless to stop him doing any number of horrible things. It had been a huge gamble already to leave Rosie alone with him.

'It's okay, I was just surprised to see you. I'm sorry I overreacted,' she said.

Harry put his arm around Rosie. 'Oh I understand,' he said, graciously. 'Don't think anything of it.'

Shannon closed her eyes. How she hated him. All she needed was one nugget of information. Please, please, if her mother and father were listening, could they help her get what she needed to nail him.

Chapter Forty-nine

Natasha

Natasha realised Harry was pushing Shannon too far. It would have been wiser for him not to go to the cemetery. If he wasn't careful she would lose the baby and then she would go right off the rails. Likely the woman would end up in psychiatric care if that happened. Harry was too blinded by his own agenda to listen. The idea of making Shannon squirm was too much for him and he could not resist. He was besotted with the goal of bleeding the Kavanis for millions. What had made him become so unhinged?

He planned an exotic vacation in Hawaii to celebrate their win. It was odd because it was somewhere she had been asking to visit for years but Harry had always refused.

Too late of him to think of it now. It was typical of Harry to be blind to the fact there was nothing left to save of their relationship.

On her morning run that day, the back of her neck had prickled, just like it often did when she felt she was being watched. For the first time, it had occurred to her that it could be Harry who stalked her. How was that possible? Harry the sloth? The man who could not even open his eyes before midday? He had told her he was spending time with Rosie and then taking her to the cemetery but why should she believe anything which came out of his mouth?

She had gone for a run and afterwards she had taken the underground to Kensington and gone to the house with the red door again.

She didn't care about Harry anymore. However, it was useful to know his plans so she could make her own.

Chapter Fifty

Shannon

Shannon sat on the edge of the bed, still wearing her black dress. Jared was changing into his shorts.

'Would you like me to help unzip your dress?' he asked.

'No.'

They had not been back long from the cemetery. What she wanted was for Jared to leave because Rosie had been chatting to Harry. Rosie got plenty of inconsequential information but she had also got one name. Apparently, the last time Harry visited a cemetery was with Natasha and it was to lay flowers at the grave of an elderly man. Harry had told Rosie that they had become friends with this man and his wife, and that Natasha had been very upset when the man died.

He had also told Rosie that they had missed the ceremony and had gone later to lay flowers. It was an odd detail and it had struck Rosie as strange because when she had probed, Harry side-stepped giving an explanation for why they were absent. When Rosie told Shannon this, that little detail interested her and when she heard the widow's name, Lady Pemberton, she was even more interested. It was one of the people she had identified from Natasha's Facebook page.

Shannon had scanned her notes. She had already found out that Lord and Lady Pemberton had been lifelong donors to a children's hospital and that Harry and Natasha also became donors about five years earlier. Natasha had posted a picture of them with the Pembertons at a charity event. So what? There was nothing suspicious about that. Except, according to Rosie, Harry and Natasha had *become friends* with the Pembertons. Just like they had done with Shannon and Jared.

It could be nothing, she told herself. Lord Pemberton likely died of natural causes and there was nothing murky going on. Or it could be important. Why had Harry and Natasha missed the ceremony? Why had Rosie felt Harry fobbed her off and didn't give an answer? Was she clutching at straws? Shannon had closed her eyes. *The devil is in the detail,* she whispered to herself. A shiver went up her back because it was one of her mother's favourite sayings.

She should talk to Natasha about the Pembertons. No, because Natasha might then warn Harry. It would be better to speak to the widow.

'I'm going to take the electrical equipment out of the cinema room,' Jared said. 'I was thinking that tomorrow we can choose some paint and I'll start the redecoration.'

'Don't bother.'

'I know today is a difficult day, which is why maybe it would be best to focus on the good things.'

'Shut up, Jared! You don't understand.'

In response to her shouting at him, a hurt look flashed across his face, which cut her like a knife.

'Then help me to,' Jared said. 'All you've done recently is shut me out. I'm here for you. Whatever is troubling you, we can work it out.'

His calm tone infuriated her.

'Oh yes, well how do you plan to work this out? I - killed - a - man!'

'W-what?'

'I said, I killed a man.'

'You're not making any sense.'

'Are you deaf? I - murdered - somebody. He was one of Donald's clients and he had been harassing me. Then he followed me and came to Sussex Abbey and I lost control. Aleksey had an allergic reaction to nuts and I threw away his medication. He died on the spot. It was the night of the gala.'

Jared shook his head. 'I don't believe you.'

'Well you should. Harry got rid of the body and now he's blackmailing me. That's what the half a million is for – so Harry will shut up and leave me alone.'

'That's not possible.'

'Why the hell aren't you listening to me?'

'I *am* listening. I think we need to take you to the doctor.'

'No fucking doctors and no psychiatrists. I'm not crazy, Jared!' she screamed. 'I'm telling the truth but the problem is you can't take it.'

Chapter Fifty-one

Shannon

After she screamed at him, Jared had stormed out of the bedroom. A few moments later she heard the front door slam.

What she told him about Aleksey and Sussex Hotel had finally rendered Jared speechless. She had wanted him to shout back. To be angry. To be furious. Instead, it was like he had imploded.

This was it then, the end of them. She had not only killed Aleksey, she had killed her marriage.

It was the only way, Shannon told herself. She knew she had cracked under the pressure. What if she had driven Jared away for good? *Don't think about it. You can only save your marriage if you can get rid of Harry.*

She quickly changed her clothes and left the house. The devil is in the detail, she repeated to herself like a mantra. Lady Margaret Pemberton lived in Kingston-upon-Thames, which was about thirty minutes' drive by taxi. She only hoped Lady Pemberton would be at home.

Lady Pemberton's property had a long drive bordered by trees. It was an expansive estate and an elegant house, almost as impressive as Sussex Abbey.

'Please can you wait for me?' Shannon asked the taxi driver.

He gave a sigh. 'I'll have to charge you for it.'

'Of course.'

'I suppose I can have a look at the races. I've got my eye on a horse this afternoon.'

She was hardly listening. Had she finally lost the plot? She would soon find out. There was no space for nerves or embarrassment, she had to get in there and talk to Lady Pemberton.

The taxi driver scratched his beard. 'I'm not sure whether to punt on it or not. The odds are nineteen to one.'

Nineteen. A cold tingle ran up her spine. Was this a sign she was on the right track? *Thanks, Mum.*

She got out of the car and then called back to the driver.

'If I were you, I'd take that bet.'

Given the grandeur, she expected to be met at the door by a uniformed butler. Instead it was an elderly and spritely Lady Pemberton herself who greeted Shannon.

'How can I help you, young lady?' Lady Pemberton asked.

'I'm sorry to bother you. My name is Shannon Kavani and I know this is very unusual and you don't know me but I really need to talk to you. It's about Harry and Natasha Forrester. I think you might know them. I'm in a lot of trouble and I don't know if you can help me but I believe you might be able to.'

Lady Pemberton narrowed her eyes. 'I don't think I recognise that name.'

'Please. You know them, don't you, I can see it in your face. Please can we talk? Harry's making life very difficult for me. I'm expecting a baby and the strain is ruining my marriage and ruining my health. I can't go on like this.'

'You really are in a state, aren't you.'

Shannon nodded. 'He's blackmailing me.'

Lady Pemberton shook her head. 'I don't know how you got my name but yes, we did know them. We were so attached to Harry and my husband adored Natasha. They broke his heart with their nastiness though I really don't see how I can assist you. I'm sorry, I think you've come for nothing.'

'Could we just talk?'

'What will it do except bring up bad memories?'

'You're the only person who might understand. I'm desperate.'

Lady Pemberton sighed. 'I know that feeling, thanks to them. All right. Why don't you come in and we can chat over a cup of tea, but I'm not making any promises.'

Shannon almost wept with relief. 'Thank you so much, Lady Pemberton.'

'Come in, my dear. And you'd better call me Margaret.'

They sat in a room with a grand piano. Several framed photographs were arranged on a side table. Margaret showed each of them to Shannon and most of them featured her late husband.

'His name was Arthur. He was reserved and dignified. A lot of people thought he was aloof but he was really very timid. We had no children and he had always wanted a son or a daughter. I think that was how Harry Forrester was able to gain his trust so easily.'

Margaret told a sad story of how Arthur had met Harry at the golf course and the two of them started playing regularly together. Then Harry and Natasha became donors to a special hospital for children for which Margaret and Arthur had been patrons for years. From that point on they had practically adopted the young couple. Harry and Natasha had been invited to their villa in Italy that summer and then they had holidayed together in the Alps at Christmas. The four of them became so close, Margaret said it had felt as if Harry and Natasha were family.

Arthur had a priceless Egyptian artefact which had been handed down from his great-great-grandfather. Since the estate was in dire need of funds for maintenance, Harry had come up with the idea of auctioning it off through unofficial channels.

'You see,' Margaret said, 'the artefact couldn't be sold through official channels because it really should have been returned to the Egyptian government. We didn't know the full details, but the story was it had been smuggled out from a dig in the old days. Arthur should have given it to a museum long ago but he never had. Then Harry came up with this bright idea. I know it looks like we have a lot of wealth, and we do, but it's all tied up in land. What we needed was cash, and an awful lot of it, to stop this place falling apart.'

'Harry is clever. He knows how to play on people's vulnerabilities.'

'Yes he does and Natasha does too. She really fooled Arthur and that was the part which broke him.'

Shannon sat up straighter in her seat. 'What happened?'

'When I think of it now it sounds silly. We trusted Harry with everything. We let Harry handle the sale because he was so enthusiastic about it and it seemed he really wanted to help us. Harry did all the research online. It wasn't long before he found a buyer. The new owner wanted discretion as much as we did, and the artefact was bought for a colossal sum. Harry organised the shipping and it was the night after that Harry and his wife went missing and so did the money.'

'Oh no.'

'We felt so silly. At first Arthur believed it must be some kind of mistake. It took a while for the horrible truth to sink in. He kept making excuses for Harry and waiting for him to get in touch. The truth was we had been conned, well and truly. All the money was gone and we had no recourse, because we should never have been selling it in the first place and Harry had all the records. The whole thing was so stressful and upsetting.'

Margaret choked on emotion and Shannon nodded sympathetically. 'I'm so sorry.'

'It wasn't long after that Arthur had his first heart attack. I know I can't say if one caused the other, but I can tell you honestly that in my heart I know Arthur was broken by what those people did to him. He never recovered. He had the fatal heart attack a few months later.'

'I am so so sorry. They're such evil people and they come across as completely believable. I thought Harry was helping me. When all along he was putting me in his debt so he could extort money from me and my husband.'

'Is that what's happening to you? My dear, you are very smart to have understood his game. The truth is, I don't see how I can be any help. Arthur told me I must never go to the police. The thought of being seen as dishonest and of being cheated by someone like Harry was too much for Arthur to bear.'

'I understand.'

Why should Margaret help her? The woman was under no obligation and she had already been through so much pain. But Shannon could feel the connection between them, one who had suffered because of Harry to another, and she was sure Margaret felt it too.

Shannon nodded. 'That's how he gets away with it. He makes it so no one wants to challenge him. All his victims are scared to do it because we get exposed. But what about your husband? You've told me that what Harry did led to your husband's death. He might even succeed in killing my baby.'

'Oh please don't say that, my dear.'

The tea had been poured and it sat going cold. Margaret stared at the cups. 'I'm not strong enough to go to the police. I'm sorry.'

'Please don't apologise, I know exactly how you feel. But it would really help me if I could use your name when I speak to Harry. I'm going to confront him. I could lie and tell him we're both going to report him. There must be other victims too and if he thinks we'll both speak out then it might have an impact.'

'I'm not sure he'll fall for it.'

'But I have to try!'

'You're very brave. Yes, all right, you can use my name and tell him we've spoken. There's no reason for him to realise I wouldn't see it through.'

'Thank you.'

'I wish I was as courageous but all I want to do is cushion myself from more hurt. I should also tell you I hired a private investigator.'

'You looked into Harry?'

'Absolutely, though don't get your hopes up. She didn't find out much. There are only two bits of information which might be useful. She discovered Harry has been questioned by the police. It was some years ago, during the investigation into the death of a man who killed himself after losing a lot of money. Harry Forrester was a friend of the deceased, and they had spent a lot of time together in the months preceding the death, but no charges were brought against Forrester. The second thing concerns Natasha. Apparently, she attempted to train as a nurse and dropped out. My investigator discovered that Harry pressurised a key member of staff to make certain Natasha failed.'

'You're sure about that?'

'Positive. I can give you names and details. I've got the file in my study.'

Shannon's hands were shaking and she clutched them in her lap. 'Thank you, Margaret. You might have given us a chance.'

Chapter Fifty-two

Natasha

Natasha heard Jared thumping his way down the stairs and then the front door slammed as he left the house. A few moments later, Shannon left too. What was going on? There had been shouting and screaming so something had happened between them. Oh good, perhaps they had broken up.

Soon after, Harry returned from dropping off Rosie after the graveyard visit and he was in a cheerful mood, whistling one of his favourite songs. 'Where's our little Shannon?'

'She went out.'

'Where to?'

'How should I know?'

'Oh come on, darling,' Harry said. 'You're supposed to be keeping your eye on her. We can't have her collapsing out on the street, can we, not when I'm about to tell her I want five million.'

He was obviously expecting a reaction so she stopped herself from rolling her eyes, giggling instead. 'I love it when you talk dirty.'

He slapped her backside and she wriggled it and laughed.

'How about if we mix up some cocktails, and go and relax in the jacuzzi,' she said. 'Then when Shannon gets back you can pop the question.'

Harry grinned. 'Good idea. I'll whip up a big batch as a celebration.'

Some time later, to Natasha's surprise, Shannon joined them. Natasha and Harry were reclining on loungers.

'Oh dear, someone doesn't look very happy,' Natasha said.

'Jared's left.'

The way Shannon said it had a finality to it. Natasha felt a flicker of hope.

'You mean, he's gone out, right, and he hasn't come back yet?'

'I mean he's left.'

'Shannon you're not making any sense. If you guys had an argument or something then don't worry.'

'It's over between us.'

That's fantastic news. 'I'm sure that's not right. Jared will be back when he's ready. Why don't you sit with us and have a drink.'

Harry opened one eye and patted the lounger beside him. 'Natasha's right, you need to chill out. Besides, I've got a proposal you're going to find hard to refuse.'

Chapter Fifty-three

Shannon

Shannon shrugged off her robe and sat on the lounger. Her mind was clear, not floundering in the brain fog she had been fighting the last few days. She knew exactly what she was going to say to Harry. He had been drinking and he was in a merry mood. He grinned at her and she gave him a look filled with loathing.

'Now, now, Shannon, let's not get twisted up. Like I said, we can do this the friendly way,' Harry said.

Natasha passed a fruit juice to Shannon. 'Here take this. It might help you feel better.'

Nothing would make her feel better. Except perhaps Harry being dead.

'Go on, Shannon, taste it,' Natasha said. 'I mixed it myself, especially for you.'

She took the drink. 'I'm glad you want to talk, Harry, because I've something I want to say to you too.'

Harry finished his cocktail in a couple of gulps and wiped his mouth with the back of his hand. He held out his glass for a refill. 'Oh, what's that then?'

It was amazing that she wasn't even frightened anymore. All she felt was focused and lucid. 'I just had a very helpful meeting with Margaret Pemberton, you know, the woman you swindled out of a fortune. She blames you for the death of her husband. She and I had a nice cosy chat and we've decided you're a problem we want to get rid of.'

Harry was in the process of slugging down half his drink. He almost choked and turned it into a guffaw. Liquid spurted out of his mouth. 'Well, well, I didn't think you had it in you, what with your pathetic attempt to pressure me over my sexual exploits. You've been doing your homework, haven't you. Clever girl.'

Harry didn't seem bothered but that didn't mean he wasn't. She turned to Natasha. 'Arthur Pemberton loved you like a daughter and you betrayed him. How could you? His wife told me he died of a broken heart.'

Harry jumped to his feet and so did both women. 'There's no such thing. Who cares anyway? I certainly don't give a damn and neither does Natasha. He was old and he was gullible. He got what was coming to him.'

From the look on Natasha's face, Shannon knew she had hit a nerve. 'What you do to people is filthy and nasty. Margaret's prepared to go to the police and so am I. You could join us, Natasha. I know you're not like Harry.'

'Shut the fuck up,' Harry shouted. 'We're a team. We work together. Or haven't you managed to get your tiny brain around that yet? Natasha and I are closer than you and your stupid husband will ever be. We've got the special ingredient.' He tried to move towards Natasha to put his arm around her and he almost tripped over the lounger.

'Listen to me, Natasha,' Shannon said. 'This is your chance to get out.'

Harry must have drunk more than she realised because he made a grab at the back of the lounger to steady himself. 'Why would she want to do that when you're about to hand over five million? Oh don't look so surprised, yes, five big ones or you're the one who'll be facing a life in the cells. Mrs high-and-mighty

Pemberton wouldn't go to the authorities in a million years. I know you're bluffing.'

Shannon backed away. 'You call yourself a team? Is that why you pressurised Nurse Golding? You remember her, Harry? She was Natasha's supervisor, and you manipulated her to make sure Natasha failed her nursing placement. Is that what you call teamwork? I've got evidence. I've got details. Nurse Golding did it because she thought it was the only way to save her brother. Apparently he was beaten up pretty badly and was expecting more. She felt terrible about what she did afterwards, but it was too late. You made Nurse Golding do it. You're the one who threatened her brother behind the scenes so you could force Golding. You set Natasha up to fail.'

'That's a bloody lie!' Harry stumbled towards her, almost tripping over his own feet.

'Margaret Pemberton hired a private detective. Nurse Golding's apology is in Margaret's file.'

'Is that true?' Natasha said.

'No,' Harry shouted. 'You know she's lying.'

Natasha's cheeks were red with anger. 'Did you? Did you make sure I failed?'

'Of course not, don't listen to her. She's making it up.'

'I think Natasha knows that's not true. You ruined her dreams. You went behind her back and stuck the knife in. Just like you do with all your victims.'

Harry shook his head. 'No.'

'You fucking bastard!' Natasha screamed it into Harry's face. 'You did, didn't you. You spoilt it for me.'

Harry was losing his coordination. What the hell was the matter with him? For a moment, Shannon thought he was about to fall flat on his face but Natasha had other ideas. She had him by the shoulders and was forcing him towards the pool. Harry didn't seem to be able to control his limbs nor did he seem able to resist.

236

'I hate you!' Natasha shouted, as she toppled him into the
water.

Chapter Fifty-four

Jared

Jared had to get out of the bedroom. He couldn't breathe, he couldn't think straight. He didn't trust himself. It was as if he might explode at any moment and do something totally crazy.

His wife had killed a man? Murdered him in cold blood? And now Harry was blackmailing them? He took the stairs two at a time, his breathing jagged.

He slammed the front door. So violently, the glass could have shattered.

This was madness. Shannon must be lying. Or else she had lost her mind. But a voice inside his head told him to slow down. Told him she could be telling the truth. That it made sense of her strange behaviour and of his misgivings about Harry.

He wanted to scream at the sky. In a few seconds and in the space of a few sentences, his whole world had been destroyed. Worse and much more agonising, Shannon had pushed him so far away, he didn't know if he would ever be able to go back home.

He wanted to inflict pain. On Harry. And on himself.

He was not a violent man, but he wanted to go back there and punish Harry, push him against the wall and force the truth out of him. But if Harry really were blackmailing Shannon, attacking him would be a very bad strategy. He had to think straight. He had to work out what to do.

He walked the streets trying to get a grip on himself. His mind refused to accept his wife was a murderer. That the woman he loved, and the mother of his child, had killed a man. Surely there must be more to this? Shannon had said Aleksey was harassing her, so why had she never mentioned Aleksey before? Why hadn't she told him? Why hadn't she gone to the police? Sought out help? It didn't make sense.

He came to a park and sat on a bench. People moved away from him, which was a sure sign he looked as terrible as he felt. Jared knew he must sort himself out. He could not go to his parents nor to Lilith for help, that would be asking too much. No, he had to deal with this himself. What if his wife was going through some sort of breakdown or suffering a mental collapse? Should he bring in specialist help?

Time passed and the sun started sinking towards the horizon yet he still had no idea what to do. Should he go back and try to calm her down? Talk to her in a rational manner and find out more? But what if she were telling the truth? What would he do then? He couldn't turn in his own wife.

A jogger went past, her ponytail swinging with each step. It reminded him how he had tailed both Harry and Natasha. After his meeting with Lilith and her warnings, he had hoped to find out more about what they might be up to. Harry had done nothing other than walk to and from the local shops, whereas Natasha's only trip out had been on her morning run.

Rage and powerlessness threatened to overtake him. He had to do *something*.

When he'd followed her, Natasha had gone for a short run and then she had taken the underground. She had gone to Kensington High Street and then to a red door in an exclusive mews where she had disappeared inside. Was there any point in taking it further? Should he go to that red door and ring the bell?

He had dismissed it as being unimportant. But now he wanted to know who she had been visiting. It might be one way of proving Natasha's innocence. Or her guilt and involvement in this nightmare.

Whoever lived behind that door might give him the answers he needed. Or was he simply delaying the moment he had to go back and face his wife? He didn't know and he didn't care. He went to the end of the street and hailed a taxi.

Chapter Fifty-five

Natasha

Natasha backed as far away from the edge of the pool as she could. Harry was treading water, or he was trying to. Blond curls kissed the nape of his neck. His skin was bronzed from sunbathing at Sussex Abbey.

What a shame it had come to this, but then again, he had given her no choice, had he? It hadn't been her plan to kill him. She was going to incapacitate him and use his phone to transfer funds to her name and then go somewhere far away where he would never find her. Harry guarded access to their savings. All she had wanted was her fair share. And then Shannon turned up.

Natasha felt no remorse for pushing him in. He had used her the same way he used everybody.

Harry often swam when he was drunk so maybe he didn't realise what was really wrong. He managed a few strokes, which was a miracle, considering the drugs she had put in his drink. He got to the side and grabbed a hold but his fingers slipped. He went under again, struggling in the water. The Rohypnol, better known as a date-rape drug, was hitting him hard. She had been putting doses in his cocktails and with the amount she had given him, she was surprised he hadn't slipped unconscious in his lounger. He was drowning because he couldn't control his muscles.

She was a bit breathless and she wiped the hair out of her face. Before she pushed him in she had taken the phone from his pocket. Now she tapped the screen to open up the bank account. In a few seconds, she had given herself the whole of the funds. *It's what you earned*, she told herself. *And Harry won't need it now.*

She ignored Harry's splashing as he tried again to get a hold on the side. It was obvious he wouldn't make it. She stared dispassionately at his efforts.

It took a while for Shannon to realise what was going on. When she understood Harry was drowning, Shannon got ready to go in.

Natasha put her hand on Shannon's arm. 'Don't. We should leave him.'

Shannon opened her mouth to say something but nothing came out.

'You know it's the only way. It makes sense for both of us,' Natasha said. 'After what you just told me I can't stand the sight of him. Let him go under. Then you can be free and so can I.'

What Natasha didn't tell Shannon was that she had also put date rape drug in Shannon's drink. So if Shannon was stupid enough to try to save him, Natasha was counting on Shannon drowning too.

Chapter Fifty-six

Shannon

Shannon could feel her heart accelerating. Harry was floundering and he kept losing his grip on the side. It didn't make sense.

Natasha was a poor swimmer. Besides, it was obvious she had no intention of trying to save her husband.

'No Shannon, let him drown,' Natasha repeated. 'He deserves it.'

'What's wrong with him? What did you do?' Shannon asked.

Natasha was so calm it was surreal. 'You're going to thank me for doing it.'

'You drugged him, didn't you?'

'It's the best way. Just let him go under.'

I'm edging towards the pool. As I'm going down the steps I wobble a bit and then I steady myself.

'No, don't help him,' Natasha calls to me.

Should I let him drown?

He's gone under and it's too late to pull him out from the side because I can't reach him. When I'm up to my waist I kick off and head towards him. There's not much time left.

Drowning is not a pleasant way to die. I can see the terror in his eyes as he sinks towards the bottom. The water churns as he desperately claws for the surface. Air billows from his lungs. I can see his arms and legs aren't working properly.

I take a breath and go under water. The bubbles coming from his mouth are huge but it doesn't take long for them to become smaller, almost delicate. Despite the flailing arms, that body is going nowhere but down.

I could help. The pool isn't so deep and the water is perfectly clear. I could take a breath and go to the bottom and reach out my hand. Should I? Should I save someone who has taken away everything I hold dear?

Harry has no conscience. He ruins people and he makes them suffer. People like Margaret and Arthur Pemberton, people like me. Why should I risk myself and my child for him?

The poolside security camera is very discreet. Probably our guests haven't noticed it but I know it's there. Taking a deep gulp of air, I dive. But something is very wrong. Both of my legs are numb.

Chapter Fifty-seven

Jared

The taxi dropped Jared at the red door. The street was called Petersham Mews. It was a pretty little cobbled lane a short distance from the lovely Kensington Gardens. Now lined with top end residences, in the past, mews were courtyards with stables and carriage houses with simple living areas above them. They were built behind large city houses and catered for the horses and stable-servants of prosperous residents. He was sure the properties here must be valued at several million each. Who was it Natasha had visited?

The door had a gold letterbox.

He rang the bell and when no one answered he banged on the door. He had lost his wife and his marriage. What else could he possibly lose?

Chapter Fifty-eight

Shannon

Shannon's lungs were bursting for air and she had no sensation from the waist down. Were her legs even moving?

With one arm she had a grip on Harry and was dragging him up from the bottom, pulling herself through the water with her other arm. He was so heavy. She fought for the surface, ignoring her own instincts which screamed at her to let him go and save herself.

He had stopped moving.

She didn't have much left in her lungs. Her legs were lifeless and she was never going to make it.

No one would blame her for letting him go. The pool camera would be her witness. It would show she had done her best. It would tell everyone she had tried. That she did all she could and it was Natasha who pushed him in.

She had lost Jared. Aleksey was dead because of her. Natasha was right. With Harry gone all of Shannon's problems would disappear. No more blackmail. Her baby would be safe. No one would blame a pregnant woman for giving up, would they?

Don't think about it. Just do it.

Slowly, she opened her hand and Harry slipped from her fingers.

Harry sank back down, his hair wafting gently. As his gaze locked onto hers she knew he had understood. This was the end. She forced herself to watch until his eyes started to lose focus and his hands relaxed. Then she broke the surface, gasping for air.

Shannon struggled to the side. She got one hand on the bottom step and was able to haul herself halfway out. Wheezing and coughing she spewed up water.

Natasha had backed off towards the wall. Shannon tried to focus on the other woman but could not see her properly. Oh God no, what was happening? Her body was shutting down. She put a hand on her belly, terrified by what was happening to her.

It was getting more difficult to breathe. 'Something's wrong, please, my baby.'

'You stupid bitch, why did you go in for him? Don't you realise what he did? At Sussex Abbey Harry knocked you out, you know that?' Natasha said. 'You wanted to stay with Aleksey in the garden, do you remember? But Harry wanted you out of the way so he bashed you on the head. I didn't see him do it. But it's the only explanation for how one moment you were talking to Harry and the next you were unconscious. And of course, there was the mark on the side of your head, which was easily explained away to the paramedics as being caused by you falling. Except I know you already had that mark and it was bleeding when we carried you inside. The only explanation is that Harry did that to you.'

Shannon tried to focus on a blurry outline of Natasha, set amongst a sea of blue tiles.

'Harry and I carried you inside. He never called an ambulance, he made you believe he did but he didn't. He didn't call the paramedics and he didn't search for the epi-pen until later. He deliberately left Aleksey to die. That's why he wanted you out of the way.'

Shannon had worked out most of that already.

'You're so gullible. He's the one who killed Aleksey and then he made you think it was *you* who did it.'

Shannon was rolling slowly onto her face and she tried to prevent it and stay on her side. She couldn't. Panic gripped her.

'You know why Harry left Aleksey to die? It's because he had already worked out that he could use Aleksey's death against *you*. Harry has always been a monster.'

'Help me,' Shannon whispered.

'Now look at the state you're in. You were stupid to try to save him, Shannon.'

Chapter Fifty-nine

Jared

Jared closed the red door behind him. He took another taxi and rushed back to Barnes. Now he knew every part of the puzzle and it was time to put an end to it.

There was no sign of anyone at home. Where the hell was everybody? He found cut fruit and open bottles in the kitchen, which must mean that Harry was on a cocktail spree. Likely he had taken his drinks to the spa.

Jared ran down to the basement. When he reached the spa and yanked open the door the scene in front of him was so violent that for a moment he couldn't breathe. Oh God, no. Shannon was lying on the steps, half in and half out of the water, not moving. Harry was lifeless in the pool. Natasha was standing as if frozen by shock.

'What the hell!'

He ran first to Shannon. No, no, she could not be dead. Not Shannon. Not their baby.

When he saw her eyes were open, he fell to his knees.

'Get over here and save my wife,' he called to Natasha.

He checked Shannon's pulse. It was very slow. Natasha knelt by his side but she made no move to help. He took Natasha by the shoulders. 'Do something,' he shouted. 'For God's sake what's wrong with you?'

He did not want to leave Shannon but he had to get to Harry. Jared dived into the pool.

A few moments later, Jared cursed as he dragged Harry out of the water. 'He's not breathing.' Then he fumbled for his phone, hoping to god it was still working. When he punched in the numbers, Natasha took his hand.

'Please don't call for help, not before you've listened to me.'

'Are you mad? Get off me.'

She tried to snatch his phone but he pushed her away. It took a few seconds to connect to the emergency services and he gave the details.

'Please, a man has drowned,' he said. 'And my wife is pregnant. She's not moving. I don't know what's wrong with her.'

He hung up and rounded on Natasha. 'Jesus Christ, do something! They need help.'

'You've got to trust me. Please Jared, I saw your wife kissing a man at Sussex Abbey. It was the night of the gala while you were on the phone speaking to your father.'

He put Shannon into the recovery position. 'It's all right, darling. Try to hang on. Help will be here soon.'

Natasha started crying. 'I'm so sorry. I didn't want to tell you before because it seemed so... unfair. Your wife had an affair with a man called Aleksey. She kissed him in the garden and then she murdered him.'

'What?'

'I saw it happen. Aleksey had a nut allergy and Shannon deliberately fed him nuts and then she threw away his epinephrine. The poor man died before an ambulance could arrive.'

'No. The ambulance came for Shannon that night. I called for it myself. You said she fell.' Jared tried to clear the water from Harry's lungs. 'Come on man, breathe.'

'That's not what happened,' Natasha said. 'Shannon killed Aleksey and then Harry covered it up for her. He's been blackmailing her with it ever since which is why you have to let Harry die.'

Jared shook his head. And then he rolled Harry onto his back and began artificial respiration and heart compressions.

'Don't you see? The baby isn't yours. That's why Shannon was prepared to murder Aleksey. So you didn't find out the truth about the pregnancy. She had an affair and Aleksey is the father, not you.'

Chapter Sixty

Shannon

Shannon could no longer move her arms. As she listened to every word Natasha told Jared, she tried to talk to Jared but it was a whisper and he didn't notice. Though she fought as hard as she could, more sound would not come out of her mouth.

'Don't you see?' Natasha had said. 'The baby isn't yours. That's why Shannon was prepared to murder Aleksey. So you didn't find out the truth about the pregnancy. She had an affair and Aleksey is the father, not you.'

Shannon felt her heart falter. This was the end then. Though she had told Jared about Aleksey's death, she had not talked about the baby.

'How do I know you're telling me the truth?' Jared said.

Shannon felt as if she was dying inside. She tried to move her fingers. Tried to get Jared's attention. He mustn't listen to Natasha.

Natasha was eager. 'Harry has proof. He took a video of your wife with Aleksey and of her throwing away his medication. Harry has the epi-pen with Shannon's prints on it too because he found it in the garden later.'

It was hard for Jared to carry out artificial respiration and to talk and it took a while for him to answer. She could see it all and she was powerless.

'What about Aleksey?' Jared asked.

'Harry put his body in the river.'

'Oh my god.'

'I can get the proof for you,' Natasha said. 'I know where Harry has stashed it.'

'All right.'

While Natasha ran off, Jared continued artificial respiration on Harry. That was the sort of person Jared was – an honest man, full of integrity. He would not even let his worst enemy die in front of him.

After the rape, she had tried so hard to put it behind her. Then she had taken the pregnancy test and it had been positive. She knew Aleksey could be the father and she had ignored it. She and Jared had wanted a baby for so long and now they had one. It had been easy to convince herself that she could keep it secret.

The agony of not being able to reach out to Jared was torture. Her energy was draining away. She screwed up the last of her strength.

'It wasn't an affair,' she whispered.

Jared blew a breath into Harry.

'I was raped.'

She moved her hand, and it swished in a little puddle of water. Jared looked her way. She moved her hand again. He came close and put his ear to her mouth.

'It wasn't an affair. I was raped.'

'I know.'

Shannon felt herself hovering on the edge of consciousness. She didn't know if she was dreaming.

'It's all right and everything is going to be okay,' Jared said. 'I already knew about Aleksey and I already knew about the baby. This will be over soon. Please darling, just hang on.'

Chapter Sixty-one

Jared

Jared had been working on Harry for a few minutes before Natasha came back. As far as Jared could tell, Harry's heart had stopped.

'Why are you bothering with Harry? It's too late,' Natasha said. 'Here's the epi-pen. The recording is a video clip on Harry's phone and I know just what to do with that.' She held Harry's phone out and dropped it into the pool.

He smiled at her, though he did not stop his work on Harry. 'Good, thank you, and before the police arrive perhaps you'd better tell me the truth.'

'I've told you everything.'

'Natasha, you've not been honest with me and I really wish you had been. Aleksey was never killed.'

Confusion and then concern passed across Natasha's face. She really was a good liar. Jared took a pause from doing the artificial respiration.

'How do I know Aleksey isn't dead? Because I talked to him about fifteen minutes ago. He told me you injected him with epinephrine. You saved his life and then you told him Harry was dangerous and that he should pretend to be dead otherwise Harry would really kill him. Aleksey was in shock and he played along with it. He said you told Harry he was dead and Harry believed you.'

Jared could hear the sound of a siren outside. He wished Natasha had told him the whole truth and then he would have been more kind to her.

'Aleksey told me he waited until Harry dumped him in the water. Then Aleksey swam away. I saw Aleksey isn't looking so good. He told me he managed to swim to safety but he suffered a stroke afterwards. The doctors think it was a consequence of the anaphylactic shock and then the exertion. One side of his face and body are partially paralysed, but still, you know that don't you? You're not all bad, Natasha, are you? You saved Aleksey. You've been visiting him. At least that means you're not as bad as Harry but you were prepared to let Harry make my wife suffer, weren't you?'

'I did it for you.'

'I don't think so.'

'I knew what she'd done and how she had cheated on you and you deserve better! You and I, we're good together, aren't we?'

Jared took a few deep breaths. 'Where did you get the medication from to save Aleksey?'

'From Clarissa, you know, the older woman who always wore pearls. She and I got friendly and she told me her husband had liver problems and she was really worried because he also had serious food allergies. He carried an epi-pen at all times and Clarissa did too. She gave hers to me when I told her it was an emergency.'

'And you rushed back outside and used it on Aleksey without Harry knowing.'

'Harry didn't want to watch Aleksey die. But he thought it was okay to tell me to stay to watch, even though he knew it would be torture for me. That was my chance to inject him.'

What a crazy, twisted story. Though it didn't explain how Shannon came to be lying on the steps of the pool, with Harry drowned. Jared blew a few more breaths into Harry and he was still keeping Harry going when the paramedics arrived and took over.

The police were there too and Jared didn't hesitate.

'Officer, you need to question that woman.' He pointed at Natasha. 'There's no way Harry drowned by accident and I'm pretty certain that if you test Harry's drink and my wife's glass, you'll find traces of poison. My wife whispered to me that Natasha drugged them.'

'That's a lie!' Natasha screamed at him. 'Your wife's lying because she doesn't want us to be together.'

She was still screaming when the police led her away.

Chapter Sixty-two

Shannon

When Shannon woke up in a hospital bed, Jared was by her side. The last thing she remembered was lying by the pool listening to her husband talk about Aleksey being alive. But had that been a dream?

He kissed her. 'You've been thoroughly checked by the doctors and the baby is fine. How are you feeling?'

'Dreadful.'

'I bet you are. That stuff Natasha gave you knocked you out.'

What could she say to him to make this right? Did they still have a chance? She took his hand. 'Jared, is it true that Aleksey is alive?'

He nodded. 'I wish you had told me.'

'About the rape?'

'Yes, and about the baby and what happened at the hotel.'

'I wanted to. I just couldn't find the words and then Harry had me in a corner.'

'Jesus.'

'I didn't tell anyone because I felt so ashamed. Aleksey was a client and I went for a drink with him. I think he drugged me but I don't remember. Then I realised the baby might be his and I didn't tell you because... because we so wanted a child. I'm sorry.'

'You haven't got anything to be sorry about. He's the one who-' Jared's voice broke.

'Aleksey is mad. He believed he loved me and he kept telling me we could be together. It was crazy talk. I didn't mean to kill him. It was an accident. All I wanted was to keep him away from us.'

'I know. And I know everything Natasha said was a lie.'

'Aleksey is alive? I can't believe it.'

He stroked the hair back from her face. 'It's incredible but it's true.'

'What did he tell you?'

'He told me you went willingly to his house after a few drinks and that you wanted to have sex with him. I knew he was lying.'

Shannon cried. 'How can you be so sure?'

'Because I know you and I love you. That man was a lying hound. I knew it as soon as I set eyes on him. He's not right in his head.'

'He drugged me.'

'That piece of shit deserves to go to prison.'

Jared gave her a tissue and she dabbed her eyes.

'I know you acted on the spur of the moment at the hotel and then you regretted it,' Jared said. 'The thing is, Aleksey deserved it. From what Aleksey told me, it was Harry who was prepared to leave Aleksey to die, not you.'

She would never in a million years have believed Natasha would save Aleksey.

'I'm not pleased Aleksey had a stroke,' Jared said. 'But I'm not sorry either. It was a good job he was incapacitated otherwise I wouldn't have been able to control my rage. We can call it poetic justice. For what he did to you.'

Jared went on to tell her the full story of how he had followed Natasha on her morning run. Then, after he and

Shannon had argued, he had returned and spoken to the man behind the red door – Aleksey.

Jared was so understanding. He told her he felt raw and powerless about the rape. Shannon understood, but for her, the baby was all that mattered.

The effects of the Rohypnol were slowly wearing off and she felt much better. One thing she did understand was that the drugs Aleksey used on her had been like the one Natasha used, because she felt the same. It was a validation of her suspicion Aleksey had drugged her.

As soon as she felt better she would be filing a report against Aleksey for rape. Right now, she was just happy it was all over.

Chapter Sixty-three

Shannon

Later that day, Rosie arrived.

Jared kissed his sister-in-law. 'I'll go and get a coffee,' he said. 'And give you two a bit of private time.'

Shannon reached for a tissue and blew her nose. 'He's been so understanding and supportive. What would I do without him?'

'I could not believe it when Jared phoned to tell me what happened.'

'I'm sorry I didn't tell you the full story.'

'Don't be silly.'

'When I believed I had killed Aleksey I didn't know what to do.'

'Aleksey is alive and you did your best to save Harry which, considering what Harry was doing *to you*, was more than heroic.'

The ambulance crew had not been able to revive Harry and he was pronounced dead on arrival at the hospital. The pool camera had captured it, meaning Natasha was the one on the line for Harry's death. *No one would ever know the real truth*.

'He died anyway,' Shannon said.

Rosie shrugged. 'We can't pretend it isn't for the best.'

'You going along with Harry's friendship advances was vital,' Shannon said. 'Without talking to Margaret Pemberton I would never have had the courage to confront Harry. When I told Margaret Harry was dead, she cried on the phone. She said she's at last got justice for her husband. I think she's right. I'm glad he's gone.'

'I can't believe you kept all that pain and anguish to yourself. The rape, Sussex Abbey, I wish you had let me help you.'

Shannon sniffed. 'I was in a very bad place. I felt so naïve about trusting Aleksey and I was caught by my loyalty to Donald and what it would mean if I went to the police. It would have been Aleksey's word against mine. The crazy thing is, I spoke to Donald just a few minutes ago and he immediately cut Aleksey off as a friend and as a client.'

'I can't believe you lived through that.'

'Too many women do. Rosie, please don't cry.'

'I can't help it.'

'It's over. Harry is dead. It was Harry who made me believe that I killed Aleksey. I didn't feel I could turn to anyone, not to you and not even to my own husband.'

'I'm so sorry.'

'You were there for me when it mattered. And I'm sure Mum was helping me.'

'Do you think so?'

Shannon smiled and squeezed Rosie's hand. 'Yes, I do.'

They were quiet for a few moments.

'You're safe now,' Rosie said.

Shannon could still not believe how completely she had been fooled by Harry. He had managed to convince her Aleksey was dead. Well, Harry had believed it too, apparently. It was only Natasha who had known Aleksey was alive. The scheming bitch.

'Natasha was part of it. She let me suffer even when I had gone to her asking for help.'

'You did?'

'Yes, I thought she was a friend and I asked her to help me get Harry off my back. I wanted to know if she knew anything I could use against him. She played the victim and showed me her bruises and cried about how Harry physically abused her and controlled her every move. I'm sure she'll be using that in her defence when she's on trial for Harry's murder.'

'Good luck to her,' Rosie said. 'I don't think she stands a chance.'

'Oh, I don't know about that. Natasha can be very convincing when she wants to be. In her own way she was just as manipulative as Harry.'

'Jared told me she was the one to drug Harry and you, and she pushed him in the water. What a vile couple.'

Shannon sighed. She was so relieved to be free of them.

Her husband had brought her flowers and she brushed them with her fingertips. They were her favourites and they had a lovely sweet scent. She and Jared were going to be okay.

'All that's important is the baby,' she said.

'Thank goodness the pregnancy wasn't affected,' Rosie said.

'The doctors told me that at the pool, when my heartbeat slowed so did the baby's, but we've since both recovered from the effects of the Rohypnol. I had much less in my blood stream than Harry did. They told me there's no reason for it to have any effect on the baby's development.'

It had been such a relief to hear this that Shannon had found it hard to stop crying and so had Jared.

Shannon lay back and closed her eyes. Harry was gone. And men like Aleksey and Harry would never get the better of her again.

Chapter Sixty-four

Jared

After Rosie left, Jared had gone back to sit by Shannon's side. He stayed until the nurse told him it was time for him to leave. Then he came home to an empty house and sat in the living room, staring out at the River Thames. He recalled the moment he had knocked on the red door and it had been opened by a pale-skinned stranger. The stranger had been unshaven and bleary eyed and one side of the man's face was sagging. Though he was around the same age as Jared, he used a walking frame to get to the door. The man had recognised Jared.

'You must be Jared, the wonderful husband of the wonderful Shannon.'

There was bitterness in the man's voice.

'I'm at a disadvantage here,' Jared had said. 'I'm sorry but do I know you?'

'You will do soon,' Aleksey had said with sarcasm. 'Why don't you come in and I can fill you in on the story? I think you'll find it fascinating.'

Aleksey had taken him to a luxury living room. The man was not shy and he was happy to talk because he didn't feel he had anything to hide. That was how Jared found out about Aleksey's infatuation with Shannon. He discovered that Aleksey was a client where Shannon worked and he had been out with her for lunches plenty of times. Aleksey had admired

Shannon for years and he had come to know her well enough that one day, out of the blue, she had broken down in front of him and talked about her distress at not being able to have a baby. Aleksey had invited her for a drink and he considered it was the spark which ignited her love for him.

'As soon as I brought her back here she was all over me.'

'You're lying.'

'I am not. Up until the moment she tried to kill me, I believed she loved me as much as I loved her.'

The man had clearly been deluded.

'Oh yes. And I understand that she's pregnant? Congratulations.'

Jared had the impression Aleksey was enjoying watching him suffer. He had gripped the arms of the chair as Aleksey launched into a retelling of the events at Sussex Abbey. First, he talked about how he had met Natasha at the public house and she had invited him to the gala. Then, at the gala, he had drunk too much and he demanded to speak to Shannon, even when he had promised her he would stay away. And then there was the part about the epinephrine – that he had ingested a trace of nuts and Shannon, who knew about his allergies, had snatched away his medication and threatened him.

'She wanted me to stay away from you.' Aleksey gave a sardonic laugh. 'And here you are knocking on my door. Then she left me to die. It was Natasha who saved me.'

That Aleksey was alive seemed like a miracle because Shannon had just hours ago confessed to Jared that she had murdered Aleksey.

Jared had realised Shannon had been played. By Harry. And by Natasha. And that Natasha had played her own game too because she had conned Harry. What a twisted mess.

The part Jared could not accept was Shannon sleeping with Aleksey. It did not ring true and he did not for a moment trust it. However, it was clear Aleksey believed it. Either

Aleksey was making it up, or if it had happened it wasn't the way Aleksey told it. Which would mean what? That Aleksey had forced Shannon? Jared's heart had gone cold.

He went upstairs and peered into the room next door to their bedroom. His legs felt shaky after having recalled the encounter with Aleksey. *It's over*, he told himself. *Now you need to find the strength to move on.*

His wife had been raped and she had not turned to him. That was difficult enough to live with, but then there was the question about the paternity of the baby.

The cinema room was not yet a nursery but it would be soon and he knew more than anything that he wanted to be a father. He wanted to be there for cuddles with a little one into the night, to have his hand gripped by tiny fingers, to live in a house with children shouting and laughing. Nothing was more important. As far as he was concerned, this baby was his, now and forever more.

Chapter Sixty-five

Shannon

Shannon was happy to be home. Quietly, and without fuss, she and Jared were picking up their life from where it had been before Sussex Abbey. They were taking it one day at a time and so far, so good.

She had cleaned out Natasha's and Harry's belongings and thrown them in the rubbish bin, which had felt very cathartic. Natasha was awaiting trial and she had disappeared from their lives.

It made her furious that Natasha had told Jared about the questions surrounding the paternity of the baby. There was no doubt in Shannon's mind that Natasha had done this deliberately in the hope that she would be the one to pick up the pieces of Jared's broken heart.

Jared was in the kitchen cooking supper. From the aromas, she guessed it was a mushroom risotto.

'That smells wonderful,' she said. 'What is it?'

'You'll have to wait to find out, it's a surprise,' he called through to her.

She smiled. Jared had taken his father to the hospital for his chemo treatment and father and son were getting on better than they had for a long time. She put her hand on her belly. It was starting to round out and she was so looking forward to when it was huge. Settling back, she rested her head against the cushions.

The only thing they had not talked about was the paternity of the baby. Jared had refused to discuss it and he told her that as far as he was concerned, he was the father. He was the one who would be there for this child, he was the one who would protect them and nurture them and love them – this baby was his.

Did she believe he could make that leap and leave all doubts behind him? She wanted to have faith he would not have regrets, she really did. Beyond that, she was putting her trust in her love for her husband.

Closing her eyes, she imagined what it was going to be like being a mother – holding her baby, caring for it and kissing its soft skin, breathing in the sweet scent and gazing into her own baby's eyes. It was a dream her poor heart had spent so long chasing and now it was becoming real. Soon it would be just her, Jared, and the baby, and they were going to enjoy every moment of their life together.

She had faith in herself too, and her ability to deal with what the future might hold. Letting Harry go had changed her. She was stronger now. She had claimed back her power.

Chapter Sixty-six

Six months later

The birth of the baby had been so emotional, Jared still felt choked up. Afterwards, there were so many procedures and checks by the midwife and the nurses and Jared didn't really register much of it. Now, several hours later, Shannon was asleep and he was the one who had the chance to sit quietly by Shannon's bed holding the baby. No, not *the* baby, *his baby*.

Up until that moment he had been willing to accept the baby as being his without needing any proof. He had not wanted a DNA test. In fact, he had been ready to welcome this child into his life with open arms.

It was a boy. He had dark eyes and a dark mop of hair and tanned skin, which in itself was a significant combination, but it was his nose which brought tears to Jared's eyes. Because it was like looking at a tiny version of Raj.

Raj had always cursed his hooked nose, which was a typical Indian feature and one Raj shared with their father. Whereas Jared had more his mother's nose, which was smaller, and as Raj often said, much more attractive.

Jared could not wait to show him to the rest of his family. He laughed quietly and cuddled his son close to his heart.

*****

You might also like…

The Couple Upstairs
The perfect home…. or the perfect nightmare?

The Couple
Ellie Mitchell is a successful writer and her husband, Rob, is a cardiac surgeon. They met after a whirlwind romance and everyone sees them as the ideal couple – happy, successful and in love.

The Lodger
Sabrina is mother to a five-year-old daughter.
A single mum who's going through a messy divorce, Sabrina is looking for a place to stay and when the Mitchell's offer her their downstairs apartment, it seems the perfect place to lie low and heal from her wounds.

A shocking secret…
The three of them form a friendship but all is not as it seems. As their lives become entwined, who can be trusted? Lies and terrible secrets lurk beneath the surface.
Someone has a sinister agenda and one of them must discover the truth, before the only way out is murder…

What readers are saying –

'Tense and thrilling'

'Nothing is as it seems'

'This was excellent, the best psychological thriller I have read for a long time.'

'A real page turner.'

'Highly recommended.'

'A fantastic thriller that keeps you guessing…lots of twists and turns.'

Grab your copy today!

You might also like,

Deadly Motives (Grant and Ruby Book 1)
Secrets never stay buried forever…

When a nurse is brutally strangled, Detective Grant recognises all too well the work of a killer called Travis. Grant's a respected veteran but early in his career Grant caught Travis for the murder of five women and Travis has been incarcerated ever since. The problem is, Travis was at the hospital when the nurse was murdered.

Young and talented, Ruby is a specialist profiler. She's been keeping herself out of the spotlight but Grant takes her under his wing to work this case. It could make her career or it could break her, because Ruby has been in hiding for a reason.

When a second woman is murdered, Grant and Ruby realise all is not as it seems.
The team must work quickly as the body count rises. Why is their suspect always one step ahead? Why does Travis keep talking about mistakes Grant made in the past? And most shocking of all, why is this case so personal to Ruby and what is she hiding from her colleagues?

Praise for Deadly Motives-

'A truly phenomenal story'

'Superb read. A must for all crime readers.'

'One that will really keep you guessing until the end.'

'Killer novel. Five Stars.'

Deadly Motives has over 1500 Five Star Ratings on Amazon and Goodreads.

Grab your copy today!

You might also like,

Good Girl Bad Girl (Kal and Marty Book 1)
The darkest crimes can't stay hidden forever…

A young body washed up by the river in London, and a matron murdered at a children's home thousands of miles away…could there be a link?

Only one person wants to find out – Kal. Why does she want to know? Because Kal's journalist mother was researching the story and now she's missing.

Kal's father was a criminal, which is why she trusts no one and least of all Detective Inspector Spinks. Kal takes on the investigation herself. She's going to need all the skills she learnt from her father, especially when she discovers a link between her own family and the crimes that have been committed.

Trafficking, deception and dark family secrets - she'll be forced to confront her own worst nightmares, and form an alliance with the police, if they're going to nail a twisted killer.

What readers are saying –

'A stunning read'

'On the edge of my seat'

'Loved the characters and the writing!'

'Great to have female leads who were strong but realistically vulnerable at times too. Can't wait to read about these characters again!'

Good Girl Bad Girl is an Eric Hoffer Book Award Finalist. Grab your copy today.

A message from Ann Girdharry –

Hello,

Thank you so much for choosing The Woman in Room 19.

I really appreciate my readers and one of the things I love about being an author is hearing direct from readers like you.

So if you'd like to get in touch, please do. You might have a question about one of my books, or maybe you have a general question about publishing. Or maybe you've spotted a typo or an error.

Whatever it is, feel free to send me an email. I'd be delighted to hear from you.

If you're an avid reader and you'd like to receive news and updates, you can join my Reader's Group. Don't worry, no spam. I'll only get in touch when I have something I think you might genuinely be interested in, like the release of a new book or offers on my titles. I offer a free gift to new members and you can find details on my webpage – www.girdharry.com

Happy Reading,
Ann Girdharry
Email – ann@girdharry.com

Acknowledgements

A special thank you to Shalini from Digital Reads Media. She is fantastic. She read through the drafts of this story and helped hone it until it was ready for readers. I know I can always rely on her experience and professionalism.

A huge thanks also to Morgen Bailey for editing and proofreading. Her attention to detail is what this author needs.

I could not have done this without them!

Titles by this Author

Deadly Motives
Deadly Secrets
Deadly Lies

Good Girl Bad Girl
London Noir
The Beauty Killers

The Couple Upstairs
The Woman in Room 19